GHOST LEGION

GHOST LEGION

A Western Story

JOHNNY D. BOGGS

Skyhorse Publishing

Visit our website at www.skyhorsepublishing.com.

10 9 8 7 6 5 4 3 2 1

Library of Congress Cataloging-in-Publication Data is available on file.

Cover design by Brian Peterson

Print ISBN: 978-1-63450-743-1
Ebook ISBN: 978-1-63450-744-8

Printed in the United States of America

For two North Carolinians:
Mike Cross, a great singer-songwriter,
and Christine Kushner, a great friend

Chapter One

"Bound for the cord," his mother had often told him. "You are bound for the cord."

Those words echoed through Stuart Brodie's head as he stared at the body hanging from the oak's sturdy limbs. *Bound for the cord*—only it wasn't Stuart Brodie who had been executed as a warning to others.

Brodie pulled his grandfather's English Sea Service pistol from his belt, cocked it, and fired over his head. The .58-caliber monster barked angrily, coughing out thick, white smoke, and the noise reverberated across the meadow, sending crows and vultures to safer climes. Still holding the pistol, he stopped his mule's nervous prancing, swallowed down bile, and stared ahead.

Younger brother Ezekiel twisted in the wind, sending a horde of flies scattering for just an instant, and Brodie's mule balked at moving any closer. His brother's hands were tied behind his back with rawhide, eyes bulging from their sockets, head tilting slightly, the neck unbroken. The killers had done a poor job, or maybe they had purposely let Ezekiel choke to death, kicking, biting his tongue in half, and trying to scream as the hemp squeezed the life out of him. Ezekiel's homespun shirt had been ripped, the shredded muslin still tucked in his soiled breeches and dancing in the wind, and they had flogged him mercilessly before his torment finally ended. Welts and dried blood scarred that broad back, the once unblemished

7

black skin. Across his chest, the murdering fiends had pinned a crudely written sign.

Tories
This is
Your
Future

Brodie slid the pistol into its saddle scabbard, dismounted unsteadily, and hobbled the animal in the meadow, upwind. His face glistened with sweat as he moved closer to Ezekiel's bloated body, and, with a rabid oath, he swung the tomahawk. The blade severed the rope those Whig brigands who called themselves Patriots had secured around the oak's trunk, and Ezekiel's body slammed into the earth. Flies buzzed furiously at the sudden movement, and a crow cawed from a pecan tree.

His fingers clenched the long handle of the tomahawk, tighter and tighter, until spasms shot up his arm, but Brodie couldn't let go, not until he choked out something unintelligible and dammed the tears building inside. Finally he jerked the blade loose, let the weapon fall, and strode angrily back to the mule, where he unfastened his woolen bedroll tied behind the cantle.

After he had covered Ezekiel's body, Brodie walked to the tavern he and Ezekiel had built along the Great Wagon Road in the South Carolina backcountry. Brodie had traveled the length of that pike, north to south and south to north, from Pine Tree Hill to Philadelphia, even venturing on the Cherokee Path to Keowee, and off the trail to the Catawba reserve. Bartering, buying, befriending Indians and whites, even some freedmen like himself, Brodie had become well known in the uncivilized settlements. He had left the innkeeping to his brother, always telling himself, as well as their mother, that Ezekiel was safe, at least as safe as anyone, white, black, or red, could be in this part of the Colonies. Innkeepers lived long lives. If anyone died, it would most likely be Stuart, murdered somewhere between the Schuylkill and the Catawba. His mother had nodded in agreement.

Well, Mama, we both were wrong.

The inn, which also served as the Brodies' home, lay in smoldering ruins. Chickens inside the coop had been killed, and not for food, and Brodie spotted one hog at the edge of the woods. At least, he assumed it was a hog. He couldn't see it clearly because of the crows pecking at the remains.

A long rifle, its stock split, the firelock broken, straddled the threshold, and Brodie picked it up with his left hand. Soot covered his fingers and palm.

Closing his eyes, he tried to picture what had happened, probably sometime yesterday. Ezekiel would have been inside when they rode up, not suspecting trouble. His brother had seen thirty summers, but his mind remained that of a boy not yet twelve. Stuart had taken him out of Charles Town to lessen the burden on his parents, although Ezekiel had earned his keep, proving time and again to be a good innkeeper and business partner, and an unquestioning brother. He would have heard the horses and stood behind the bar, ready to greet his customers with a smile and noggin of rum. When they rushed inside the tavern, he would have reacted, grabbing the Pennsylvania rifle, likely clubbing one of the assailants, breaking the stock. The rebels would have figured Ezekiel for a simpleton, but his brother had always been a fighter. Yet there had been too many—more than two dozen, if Brodie read the signs right—and they had beaten him, tied him, whipped him, then hanged him while others plundered the place and butchered his chickens and hogs. Only after they had killed Ezekiel would they have set fire to the inn, and then ridden off, drunk on Brodie rum and ale.

Elijah Clarke's Georgians, maybe. Perhaps Andrew Pickens's rebels, or even Thomas Sumter's. Or some other gang, men who had once stopped here for conversation, a good fire, and strong drink. Likely he would never know who had killed Ezekiel. Did it really matter?

He wasn't sure if he could find a shovel, not among all the rubble and ash, so he would probably wind up burying his brother with his hands.

Exhaustion overtook him at last, and Brodie dropped to the ground by the doorway. Smoke stung his eyes, and he cursed.

* * * * *

A freedman from Charles Town, Stuart Brodie had left the low country to find a place of his own in the Ninety-Six District, ignoring his mother's warnings and his father's protests.

"Men live like pigs in the backcountry," William Brodie had preached. "They are as savage as Cherokees and as rude as Baptists. What you, I fear, will find in Ninety-Six is not your fortune, but your grave. After all, you are a Negro, and your neighbors along that creek shall see you as a slave, and, mayhap, will enslave you. 'Tis no law in Ninety-Six. 'Tis no God, either."

Twelve years ago, when Brodie first staked a claim along the Long Canes, he had lived in a "potato" house, more lean-to than cabin, fit for neither spud nor spider. Bloody flux had almost killed him during his first month there. Twice, he had almost been rubbed out by Cherokees, and once, when he had dared venture over the Cumberland Gap to the bloody ground known as Kentucky, he had barely escaped a Shawnee ambush. Twice more in South Carolina, he had killed *banditti*, burying their bodies in the bowels of the forest, turning their horses loose, and covering his tracks. Not that men of that ilk would be missed, but they had been white, and Brodie remained a cautious man, untrusting of white men, white laws.

The inn started out as a rawhide affair that stank of sot weed and Sir Richard, serving only the hardest lot, but soon the denizens of that lawless district began to trust Stuart Brodie, no matter the color of his skin. Within two years, Brodie had enlisted the help of Ezekiel. Brodie's Inn, more commonly known as the Darky's Tavern, became a welcome respite for many travelers, and a profitable venture for the Brodie brothers. Six shillings would buy a gallon of rum, or some other spirit; dinner could be had for another shilling; two pence would get a weary traveler a straw bed for the night. Of course, since hard money remained scarce on the frontier, bartering was always welcome. Soon, Brodie had left the bulk of the innkeeping business to Ezekiel, while he rode up and down the Great Wagon Road, hunting, trapping, trading.

Then came the war.

At first, Stuart Brodie had no interest in either the Patriot cause or the fire-and-brimstone preached by Loyalists. This rebellion, to him and many backcountry settlers, seemed nothing more than some twisted affray between low country gentry and London Parliament. Like a forest fire, though, it soon exploded, devouring everything and everyone in its path. Neighbors killed neighbors, and answering the question—*Are you for King?*—proved deadly.

Stuart Brodie remained loyal to King George. Not that the King or British Parliament ever did much to help the Brodies, but most Patriots had little use for freedmen, although Brodie had seen some black men, and even a few Indians, riding with the *banditti* who robbed and killed for the rebel cause. Besides, Brodie's grandfather had fought for England, had served in His Majesty's Navy. Stuart Brodie carried his grandfather's pistol proudly, and he would never shame his father's father's memory by firing that weapon on British troops.

Thus, the Brodie brothers were branded Tories. It didn't hurt business at the inn, not at first. Whigs populated half the country; the other half claimed Loyalist sympathies. Yet Brodie suspected that a majority on both sides had no political leanings or objectives but merely wanted an excuse to scourge.

He cursed his stupidity. Brodie should have known this would happen. He could have taken Ezekiel back to Charles Town, out of harm's way, to wait until the world's most powerful army put down this insurrection. It wouldn't last long, not now. On his journey home from Philadelphia, Brodie had learned that George Washington's army lay in shambles, and, by the time he had reached Wachovia, word came that Sir Henry Clinton had taken Charles Town, forcing General Benjamin Lincoln's Continentals to surrender. A group of fleeing Virginians under Colonel Abraham Buford had been overtaken by Banastre Tarleton's British Legion and butchered at the Waxhaws. The way Brodie heard it, from Loyalist and rebel alike, Buford's men had tried to surrender, but almost all had been cut down by saber and spontoon. Murdered.

That little incident, hundreds of miles from Long Canes Creek, had cost Ezekiel Brodie his life. For written in dried blood on a piece of cotton tied to the chicken coop was:

Tarleton's Quarter

Brodie cursed the Patriots again. Ezekiel Brodie had never been to the Waxhaws, never even heard of Abraham Buford or Banastre

Tarleton. Two weeks ago, when the Green Dragoon was overseeing that bloody business, Ezekiel had been drinking bumbo and encouraging customers to tell their lies over pickles and whiskey.

* * * * *

How long he stared at his brother's covered corpse, he didn't know, but it must have been hours, for the crows had found their courage and returned to the oak's limbs, waiting for the opportunity to feast on Ezekiel. When a horse whinnied, Brodie reached for his grandfather's pistol—but it wasn't there.

His mule brayed in reply, and Brodie heard them, close, just around the bend, and he cursed his carelessness. The pistol was holstered on his saddle. Besides, he had not reloaded it after scaring off the carrion. Likewise, both powder horn and shot pouch remained on his saddle. Even his tomahawk lay in the dirt where he had dropped it just a few feet from Ezekiel's body. The only weapon he had was the ruined remains of the long rifle.

Maybe, he thought, tucking the weapon underneath his arm, hiding the busted stock, and placing his right hand across the destroyed firelock. He had always been a gambler, although he knew he had no hope of winning this bet.

Brodie relaxed briefly when he saw the first rider. He wore the uniform of a British officer, a regular soldier, although the men who came behind him were a mixed lot, some in red jackets and plaid kilts, others in homespun and hunting frocks. Many he recognized as patrons of his inn, Loyalists who had bought his ale, faces he remembered full of laughter, only now they looked worn and grim.

A slight man with an oval face and friendly features, the officer managed to take in everything at a glance: the butchery of animals, the covered corpse, shell of the inn, and Stuart Brodie. Sweat pasted reddish hair against his heat-flushed skin, his lips were chapped, but he remained erect in the saddle while those behind him appeared half dead. He spoke softly to the men nearest him before kicking his stallion, a beautiful bay mount, into a walk and approached Brodie alone, reining in with his left hand. His right arm hung uselessly at his side, but Brodie decided this man was anything but crippled. Yet the man's youth surprised him. Not yet forty, probably only a few years Brodie's senior.

"I am Major Patrick Ferguson." The Briton spoke in a thick Scottish accent, the tone courteous but powerful. "Of the Seventy-First Highlanders, although I am on detached service." Ferguson's head tilted toward Ezekiel's covered body. "Rebels?"

"I call them *banditti*." Brodie's voice, so hollow, dry, almost emotionless, surprised him.

"As should I. We mean you no harm, good sir." Ferguson eyed Brodie's rifle, then gestured at Ezekiel's covered body. "This was . . . ?"

"My brother. I returned home to find him hanging, whipped . . . ." Brodie stopped himself. If he kept on, he knew he would break down.

Ferguson bowed, and Brodie found him sincere. "A chaplain rides with us, and if 'tis your desire, your wishes, we can help bury your brother, speak the word of the Lord over his grave, provide a fitting funeral. Or if you wish for solitude, we shall move on. We came here to water our horses, but we will not intrude."

"Stay." Brodie's voice was urgent. He had always been a loner, but suddenly he wanted company. He stared at his moccasins, embarrassed.

"Our mission is to subdue the insurrection and protect those loyal to His Majesty from those backwater villains," Ferguson said. "Although from your face I detect that I may offer you something else."

"Such as?" Brodie did not look up.

"Vengeance."

Now he straightened, staring at Ferguson.

"Do not misinterpret my words," the major said. "I am not the leader of some lawless horde. What I offer you is a chance to serve His Majesty, but we fight like men, not barbarians, for the glory and King George. I enforce discipline. If you enlist in my army, you obey my laws, the laws of the British army. History will not remember Patrick Ferguson as a butcher, but as a soldier."

Brodie decided to test this man. "And what of the Waxhaws, Major?"

Up until now, Ferguson's face had remained a mask, but the major could not hide the revulsion. "Colonel Tarleton's actions I despise. Were I his commander, I would see him cashiered, if not hanged." Ferguson dismounted, and the ease with which the crippled man moved surprised Brodie. The Scot worked fast, unsheathing a strange rifle from a saddle scabbard, and Brodie leaped to his feet, bringing his blackened barrel up toward the major's chest, suddenly aware of at least a dozen muskets aimed in his direction.

Ferguson laughed. "As I announced, my intention is not to bring you harm," Ferguson said, "and I do not believe you could harm me . . . with that." His eyes sparkled, and Brodie pitched the destroyed weapon into the ashes behind him.

As soon as Brodie turned, Ferguson tossed the rifle sharply. Brodie caught it, noticing the major's measured smile, and stared at the strange rifle.

"It is of my own design, breechloading . . . ."

"What?" Brodie couldn't hide his confusion.

"You will learn, if you join us. If not, I will bid you good day after we see to your brother."

Chapter Two

There were times—more often it seemed, these days—when Marty McKidrict hated being a woman.

Blood trickled from her nose and over her lips, the salty taste familiar to her as she sat on the floor, body trembling, the cabin reeling as her husband towered over her, shouting in rage.

"Fraise! Is that the best you can do, woman? I come home from a hunt, bring a guest to sup with us, and you have the gall to serve bacon fraise?"

The next voice sounded almost comical, and Marty would have smiled, although without humor, were it not for the price that disrespect would have cost her.

"Seb, I like bacon fraise."

For a moment, she thought that might save her, for now her husband turned his rage on his companion.

"You like fraise. You like fraise. Glory to His Majesty, Willie Duncan likes fraise. Well, eat it, eat it all."

Sebastian McKidrict towered over most men, while Willie Duncan had to look up at Marty. The bruising man shoved Duncan toward the rough-hewn table, tossed a plate full of the pancakes, now cold, in front of the nearest table, drew his knife from the sheath, and buried the blade an inch deep beside the plate. "Eat your fraise, Willie. 'Tis probably made from hog corn."

Seb took a long pull from a clay jug, wiped his mouth with the coarse sleeve of his hunting frock, and whirled. "Up, woman!"

he demanded. "Up from the filth. Up, or by thunder I shall tear off your arm."

The drink had hold of him. Drink and the Devil. She wiped away the blood and slowly made herself stand, letting the dizziness pass before looking into his blazing blue eyes. Behind him sat Willie Duncan, devouring the pancakes she had cooked only minutes earlier and washing them down with rum from his own brown jug.

"Look around you, woman. Look at the squalor I live in. By Jupiter, I should have left you back on the Yadkin. Wife? Dogs and Cherokees make better companions than a bony little strumpet like you."

She had to guess what reaction he wanted. To fight back? To cry? To grab a broom and begin cleaning? Fight back? That had worked when she had first arrived at his place on the Tiger, the first time she had seen him when the rum brought on his rage. "Do not come in here full of kill devil and raise voice or fist at me, Seb McKidrict," she had told him. "I clean your house, patch your drawers, and feed your dogs, but I sha'n't bandy words to any man when rum is on his breath." That time, Seb McKidrict had laughed, let out a rollicking, good howl that even made Marty grin before he staggered off to the corncrib and slept till he had sobered. Yet, now that she had been his wife for fourteen months, Marty realized that perhaps he had only laughed that time because she held the Deckard rifle in her arms.

Seb McKidrict wasn't always the fool. He had seen Marty shoot, had often bragged at her marksmanship, and had won more than his share of shillings and noggins of rum on their journey from the Yadkin to the Tiger by betting that she could split a .50-caliber ball on an axe blade and drill the targets on either side of the tool. That's how they had met, on the Forks of the Yadkin, when her father had brought her to shoot against the best men of the backcountry, or at least those who had showed up at the settlement with their long rifles and an itch to prove their prowess. He hadn't been drunk then, Seb McKidrict, and his eyes danced with passion that made Marty confident. She had always been confident with a Deckard rifle, but never with boys, not even her brothers or father. Seb had doffed his cap, run his fingers through that rough black beard and thick hair, and mumbled a few words that Marty had smiled at, even if she hadn't really understood a word the big oaf said.

That had been in the spring of 1778. Seb McKidrict had taken off for the Tiger, and Marty, duly recorded champion shooter of Oliver's Settlement, had returned with her father and brothers to Sinclair Hollow. The next time she had seen Seb McKidrict was the following spring, when he came to the river with a proposal of marriage and mule laden with sundry items, rum, deer hides, and Spanish *pesos*.

Proposal? It had been more like bartering, her father and Seb McKidrict, both well in their cups, haggling over a fair price. Once they shook on the offer, her father had sent her youngest brother to fetch the Methodist preacher, even though they were Presbyterians, and Sebastian McKidrict had taken Martha Anne Sinclair as his wife. She didn't love him, but the way he talked she had expected a better life with him than serving as a scullery maid—when not hunting or target shooting—for a brood of hungry Yadkin River Sinclairs who had sent her mother to Glory before Margaret Sinclair had seen thirty-two winters.

The second time Marty had stood up to her husband, he had beaten her, had almost killed her, cracking ribs, breaking her nose, and leaving her in a pool of her own blood before storming out of the cabin and heading to Milton's Tavern. He did not show up again for more than a month.

Such became the pattern. Seb McKidrict would return, full of kill devil, looking for an argument, and the beatings would begin. Then, he would disappear, only to reappear just when Marty had begun to think that, maybe, this time he had died. For a while, she tried to please him, thinking she had done something wrong. She didn't know a thing about being a wife, couldn't ask her mother who had died before Marty turned five, and the McKidrict cabin lay in the thick of the Tiger. No neighbors to speak of. No friends, except the sorry lot that Seb sometimes brought home.

Her husband was *banditti*, the kind the Regulators had driven out of the Long Canes, the kind her brothers were bound to become. The plunder he had used to buy Marty from her father had been stolen, and the only time she had ever felt sorry for Seb McKidrict had been that fall, when he had stumbled home with a ball in his shoulder, sobbing that he would die without ever being loved. She had bathed the wound with rum, drained it, dug out the flattened piece of lead, and cauterized the ugly mess with Seb's own knife. He had left a few days later, without ever thanking her. Well, he hadn't beaten her that time.

"What's the matter, woman?" Seb goaded her now. "Did I wed a woman deaf and dumb?"

She wouldn't fight back, nor would she try to read his mind, grab the broom, start sweeping. That would just fuel his rage, for she had done just that months before, and he had broken a broomstick over her back, cursing her for stirring up dust over his breakfast.

Cry? No, Seb McKidrict had never seen her cry, and never would. She had cried plenty, from the pain, from her shame, from her own misery, but never in front of him, only after he had disappeared into the forest. Besides, she had no tears left, had not shed one in six months.

Instead, Marty McKidrict stared at her husband, not blinking, not challenging. One day, he would wind up killing her, and then she would have her revenge, if someone learned of her fate and hanged Seb McKidrict as a wife-beater and murderer.

Silence became her protector, but Willie Duncan ended the spell.

"Let's go to Milton's, Seb," he said, sliding the chair legs across the warped planks—McKidrict's idea of luxury since most homes had dirt floors—and standing as he dabbed his mouth with his bandanna. "I have a taste for geneva of mint."

"Aye." He looked at Duncan but spoke to Marty. "This place better not smell of rot and dirt when we return, woman. A husband has a right to desire a home that is clean."

With a nod—anything to be rid of him—Marty turned, testing her nose gently. She yelled when his right hand clamped her shoulder, his powerful fingers digging underneath the collar bone, bruising her flesh, jerking her back to face him.

"No one, man nor woman but especially not my wife, turns while I am speaking!" Seb shouted. He shoved her against the wall, banging her head against the logs, and she groaned, cursing her own stupidity. He had been looking for an excuse, and she had given him one. She had turned her back on him, giving him an opportunity.

He struck her again, and the trickle from her nose became a torrent. She tried to block his next blow, but wasn't fast enough. His right hand crushed her throat, squeezing tighter, and her brain screamed for air. Her eyes widened with the realization that this time he might just kill her.

Willie Duncan stood beside them now, saying something she couldn't understand, maybe pleading, pawing at Seb's thick arms. Seb shoved him aside, releasing his grip, and Marty slipped from his grasp, trying to find the door, to run. She took a few steps before Seb's fingers grabbed her and pulled. The muslin chemise ripped as she crashed against the table, overturned it, and fell to the floor.

She rolled over, groaning, on her back, blinking away confusion and pain, till she saw them staring at her, Seb McKidrict holding the torn garment in his massive hands, which he carelessly let fall to the floor. The drunkenness had left Willie Duncan's eyes, and he stared at her with a violent hunger.

"Milton's can wait," Seb said dryly.

Marty reached for the knife, still stuck in the wooden table, tried desperately to pull it out, but the handle slipped from her fingers as they dragged her away.

Her screams woke Seb's dogs from their slumber outside until their brays echoed her own, as if those hounds were screaming with her, or maybe they were simply laughing at her, mocking her.

* * * * *

Light stretched through the open cabin door when she finally awoke, warming her face. Blood had matted her hair, caked her lips and face, and she moved stiffly, grunting as the dried blood stuck to the floor and pulled her hair as she tried to sit. A spasm shot through her body, and she leaned against the wall, thinking she might retch, but the nausea passed.

She inched up the wall, pulling herself to her feet, kicking off the remains of her ripped, blood-stained clothing, discovering other injuries. A rib had been broken, and her searching tongue found a missing tooth. After staggering to the open door, Marty made herself reach up, biting back the pain until she had lifted the Deckard rifle off its mounts. It felt like a cannon in her aching arms, but she pulled the firelock to half cock and sprinkled powder from a horn hanging beside the door into the rifle's pan. She shut the pan, and stuck the stock of the rifle underneath her armpit, the curly maple cold against her skin. The Deckard was always charged and loaded, but she had learned the necessity of keeping the powder in the pan fresh.

Only a few items had she brought with her from Sinclair Hollow, her mother's wedding ring and the Deckard rifle. The ring was long gone. Seb had almost broken her finger prying it off to trade at Milton's for a firkin of ale. The long rifle, though, remained her one friend, her protector. It was light, graceful, the way she had always wanted to be, with a forty-four-inch rifled barrel and crescent butt plate that fit as if that Pennsylvania German had made it especially for her. Only she didn't know who had originally owned the long rifle. Her father had brought it home years ago, before the Regulators had chased him out of the Long Canes and the Sinclairs had settled on the Yadkin.

After slinging the powder horn and shot pouch over her bare shoulder, she grabbed an oval-eye tomahawk and stepped into the afternoon sunlight.

She must look foolish, she thought, naked except for shoes, bloodied and bruised like some disfigured ogre, carrying a long rifle and tomahawk. Marty didn't care. She scanned the yard. No horses, no dogs, and, most importantly, no sign of either Seb or Willie Duncan. Most likely they wouldn't be back, not for another month or more, if that, but she wouldn't be caught unprepared, just in case.

The sun felt good, but not cleansing, as she crossed the yard and found the path in the woods. At first, she moved with a purpose, despite the broken rib, but soon she slowed, suddenly exhausted, her muscles cramping, head spinning. For the last 200 yards, she needed to use the rifle as a crutch, moving warily past the rhododendron hells and blackberry brambles until she finally reached the pool along the cascading creek.

A woodpecker's nervous beating answered a hawk's shrill cry, and then she leaned the Deckard against a granite boulder, set the powder horn, pouch, and tomahawk on the ground nearby, and slipped into the chilling water.

She blacked out momentarily, but soon found the water soothing, relaxing, even warming. Marty bathed her face, soaked her black, tangled hair, and rested her head against a wet rock, just where the rays of sunlight crept around the menagerie of limbs and leaves and warmed her face.

Cupping her hands, Marty drank gingerly and remembered. Once, when she had first arrived, she had killed an eight-point buck at this pool, dressed it, and carted the meat back to the house, but now she could never bring herself to kill any animal, even for venison, at this place. It was her sanctuary, hallowed ground.

Briefly she cried—her first tears in months—but the ducts suddenly blocked. She wanted to escape, to get away from the clutches of Seb McKidrict, but she had no place to run. This country was as foreign to her as the revolution the King's army and so-called Patriots were fighting, far, far from the frontier.

One day, though, she'd have to run, or let Seb kill her—or kill him.

A squirrel scurried down a pine across the creek, considered her for a minute, then stood on its hind legs and began gnawing on an acorn. It stopped instantly when the hawk cried again, studied Marty as if she had made the noise, then bolted up the pine and leaped from limb to limb until it had disappeared.

Silence descended, and a cloud blocked the sun. She heard nothing now but the rushing creek, and she found herself marveling at how easy it would be to slip into the deepest part of the pool. How far, Marty wondered, would the Tiger carry her from perdition?

Chapter Three

Loyalists called Major Patrick Ferguson "Bulldog"—and with good reason. Stuart Brodie had never seen anyone so driven; the major had more fortitude than Brodie himself. He drilled his volunteers relentlessly, teaching them how to maintain formation, load, fire, and fight with bayonet, shrieking commands by a pair of silver whistles that dangled from rawhide thongs around his neck. In the blazing heat of a sultry Carolina summer, the settlers-turned-soldiers—even Brodie—cursed those whistles, yet they never showed Ferguson, Inspector of Militia in the Southern Provinces, any disrespect.

Which amazed Brodie. Backcountry folk were not used to any sort of regimen, especially military discipline. He expected his fellow soldiers to desert, half figured he would run out one night, but no one left. Those white men around him even seemed eager to learn how to fight properly. Maybe they found strength in numbers, or maybe they wanted to be loyal to Major Ferguson, if not the Crown. The Loyalists respected Ferguson, admired him. So did Brodie. The Bulldog asked nothing of his men that he would not do himself, and, one-handed or not, he often did what he asked better than his troops.

"We are the western flank of Lord Cornwallis's army," Ferguson told them. "If we fail, the King fails. Cornwallis, Sir Clinton, even King George, I dare say, think of this militia as a band of ruffians. But I know better. I believe in you, that you will do your duty." Every night in camp, Ferguson gave some variation of that speech to his exhausted legion. It worked without fail.

They drilled, and they marched over Indian trails, through thickets, fighting the brambles and heat while searching for rebels. Only those brigands proved elusive. They fought like Indians, hitting from ambush, then disappearing. It had to discourage the Bulldog—certainly it discouraged Brodie and his fellow soldiers, and not only because they hadn't caught up with their enemy. No, the way Brodie figured it, if they finally fought a battle, they wouldn't have to drill so much.

* * * * *

Muscles aching, Brodie sat near the picketed horses and mules, studying the rifle he had been trying to master in the months since joining Ferguson's army. It had a rifled barrel, in .65 caliber, and loaded from the breech rather than the muzzle. A trained soldier could fire four shots per minute while marching, Ferguson said, and consistently hit a target 200 yards distant. So far, Brodie had managed to fire, consistently, only three times a minute. Hitting his target, well, that had never been troublesome.

Closing his eyes and pulling himself to his feet, Brodie worked the rifle. He turned the trigger guard clockwise, lowered the barrel slightly, and dropped a ball inside the opening. Next, he grabbed the powder horn and pretended to pour in a charge, returned the trigger guard to close the plug, and let out a short breath. *Prime, cock, fire*, he told himself.

"When you can do this blindfolded," Captain Abraham DePeyster had told him, "I will consider you a soldier of the Crown."

Brodie's eyes opened, and his face flushed. A dozen or more weary Loyalists stared at him, and Brodie sat down.

He couldn't understand why the major had given him his invention. That crippled right arm prevented Ferguson from using the rifle himself, but why give it to a freedman, a man he didn't even know? Why not Captain DePeyster? Why not any of the other soldiers, most of them armed with Brown Bess muskets or their own fowling pieces?

After cleaning the weapon, Brodie stretched out to rest, but, as soon as he had closed his eyes, a shadow crossed his face and he looked up to see DePeyster towering above him.

DePeyster was part of Ferguson's corps of American Volunteers, mostly New Jersey and New York settlers who had served with the major since December. These were Ferguson's right hand, maybe not trained in England but more professional, better disciplined than the Carolina Loyalists.

"The major desires an interview with you," the captain said, and was gone.

* * * * *

He found Ferguson shirtless in his tent, being attended by Dr. Uzal Johnson, another one of the American Volunteers. The young surgeon from New Jersey pulled a leech off the major's crippled arm and stuck it in a dark jar.

"Brodie!" Ferguson exclaimed, and sat on the cot, dismissing the doctor while pulling on a shirt. "How well do you know this country?"

They were camped on the Enoree River at Musgrove's Mill, not far from the North Carolina border. "'Tis not unfamiliar to me, this country." He had fished the Enoree often, set traps upstream and down, and traded with the Catawbas not too distant.

"I need someone to scout, to report back to me when the rebels are in close proximity."

"They are close now, Major."

Ferguson slipped his arm into a sling and gave Brodie a hard stare.

"I can feel them," Brodie explained. "Smell them."

With a snort, Ferguson shook his head. "Negro superstitions," he said impatiently.

"Backcountry experience," Brodie shot back, adding softly, "sir. In this country I have resided since 'Sixty-Eight, Major," he went on, "and I know more than a little of the men we pursue. They are also chasing you, and our army is too big to go unnoticed."

"But they will not fight," Ferguson said. "They are nothing more than cowards, and their cause is lost, after Charles Town and Camden. Nonetheless, I desire to employ your services as a scout. Find out just how close the *banditti* are, learn their strength and location, and report back to me." His tone lost its severity. "How is my rifle?"

"I'm learning, sir."

"Good." Ferguson poured himself a drink, and did not offer Brodie the whiskey. "You can leave at first light. Is there anything else?"

He shuffled his feet. Since he had joined the militia, he had heard the stories about Ferguson, camp gossip, maybe, but some of the soldiers who had been with Ferguson up north swore it was true. Brodie had always been curious. "Well, Major, I was wondering . . . ."

Ferguson drained the whiskey, and set the glass down. "Aye?"

"Is it true?"

The laugh proved infectious, and Ferguson poured another drink and collapsed on his bed. He must have been asked that question scores of times. "I cannot say," he said. "Mayhap, mayhap not. 'Twas at Brandywine in September of 'Seventy-Seven, and I lay alongside the woods with my men, holding my rifle . . . your rifle . . . when two of the enemy appeared, one in a hussar dress, the other in green and blue on a fine stone horse of bay color, wearing a high cocked hat. I ordered their deaths, had my best three shots take aim, but I found no honor in that, no glory, and the order sickened me, so I belayed it. Instead, I advanced toward the rebel in the cocked hat . . . by then, the Frenchman had departed . . . and called at him to surrender. He disregarded my invitation, gave me a look of contempt, and turned back toward the rebel lines. I could have shot him, killed him, put three balls in his back before he reached safety, but he was such a brave man, I spared his life."

"So, it is true?" Brodie asked.

"I cannot say. The next day, while Doctor Johnson and others were working on this"—he nodded at his mangled arm—"I was informed that the man in the blue and green, the one who had acquitted himself so bravely, was indeed George Washington, that the general was attended by a French officer in hussar dress. Perhaps it was. But I am not sorry that I belayed my order, am not sorry that I did not know the brave soldier's identity. I will provide you with written orders before breakfast, Brodie. You can read?"

"Read and write," Brodie answered.

* * * * *

The owl woke him in the grayness, only it wasn't an owl. Brodie rolled to his side, grabbed the rifle, and began whistling for the sentries, trying desperately to wake the men closest him. A horse whinnied nervously, and Brodie saw the shadow, not ten yards before him. He pulled back the hammer while bringing the stock tightly against his right shoulder.

A muzzle flash blinded him in the darkness, an instant before he pulled the trigger and heard his own rifle bark, and the ball tore into the tree beside him, peppering his face with bark.

"Rebels!" Brodie screamed. "Rebels are amongst us!"

He didn't realize it, but he had already reloaded the rifle and fired a second shot, even though he could barely see. This time, he heard a man cry out in pain. "Rebels!" Brodie repeated. Screeching blasts of Ferguson's whistles answered Brodie's cry.

Brodie charged, firing, barely stopping to reload. He stumbled across one writhing body, and kicked the man's face. Blocking out the noise of the battle around him, Ferguson's whistles, the screams and unnerving yells of the attackers, the ringing in his ears, Brodie remembered Ezekiel's body and the burned inn. With a curse, he charged and fired, charged and fired.

"Brodie!"

He stopped, blinking away confusion, mouth suddenly parched, and saw Captain DePeyster not two feet from him.

"Fall in formation," DePeyster ordered. "The enemy is retreating, and we shall smash him."

Brodie stepped aside, trying to absorb what had happened. He wanted water, or rum, and ran his tongue over his cracked lips. *I must have gone mad,* he thought, watching, as if almost detached, as the line of troops, American Volunteers, and South Carolina Loyalists, marched after the fleeing rebels who disappeared in the thickets near the river.

The whistle cried, and DePeyster, or some other officer, barked out the order: "Fix bayonets!"

The New Jersey and New York troops slotted their sixteen-inch blades against the barrels of their muskets while back-country volunteers had whittled down their knife handles and made them fit.

"For the Crown!" Ferguson shouted. "For your honor!"

Realization staggered Brodie. He had almost made the mistake Ferguson was about to by charging after the handful of rebels who had stormed the camp. He could see the hint of sunlight.

"Major!" Brodie found his voice and darted to Ferguson. "It's a trap, sir!"

"A trap these *banditti* have wrought," Ferguson said, and blasted the whistle.

"Charge!"

Brodie shouted, tugging at Ferguson's good arm. He wanted to explain how men fought on the frontier, how he had fought against Cherokees and plunderers.

"Cowards I will not abide, Brodie!" Ferguson screamed. "By God, I will have you hanged!"

Staggering back, Brodie watched the army march into the dawn.

* * * * *

Ferguson's head bowed as he left Doctor Johnson's wagon, and collapsed on a fallen pine, DePeyster at his side. The screams of men echoed around them, and Ferguson lifted his gaze, shaking his head in response to something DePeyster had said, and looked at Stuart Brodie.

"I spoke words in the heat of battle," Ferguson said, his voice dry, drained of emotion, exhausted. "I withdraw them. You are no coward, Brodie, and I now order you to remind me of my

own arrogance whenever you see fit. Negro superstitions, bah!"
He turned back to the captain. "What are our losses?"

"Sixty-three dead, Major. Ninety wounded. Somewhere
between fifty and seventy missing or captured."

"And theirs?"

DePeyster shrugged. "We have found four dead, and have
three wounded prisoners."

Ferguson swore, but he stood and approached Brodie, forcing
a smile. "Belay those orders I issued last night, Brodie. I think we
have found the enemy."

"Do we pursue, Major?" DePeyster asked.

Ferguson looked again at Brodie, as if asking for advice.

"They will just scatter, Major," Brodie said, "like leaves in the
wind."

"Like brigands." Ferguson spat. "No need to give chase,
Captain," he said after a moment. "Let them run. We know
where they are going." He whirled, striding toward his tent, but
stopped and pivoted, facing Brodie again.

"The rebel prisoners will be treated humanely. You will see to
that, Brodie. Not one hair on their heads is to be harmed."

* * * * *

Gilbert Town had been settled near Second Broad Brook, a haven
for rebels and Loyalists, depending on who had the stronger force
at the time. Like many backcountry settlements, it wasn't much
to look at, just a few log cabins, outhouses, more pigs than people. Scotch-Irish and Germans had settled here, most of them
loyal to King George. A year or so back, Rutherford County had
been formed, carved out of old Tryon County, and the town
founded by William Gilbert had become something of the center

of law and order, although lately a person would be hard-pressed to find any law, and certainly not much order.

Rebels came, then fled. British forces came, then went after the rebels, who came back until word came that the King's men were returning.

Brodie rode in, weary, leading the prisoners in from the Broad Brook Road after crossing at Denard's Ford. The rebel horde had vanished again—no surprise to Brodie. What shocked him was when he learned the date: September 7th. He had been with Ferguson for, what, four months?

Ferguson's army, routed in the ambush, remained a threat to the rebels, but needed rest, needed supplies. Most importantly, the major needed new men. Rebels had bloodied the militia, and Ferguson's pride, at Musgrove's Mill. The New Jersey doctor turned the local tavern into a hospital; William Gilbert's cabin became Ferguson's headquarters.

While Brodie oversaw the handful of prisoners, Ferguson listened to any information the Loyalists might have.

John Sevier, Isaac Shelby, and Colonel James Williams had been at Gilbert Town, with dozens of British prisoners and a bunch of whooping, drunken rioters celebrating their deception at Musgrove's Mill. Then, like cowards, after learning of Ferguson's approach, they scattered, Williams taking the prisoners on to Hillsborough, and Sevier and Shelby retreating back across the Blue Ridge Mountains.

Brodie prayed Ferguson would pursue, although he knew they wouldn't, couldn't. Gilbert Town would become the Loyalist militia's camp, and Stuart Brodie groaned at what that would mean.

Manual exercise—wheeling—marching—bayonet drill—and Major Ferguson's unholy whistles.

* * * * *

Brodie hadn't seen much of Ferguson, although he had certainly heard those horrible whistles enough, since arriving at Gilbert Town, so he was surprised when he was ordered to report to Ferguson's cabin and bring along a rebel prisoner, Samuel Phillips, who had been captured at Musgrove's Mill. Phillips's face remained bruised from Brodie's savage kick during that fight.

"Mister Brodie can read, Phillips," Ferguson said when the two entered the cabin. "Can you?"

No answer. The rebel just picked at the dirty bandage that covered his bare head and bloodied left ear.

"No matter. I am paroling you, Phillips, on the condition that you deliver a message to your countrymen. If you cannot remember it, well, I have written it on parchment. I trust someone in that backwater country can read. Mister Brodie?"

Brodie took the parchment curiously, unrolled it, and read it silently, then aloud, after Ferguson's order.

To Isaac Shelby, John Sevier, and the officers on the Western waters called the Watauga, Nolachucky, and Holston:

If you do not desist from your opposition to the arms of the British Crown, I will march my army over the mountains, hang your leaders, and lay your country to waste with fire and sword.

Patrick Ferguson
Major
71st Regiment

Ferguson's handwriting was as sweeping as Brodie's own.

Brodie rolled the paper, secured it with a thong, and presented it to the paroled prisoner.

Samuel Phillips, who had stopped fingering the bandage, found his voice. "You're a fool, Ferguson. A bigger fool than that butcher Tarleton."

"You are dismissed, Phillips, and you would be wise to hold your tongue before I put you in stocks and send some other brigand on my errand."

The prisoner darted out the cabin, leaving Brodie staring at Ferguson.

"Speak your mind, Brodie," Ferguson said. "Remember your orders."

Brodie tried to find the right words. They eluded him, so he just blurted it out: "It is not something I would have done, Major."

"It was nothing I would have done were I fighting honorable men, Brodie," Ferguson replied. "But I am tired of these cowards. They fight like savages, yell like savages. Mark my words, I despise Colonel Tarleton, but perchance I see something now to his methods. You do not treat cockroaches like men. You squash them with your boot heels, and, if these fiends do not desist with their banditry, I mean what I said. I will cross the mountains and put them all to the sword or hang them as thieves."

Brodie shook his head. "You won't have to cross the Blue Ridge. Once they get your message, Major, those boys will come looking for you."

Chapter Four

September's winds and rain foretold an early winter. Already maple and oak leaves had lost their brilliance and begun turning brown, carpeting the mountains. The coolness of the morning and gray sky matched Marty McKidrict's mood as she sat near the pigpen, cleaning a half dozen squirrels with detached interest. Methodically she would slice the stiff fur around the dead animal's head and limbs, then cleanly peel back the skin and toss it on the rough-hewn bench where she prepared fish and meat, churned butter, stitched buckskins, and sometimes just sat, stared and dreamed. After gutting a squirrel, she would throw the entrails and head to the hogs, and the carcass into a bowl of water. She'd fry the squirrels tonight for supper, and what she didn't eat she would put into a stew for tomorrow.

She had taken Seb's squirrel rifle that morning, instead of her Deckard, which was too large a caliber for shooting squirrels. Besides, Seb never used the rifle, never even bothered to clean it, and the handsome piece would likely have rusted away had Marty not taken care of it. The rifle leaned against the rails of the pigpen.

A hog grunted.

"You're next," she told him, and tossed the last squirrel into the water.

Butchering hogs—that was work for a man, but Marty had grown not only accustomed to the annual slaughter, but also packing the meat in salt for winter. Her father and brothers had shunned such work, any work, for that matter. So had that no-account husband of hers, wherever he was.

After tacking the six squirrel skins on the side of the privy to dry, she dipped her hands in the bowl and did her best to wash off the blood and grime, scrubbing herself clean, more or less, with coarse burlap.

A horse whickered, and Marty turned quickly, overturning the bowl, dumping the cleaned squirrels onto the bench. She spotted the rider, moving casually, long rifle cradled across his lap, and gasped. It wasn't her husband—too wiry to be Seb—but she had never had a visitor, except the sorry lot her husband brought over from time to time.

She grabbed the squirrel rifle and ran for the house, hearing the man's greetings, but ignoring them. The door slammed behind her, and she pulled in the latch string, slammed across the bolt, headed to the window, and replaced the smaller rifle with her Deckard.

"Hello!" an Irish voice called. "I didn't mean to alarm you, Mister McKidrict."

Mister! Marty laughed softly. Well, she certainly didn't look like a woman, not in greasy buckskins and hunting frock, not with her matted hair, and not with the nose Seb had busted during his drunken riots.

"I am Flint O'Keeffe, and bring word from John Sevier. I desire just a few minutes of your time, Seb."

"I'm not Seb!" she yelled back. "And I know neither Flint O'Keeffe nor John Sevier." Actually she had heard Sevier's name mentioned by Seb and his friends, usually in contempt, which meant John Sevier was in all likelihood a decent sort.

"I . . . I thought this was the McKidrict claim . . . I . . . ."

"It is. I just ain't Seb! I'm . . . ." Being a woman alone caused her pause. "I'm Marty McKidrict." Her voice sounded raspy enough, thanks to the bruises Seb had left on her throat, plus her broken nose, that she probably didn't sound like a woman, either.

"Seb's brother?"

Marty snorted. "I wish," she whispered as a once-forgotten passage from Genesis flashed through her mind: *And it came to pass, when they were in the field, that Cain rose up against Abel his brother, and slew him.*

"Yeah, his brother. Now leave me be!"

"Mister McKidrict, please, just a few minutes. I bring news that concerns every man this side of the mountains, and, honestly, I am not one who cares to shout through closed doors."

Marty didn't reply.

"McKidrict, I am neither brigand nor fool. I can see those squirrels you shot. Head shot, it appears to me. I know when I am outclassed. My rifle is primed, but not cocked. Would you kindly, sir, open the door and allow us to converse as gentlemen?"

She smiled in spite of herself, removed the bolt, and opened the door, slightly at first, so that she could peer through the crack and make sure this O'Keeffe wasn't lying. He held the reins to a claybank mare in his left hand, long rifle in the right, although the stock had been butted on the ground. Pushing the door open with the barrel of her own rifle, Marty stepped through the doorway.

"A pleasure to meet you, Marty McKidrict," O'Keeffe said.

"Likewise." She spoke so low, though, she doubted if O'Keeffe heard.

Flint O'Keeffe's smile revealed white teeth through a black beard. He stood tall, dressed in a tan hunting frock and plain britches, Cherokee moccasins, and a black cocked hat that did its best to hide unruly, curly black hair that had been braided into a queue with a green piece of silk. His eyes looked blue, maybe green. From this distance, Marty couldn't tell, but he certainly carried himself well. He looked even downright handsome, at least better-looking than her husband or the scoundrels he brought by the cabin, or any of her brothers for that matter.

"Thank you," O'Keeffe said. "My poor voice is hoarse enough."

Her effort to reply failed. Did he want a drink of whiskey or tea? Seb hadn't left any rum behind; he rarely did. Tea had become scarce what with the taxes and boycott. Besides, this man was a Whig, and Whigs preferred coffee over tea. Drinking coffee was patriotic. Not that it mattered—she had no coffee in the cabin, either. *Where is your hospitality?* Marty thought. *Invite him in*, but she couldn't bring herself to do that. Besides, deep down, she knew what had happened to her hospitality. Marty had been living with rogues far too long, first her father and brothers, and lately Seb McKidrict. Good manners, it seemed, had died with her mother years ago. She worked her jaws again, rolled her tongue, but words again eluded her. Inwardly she cursed herself, that lack of confidence.

O'Keeffe broke the silence. "I didn't know Seb had a brother living here," he said.

"You know my . . . brother?"

"No. His acquaintance I have never made. I am new to these mountains, from Virginia originally and more recently . . . well, I know John Sevier and call him a friend. It was John . . . Colonel Sevier, I should say . . . who asked me to send word of a gathering at Sycamore Shoals."

Marty knew of that place on the Watauga, where the Doe River converged. Since colonists had first crossed over the mountains, Sycamore Shoals had been an important gathering place, and the Cherokees had treated there long before any white presence. Treaties had been signed, couples married, games played, battles fought. The great Transylvania Purchase had been brokered at the Shoals, and Dragging Canoe's Cherokees had attacked Fort Watauga there only a few short years back. Of course, Seb had never taken her to the Watauga, never let her socialize, meet other women, see children.

O'Keeffe kept talking about the duty of all men, the war against the King, but Marty didn't feel like listening to politics.

"Mister O'Keeffe," she said, "nary a whit I care about taxes, about representation, about the rights of Whigs or Tories. All I want to do is make it through the winter. This war is not mine. It's a war of arrogant . . . ." She almost said *men*.

"It's a war for justice, Marty McKidrict," O'Keeffe jumped in. "And it does pertain to you, for Major Patrick Ferguson of the British army has sent word from Gilbert Town that he will lay waste to our country and hang us all. Such threats the men and women who trekked over the Blue Ridge will not abide."

"If this Ferguson comes here, threatens me, mayhap I will fight him. Until then . . . ."

"He is coming, McKidrict. Coming with a thousand Tories, and I dare say that number is more than even you can shoot. All I ask, neighbor, is for you to join us at Sycamore Shoals on the Twenty-Fifth and hear the words of John Sevier and Isaac Shelby." He grinned. "Never yet met an over-mountain man who sent his regrets to an invitation to drink, dance, trade, eat, and listen to some stumping."

"Never been to the Shoals," she heard herself saying. "You'd have to draw me a map."

He eyed her curiously, but walked to his horse, tucking the long rifle underneath his arm, and opened a bag behind the saddle. O'Keeffe worked, his back to her, and Marty wet her lips, wondering what this Irishman was doing. After a few minutes, he turned, placed the rifle on the ground, and approached the cabin. He held a piece of paper in his hand. A map.

Marty stepped back, feeling tricked. Now he had reason to be close to her. She thought about raising the rifle, but couldn't. Her throat turned dry as he stopped a few feet from her and held out his hand. She jerked the map from his fingers and shoved it inside her hunting frock.

"I thank you," she said.

O'Keeffe didn't move. His hand remained outstretched.

"I am Flint O'Keeffe," he said again. "It is a pleasure to meet you, Marty McKidrict."

The hand still didn't waver, even as O'Keeffe let out a riotous laugh.

"You are the most singular individual I have met since leaving Williamsburg." He shook his head, but the hand still remained, waiting.

Marty clasped it, and felt his strong grip. The handshake was curt, but friendly.

"I hope to see you at Sycamore Shoals," he said. "The cause of liberty could use one whose aim is as true as yours."

She thought about inviting him to supper, but elected not to. Maybe he was a gentleman, but she didn't trust him, didn't know him, and, well, it wouldn't be pleasant for anyone if Seb came home and caught them alone.

After he left and she made sure he had indeed gone, Marty stared at the map he had drawn. With a snort, she crumpled it in her fist, tossed it on the floor, and went to gather the squirrels. As if she'd ever go to Sycamore Shoals.

* * * * *

Two nights later, she gathered kindling and dry leaves to start the fire, and looked at the wadded piece of paper beside the door. It would burn as well as straw, twigs, or leaves, but Marty couldn't bring herself to jam it in the cabin's stone fireplace.

After placing the cast-iron pot over the coals to heat up leftover stew, she picked up the map Flint O'Keeffe had drawn for her, smoothed it out on the table, and sat down, studying it.

She couldn't read—maybe had her mother lived. The Sinclairs, with the exception of Margaret and her nightly Bible readings that Marty vaguely recalled, never saw a need in reading or writing, and, if Seb McKidrict had any education, he kept it well hidden. Yet the map seemed plain enough: northwest through the gap, over the knob to the Piney Flats pike, and to the convergence of the Doe and Watauga. On foot, with good weather, she could make it there in two days.

"'Dreaming does nobody no good,'" she said out loud, quoting her father, and snatched the map. She planned on wadding it up one final time and tossing it into the fire, yet again something stopped her.

Months ago, after Seb's most vicious beating, she had dreamed of escaping her husband's clutches. What had stopped her? She had nowhere to run, only here was a map, a way out of a bad marriage. Stay here? And do what? Wait for Seb McKidrict to kill her? It wouldn't hurt, she thought, just to walk to Sycamore Shoals and listen to what this John Sevier had to say. Meet other wives. In all likelihood, she would return to the Tiger before Seb came back from one of his raids or drunken forays. If she did return. Maybe even find someone who would take her . . . where? Back to Sinclair Hollow? Her brothers and father might not beat her, but living with those outlaws, who considered her more chattel than sister, had no appeal. Charles

Town, perhaps, or back to Ninety-Six. John Sevier's army might need a laundress.

She laughed at that idea. When was the last time she had bathed? Her clothes reeked of animals, sweat, and dirt. Dirt covered her face. Even Flint O'Keeffe had failed to recognize her as a woman.

Go as a man.

"Bah," she said of that fleeting idea, and went to the fireplace to fetch her supper.

* * * * *

Sleep came hard, and, when exhaustion finally overtook her, it proved a fitful sleep. She woke, still tired, before dawn, pulled on her buckskins, got the coffee boiling, and began prying up loose floorboards, working at a furious pace to keep from thinking about what she was doing. For Seb McKidrict, wooden floors were not really a luxury, but a hiding place. Despite his claim, he hadn't floored the cabin to woo Martha Anne Sinclair. She found the escape tunnel, in case Regulators arrived, and his stash of plunder: jewelry, a few gold teeth, a watch, silver cross, buttons, and three Cherokee scalps, but no hard money. She did see a powder horn—five, in fact—lead bars, cartridge boxes, leather pouches, molds, one broad sword, and three pistols. She chose the lightest pistol, long-barreled, probably French-made, maybe weighing a pound and a half, and found a pouch containing two dozen lead balls that matched the pistol's caliber.

She hurriedly packed jerky and biscuits into a sack, along with a fairly clean extra shirt, awl, sinew, pewter cup, hairbrush, and one of Seb's clay pipes. She tried to braid her hair into a queue in the fashion of these backcountry colonists, pulled on a wide-brimmed hat, and took her own hunting equipment, canteen, and the Deckard rifle.

After opening the gate to the pen and letting the pigs free, Marty went back inside the cabin and caught her breath. She picked up Flint O'Keeffe's map, slid it into a pocket, and walked outside. *Last chance to let your cowardice show,* she thought, *and stay here.*

Marty spit on the cabin's floor before slamming the door.

Chapter Five

Wading across the shallows of the Watauga River, Marty McKidrict stared in disbelief.

Even had Flint O'Keeffe not drawn her a map, she would have found the gathering spot, for Marty had smelled smoke from all the bonfires and cook fires since yesterday, and heard the rambunctious noise the past couple of hours. Only now, the smoke didn't smell so pungent, but carried the aroma of fry bread, bacon, and beef, and the noise, while louder, sounded of frivolity—music, laughter, and long rifles fired not in anger, but to win bets. The scene reminded Marty of the shooting contests back on the Yadkin, only those affairs, although closer to the larger settlements, had never attracted this many people. It seemed as if thousands of backcountry pioneers had swarmed to Sycamore Shoals.

Tents, lean-tos, and cabins dotted the ground. Hastily built corrals held hundreds of horses, and cattle grazed in the distance. People were everywhere. Marty doubted if the streets of Charles Town were this busy, at least not since that continental general surrendered his army to the British this past spring.

A beaming backwoodsman helped her onto the bank, pumping her hand vigorously with a grip that almost crushed Marty's bones. "John Crockett," the man introduced himself. "Are you a Sullivan County man or a Washington County man?"

Marty told him her name, but had to think before answering Crockett's question. "Washington County," she said after a minute, although it was as much a guess as anything.

"Then you'll need to see Chucky Jack, or do you know Colonel Sevier?"

Her head shook meekly.

"Well, he sha'n't be hard to find," Crockett said. "He'll be the one cussing the mostest, spitting the farthest, and riding the hardest. That's a right handsome rifle, McKidrict."

She glanced at the Deckard.

"No offense, but you don't look big enough to tote it."

"I've toted it from the Tiger," she said. "And I hit what I aim at."

Crockett grinned. "You'll get a chance to prove that, McKidrict. Chucky Jack says too many folks have answered the call of duty. We can't take everyone with us to kill the Tories. Need to leave some militia to protect our womenfolk in case the English try to sic the Cherokees on us again." Crockett's eyes hardened. "Savages done kilt my father, backed by British swine."

They turned at the sound of splashing behind them to see another buckskinned figure crossing the Sycamore, and John Crockett waded into the water to shake the man's hand. Marty walked from the Sycamore into the crowd, hearing Crockett ask: "Are you a Sullivan County man or a Washington County man?"

She wasn't the only woman here, either, although, as far as she could tell, she was the only one passing herself off as a man. Underneath a clumsily constructed lean-to, two women sat spinning their looms, while Marty spotted a buxomly redhead saddle-stitching a pair of deer leggings. Others cooked, including a stout black woman who served her husband a plate full of cornbread and ham. The aroma sent pangs through Marty's stomach. She had eaten the last of her biscuits and jerky late last night.

Two heavy-set men almost knocked Marty down as they rolled across the wet ground, and a handful of others shoved her out of the way, cheering on or cursing at the two dirty, smelly wrestlers.

An ear-splitting whistle stopped the tumult, and Marty looked at a woman in muslin, her dark hair streaked with gray, standing in the driver's boot of a wagon.

"This ain't no jollification!" the woman shouted. "You boys come over here. There's work to be done."

Most of the men took off running, the woman's curses peppering the air as they fled, but the two wrestlers pulled themselves off the ground and, cowering, approached the woman, as did the black man, after handing his empty plate to his wife.

Marty turned to go, but the woman's deafening roar caused her to tremble and spin around.

"I said come here! I got work for you to do."

Marty just blinked.

"You aim to fight the Tories, don't you? Shoot a mess with that long rifle in your arms?"

Another blink.

"Well, you won't be killing nobody without me. Move. Get these barrels out of this wagon." She glanced at the sky. "Rain, or something worser or wetter, will be commencing shortly. Move!"

After resting the Deckard against the lean-to, Marty hurried to the wagon, grunting at the weight of the barrels as she helped the black man carry one and stack it in another tent. The two wrestlers carried one barrel each, and neither snorted nor complained as they stacked containers on the ground.

"Put that pipe down!" the woman shouted. "What the blazes are you, a Tory spy? That's four hundred pounds of powder I've brung, plus the makings for another hundred, and I didn't make it meself and haul it to the Shoals to get blown back to Buffalo

Creek. Get away from here, before I shove that pipe down your bloody throat!"

"Milling gunpowder is illegal, Mary McKeehan Patton!" a smooth voice called out. "Why, Major Patrick Ferguson will have you in stocks, if not drawn and quartered as an example to the rest of North Carolina."

"Patrick Ferguson can kiss my rebel arse," she replied. "As can you, Chucky Jack."

Colonel John Sevier laughed, then cursed and ordered a half dozen others to help unload the barrels.

"I ain't finished all of it, like I said," the woman told the colonel. "But I'll have the rest of it done before you and the boys take off. My powder burns fast, and hot as the fires of hell."

"Just like your tongue," Sevier said.

The last of the barrels unloaded and stacked, Marty walked to Sevier with trepidation. She matched his height, but couldn't equal his stare, or tongue. His chest was built like one of those kegs of gunpowder, but he moved like a panther, and, although he smiled and laughed often, Marty detected a seriousness about him, and a savageness.

"Mister . . . Colonel Sevier?" Marty tried to lower her voice an octave, but didn't think she succeeded, nervous as she was.

He studied her, but said nothing.

"John Crockett said I should make your acquaintance, er, report for . . . duty. I am Marty McKidrict from Tiger Creek."

Sevier frowned. "I know of a Seb McKidrict."

"My . . . brother."

He just stared.

"Flint O'Keeffe brought word, Colonel. I am here."

"Where's your rifle, McKidrict?"

She nodded toward the lean-to.

"Good. We need men to guard the settlements when we leave to find Ferguson. We shall muster you in for the home militia. Keep an eye out for Cherokees whilst we are gone. Daniel Andersen will be your commander." He spun on his heels and began marching away.

Marty's mouth trembled at this . . . this . . . *demotion*. When she heard Mary McKeehan Patton's laugh, and realized she was laughing at her, Marty grabbed her rifle and ran to catch up with Sevier.

"Sir!" She grabbed his shoulder, and Sevier whirled, unleashing a series of oaths, his face reddening, face masking in anger.

"I didn't walk two days to be told I ain't needed, Colonel Sevier!" Marty fired back.

"Damnation, I give the orders here!" Sevier thundered.

"Yes, you do. And I can shoot better than any man out here, I'm wagering."

"You're nothing but skin and bones."

"And I don't eat much." It was the only thing she could think to say. "Means more grub for the rest of you."

"Let me be blunt." Sevier placed both hands on his hips and leaned forward. His breath stank of rum and tobacco. "McKidrict is not a name I care much for in North Carolina."

"It sank like a stone with me, too, Colonel, but folks ain't got much of a say in their names, do they, Chucky Jack?"

Sevier's laugh surprised her, and he shook his head. "Washington County, you say?"

"Yes, sir."

"That's a good thing. If you hailed from Sullivan County, you would be under Colonel Shelby, and he is much more serious than I. One shot, McKidrict. We shall see if you speak the truth or brag. O'Keeffe!"

Her heart pounded as Flint O'Keeffe stepped into her line of vision and handed John Sevier a beautiful long rifle. "The knot on that elm," Sevier said as he aimed the rifle.

Quickly Marty followed the barrel and found the tree less than thirty yards away. Only thirty yards? Sevier must be joking. Even Seb McKidrict could hit a target as big as a knotty trunk from that distance. Marty had killed deer at better than 300 yards. The rifle boomed, and Sevier tossed it back to O'Keeffe.

"All right, McKidrict," Sevier said. "Cover my ball."

"What?"

"Vance," Sevier told another soldier. "Run to the tree, and point to where my ball struck. McKidrict, you will then cover my ball, hit that same mark. Do that, and I shall be happy to have you serve under me. Miss, and I shall buy you a noggin of rum after we whip Ferguson and his lot."

The pockmarked man named Vance took off running to the elm, and Marty waited, holding her breath. Vance, panting, examined the knot underneath a fork in the trunk. He looked harder.

"Quit dawdling!" Sevier yelled.

Another minute passed, and finally Vance looked up, cupped his hands, and shouted. "No hole can I find!"

John Sevier cursed Vance for a fool, but Flint O'Keeffe laughed.

"What amuses you so, Flint?" Sevier demanded.

"That you missed, Colonel."

Sevier cursed O'Keeffe, and stormed toward the elm.

O'Keeffe found the hole, not in the elm, but in an oak about ten rods beyond the target. Sevier's shot had gone high, missing the knot and passing between the forked trunk before thudding into the center of the oak.

"I shall shoot again," Sevier announced, but Marty was already walking away.

"No need," she said.

"What?" someone asked.

"Cover the ball," Marty said. "I believe that was the challenge. Have O'Keeffe stick a wad of cotton in the hole, give me something to see."

Sevier started to say something, probably to object, but Marty kept talking. "Just for a second. That's all I need."

She had reached the original firing position, and turned, butting the Deckard at her feet while watching, trying to look relaxed. She made out Flint O'Keeffe between the elm's knot, saw a bit of bright calico sticking out of the bark, and then O'Keeffe jerked it out and moved out of the way. Marty didn't blink, kept her focus on where the calico had been, as she shouldered the rifle, aimed, and fired.

John Sevier repeated one of his curses after Flint O'Keeffe, using his knife, dug out two chunks of flattened lead from the hole in the elm and placed the mangled balls in Sevier's opened palm. Then Sevier howled, flinging words and phrases Marty had never even heard her brothers use, at least not in the presence of a woman.

"You may out-shoot me, McKidrict," he said, "but I remain top dog in Washington County for cussing and riding. Consider yourself mustered in, with O'Keeffe's company. Now, go help Missus Patton mill her gunpowder."

Beaming, Marty thanked O'Keeffe and Sevier and made her way through the crowd of admirers, feeling their slaps against her back, enjoying their huzzahs. She felt an excitement, almost a giddiness that she had not experienced since winning her first match on the Yadkin years ago. Scarcely could she believe what she had done, had out-shot John Sevier, had won a place in the militia that planned on marching over the Blue Ridge to fight the enemy. She wasn't even sure she believed in the cause of the Whigs.

Suddenly she stopped, and found herself sweating despite the chill of autumn. Reality frightened her. She was doing it, leaving Seb McKidrict for good.

* * * * *

Sweat poured off Marty's face as she stood over the cast-iron pot, stirring the concoction Mrs. Patton had placed over the blazing coals. The unkempt woman assured Marty she had nothing to fear milling the black powder, but Marty wasn't sure. Maybe they wouldn't be blown to bits, but the rotting smell of the sulphur twisted Marty's stomach into knots. Mrs. Patton just stared at her, dipping snuff while filling kegs with the powder, unaffected by the stench. She hadn't spoken for an hour. Marty wiped her forehead with a rag, offered Mrs. Patton a weak smile, and stirred some more.

Mary McKeehan Patton wasn't the only person helping out the militias of Colonel Sevier and Colonel Shelby, who Marty had yet to meet. A settler named Baptist McNabb and another man named Mathew Talbot had brought ground corn and grain from their grist mills, donating wagonloads so the volunteer soldiers could make bread during the upcoming march over the mountains. Over around Bumpass Cove on the Nolichucky River, lead had been mined for rifle balls by a handful of John Sevier's neighbors. Practically any farmer with an extra cow or horse—and, in some cases, the farmer's only cow or horse—had been donated to the cause of liberty. Perhaps, Marty thought, she should have paid more attention to the talk of revolution, tried to understand what exactly was going on in the low country and other colonies, and why it was happening. Perhaps the colonists needed to separate from England. Certainly everyone at Sycamore Shoals thought they were in the right.

"What in the name of Jupiter are you doing here?" Mrs. Patton finally said.

"Ma'am?"

She spit. "Does your husband know what you're up to, *ma'am*?"

Marty dropped the stir stick, felt the color draining from her face. "I don't know . . . ."

"I am no fool. I be a woman, and a mother, a mother of sons and daughters. More than you have fingers on your hands, and that's only them that lived. Mayhap these men don't see through your hunting frock, but I do. And they will, too, soon enough."

"I am . . . ."

"Where do you think you will answer nature's call, McKidrict? It's a long march to Gilbert Town. Some of these men are decent, but some . . . ." She spit again. "Now, are you doing this fool errand to please your man?"

"Not hardly." This time it was Marty who spit.

Mrs. Patton grinned widely. "To get away from him, then?"

No answer. Marty felt weak, from the heat, the stink, the interrogation, her own stupidity. How did she think she could get away with such deception? She couldn't even fool this backwater matron.

When Mrs. Patton stood, though, Marty shot to her feet. "Please!" Desperation accented her voice.

"Keep your voice down," Mrs. Patton snapped. "And don't get to crying. That would give you away, sure enough." Her head shook as she chuckled. "You have backbone, sister. Or should I say something indelicate? Wisht I had your gumption."

The woman walked closer and used her forefinger to hook out the mass of finely ground tobacco between her gums. Brown flakes stuck between her nearly rotten teeth. "I've heard of Seb McKidrict," Mrs. Patton said. "Never knowed him to have a brother. Not one that would claim him, no how. Best be careful, Marty McKidrict. I shall give you a pouch of snuff. Don't swallow the juice or you'll be sicker than a dog, but it might help you pass muster. At least, no man will want to kiss you. Take a pinch and put it between your gums. Curb hunger, too. Look everyone in the eye, and don't lower your voice. That will betray yourself. You talk raspy enough, like a saw, and there's enough dirt on your face. Ain't got much to your chest." Mrs. Patton snorted. "That means you ain't nursed no dozen kids."

Actually Marty had wrapped her breasts tightly with strips of linen. It wasn't exactly comfortable, but it did the job.

"Watch the way you walk," Mrs. Patton continued, "and keep them slender hands in your pockets. Don't wet your britches, neither. Now, stir that bloody pot. I shall be back directly, *Mister* McKidrict."

Chapter Six

For the past two weeks, Stuart Brodie had forced down the bile rising in his throat. He rode along the Carolina border with ten of Major Ferguson's militia, and at least three score Loyalists commanded by a swarthy, coarse creature called Bloody Bill Cunningham.

At first, Brodie thought he would like, or at least respect, Cunningham. Indeed, he guessed the reason Major Ferguson sent him to patrol the country for rebels with Cunningham was because of a common bond between the two men. In 1778, a band of partisan marauders had captured Cunningham's younger brother, a cripple and epileptic, and murdered the poor lad. Like Brodie, Cunningham's home had been burned, and he and most of the men that rode with him had been driven out of the Ninety-Six district. Many had spent the past two years living in Florida, hiding, waiting for their chance to retaliate. Now that the British occupied South Carolina, they had returned, riding for the King, killing anyone who opposed them, anyone they branded a rebel.

Cunningham called himself a captain, and his men legionnaires, but Brodie labeled every sorry one of them a brigand. Thieves and cold-blooded killers comprised Cunningham's legion. He hated riding with them, but Major Ferguson had ordered it, and he would never betray the Bulldog.

"'For they sow the wind,'" Brodie told himself, "'and they shall reap the whirlwind.'"

"What's that you say, darky?"

He glanced at the pipe-smoking hydra standing beside him, a filthy, red-bearded leviathan with fewer teeth than he had brains. They stood outside a farm on the Pacolet River, holding mounts while Cunningham, mounted on a black stallion, watched like some despot as his men searched the cabin, barn, and corncribs. A woman stood in front of Cunningham, makeshift bayonets at her throat, ringing her hands and crying out her loyalty to King George III.

Tethered to a post near the well, a dog barked loudly, digging the ground with its claws, straining against the rawhide collar until it almost choked.

"It's from the Old Testament," Brodie made himself answer, although he loathed talking to this man. "The Book of Hosea."

The brute, named Pinckert, removed his pipe, spit, and eyed Brodie quizzically. "Aye, mayhap I have misjudged ye. Ye be a preacher. The darky preacher." With a chuckle, he returned the pipe to his mouth. When two boys tumbled out of the barn, prodded by broken sabers carried by four of Cunningham's men, Pinckert spoke again. "Likely ye will have opportunity to preach a funeral before noon."

The woman wailed again, tried to stand, but one of the guards brought a bayonet closer until blood trickled down her throat.

"They're just boys!" she pleaded.

"As was my brother, wench," Cunningham replied.

The dog barked louder.

One of Cunningham's lieutenants spoke: "Molten pewter was in a pot, Captain. Molds in the hay where we found these two traitors."

"For hunting!" the mother cried. "For meat."

Cunningham dismounted, handing the reins to the lieutenant, and ordered the woman's two sons, the oldest maybe fourteen, brought forward.

For several minutes, Cunningham stared, right fist tightly gripping the hilt of his broad sword, the only sound coming from the angry dog, which drowned out the woman's sobs.

"Empty your pockets," Cunningham ordered the youngest boy.

The boy didn't move until one of the men struck the back of his head with the flat of a sword. Timidly he turned the pockets of his trousers inside out, spilling musket balls over the ground.

"For hunting!" the woman begged.

"Aye," Cunningham said. "Hunting men loyal to His Majesty."

The youngest boy began sobbing, but the other just stood there, unblinking eyes glaring at the Loyalists.

"Where is your father?" Cunningham asked the second boy. "With that damned gamecock, Sumter? Answer me!"

"He's dead!" the mother screamed.

"Indeed." Cunningham snorted. "Then these two violent rebels will join him in Hades."

"Please!" The mother's voice broke, and the dog stopped barking, began wailing, as if it knew what was about to happen.

"What say you?" Cunningham asked the first child, who fell to his knees, amid the freshly molded musket balls, blubbering.

The butcher enjoyed this, Brodie thought, as the bitterness rose once more. *You shouldn't feel any sympathy for these rebels,* he told himself. *Remember Ezekiel. These two children might have molded the balls used by those traitors who burned our inn, who left Ezekiel hanging from that tree.*

"And you?" Cunningham addressed the second boy. "Will you admit to God before you die that you are a rebel hound?"

The boy spit on Cunningham's boots. "Aye," he said, his voice trembling. "My father is a Patriot. He rides with Elijah

Clarke. I only regret that what we made will not kill you. My uncles are Patriots. My brother is a Patriot. My dog is a Patriot. And you, Bloody Bill, are nothing but a Tory swine and bloody coward."

Cunningham laughed as he drew his sword, and Brodie dropped his gaze. A *thunk* silenced the mother's piercing shriek, and Brodie wished that dog would start barking again, instead of its pitiful howls, anything that would keep him from hearing the slashing and chopping of Cunningham's sword.

"Burn this nest of sedition!" Cunningham bellowed as he mounted the stallion. "Take what you like. And kill that rebel dog, too."

"What of the woman?" the lieutenant asked.

"Leave her to bury her rebel family when she wakes!"

* * * * *

Bloody Bill Cunningham cut a wide swath, and his legion grew.

He conscripted men into service for the King, farmers who feared that, if they did not join him, they would be hanged as rebels. They rested briefly at Fairforest, then crossed the Pacolet and rode hard into North Carolina.

Brodie hoped they would continue north, over the Broad River and on to Gilbert Town, where he would be relieved of having to ride with this lot, but instead Cunningham turned the command eastward, toward Charlotte Town, their progress slowed by unseasonal warm temperatures but mostly by the carts and saddlebags filled with plunder taken from those they had terrified or murdered.

Past Buffalo Creek, they dipped south again, cutting through the forest and hills, back across the border.

"What be that mountain over yonder, Preacher Darky?" Pinckert asked.

Brodie followed Pinckert's outstretched arm and found the ridge that aroused the ruffian's curiosity. Mountain? Brodie tried not to scoff. He had been over the Cumberland, had seen the Blue Ridge, had trapped and traded in Cherokee country. He wouldn't even label what he saw much more than a hill. It rose maybe sixty feet over the forests, running southeast to northwest perhaps 500, maybe 600 yards, and no more than 300 yards wide. Heavily wooded at the base, the rocky ridge was bald on top.

"King's Mountain," Brodie answered.

"Appears to me that it would be a fine watchtower," Pinckert said. "Why, a man would not even need a prospect glass to see if any rebel be chasing us."

Brodie stared at Pinckert, measuring the man. He had misjudged his intellect, his military resourcefulness. "Ride on," Pinckert said. "I shall tell the lieutenant our intentions."

* * * * *

Rainfall had soaked the fallen leaves, allowing their mounts to climb the hill without much sound. King's Mountain deceived a man, Brodie thought, as they moved through the ravines and creeks, circling moss-covered boulders, making their way to the treeless summit. What it lacked in height, it more than made up for in ruggedness. Brodie slapped at a mosquito buzzing his sweaty neck.

When they finally cleared the brush and reached the top of the knob, Brodie and Pinckert dismounted. Shielding the sun from his eyes, Brodie looked northwest. Pinckert had been right. You could see for miles up here. Suddenly Brodie shivered.

"See something, preacher?" Pinckert asked urgently.

"No . . . just . . . ." He shuddered again.

The big man laughed. "Ye must have just stepped on ye grave, Preacher Darky." He fished pipe and pouch from a possibles bag that hung around his neck.

Then Brodie saw the flash of brown, off there, to his right, in the trees below the summit. A deer? No. It moved again, from tree to tree, a rifle, knife, or something metal reflecting sunlight, and Brodie brought Ferguson's rifle up, tightened the stock against his shoulder.

"What . . . ?" Pinckert began, but the explosion of the rifle silenced him.

Brodie stepped out of the smoke, reloading as he moved, as his squealing mule bolted across the ridge top. "Halt!" Brodie yelled. The man, slender, red-headed, screamed, and ran down a deer path, not bothering now to hide in the trees.

Brodie cocked the rifle and aimed again, but, before he could pull the trigger, Pinckert thundered past him on horse, charging down the hill, ignoring the brambles and bushes. Brodie caught his breath, turned, looking for his mule, but it had stopped sixty yards away. He took off running, chasing Pinckert and the fleeing stranger.

The runner slipped on wet moss, tumbling over a boulder, crashing against a dead tree, and Pinckert reined his horse to a sliding stop. For a big man, Brodie marveled, he rode amazingly well.

By the time Brodie reached them, Pinckert had straddled the fallen figure, had jerked up the red hair and held a knife at the throat.

"For God's sake, Pinckert!" Brodie called out, although almost out of breath. "Stop! It's a woman!"

Her face crashed against the wet leaves when Pinckert released her hair. The big man just blinked stupidly, staring at her. She rolled over, eyes filled with fright, and crawled from beneath Pinckert, backing away until a boulder trapped her progress.

After sheathing his knife, Pinckert faced Brodie.

"Preacher," he said heavily, "me thinks we've lugged the wrong sow by the ear."

* * * * *

"Who are you?" Cunningham asked the woman.

"Virginia Sal," she answered.

"And what, pray tell, were you doing on King's Mountain?"

"I was lost. Trying to reach Gilbert Town."

"Far off the trail, you rebel harlot."

The slap caused Brodie to step back. He found himself bringing up his rifle while Bloody Bill Cunningham rubbed his stinging cheek. The woman looked like she would slap the captain again. She was buxom, blue-eyed, and fair-skinned, and Brodie could not help but notice the looks the rogues, including Captain Cunningham, had given her since he and Pinckert had brought her down from King's Mountain. Some had blushed at the glimpse of her bare ankles, and a few had rushed to bring her clothing, shoes, water, biscuits, and rum. Most, however, eyed her wickedly, and Brodie figured maybe Pinckert had been right. Perhaps he had stepped on his own grave up on King's Mountain. So far, Cunningham's men may have threatened or beaten a few rebel mothers, daughters, and sisters, but they had never done anything disgraceful. This seemed different. A beautiful woman alone in a camp full of ruffians. Brodie would defend her if need be, only he knew they would both die if it ever came to that.

"Rebels killed my husband at Thicketty Fort back in July," she said icily. "And you will withdraw that insult immediately before I claw out your eyes, you whoreson."

Cunningham laughed so hard he doubled over, and, wiping tears from his eyes, he gave a mock bow. "I beg your forgiveness, Widow Sal, and kindly hope you will allow Captain Cunningham's Legionnaires to escort you to Gilbert Town."

Brodie lowered the rifle and wet his lips. He prayed they would make for Gilbert Town with all haste.

* * * * *

They didn't, of course. Once again, the disgust rose in Stuart Brodie's throat.

This time, he stood inside the cabin with Pinckert and Cunningham's lieutenant, Abel Hart, as they questioned the lone woman in the cabin on Brush Creek, while Cunningham's legion waited outside or searched the property. Brodie longed to be back with Ferguson, to be as far removed from Cunningham as possible. Rebels had hanged Brodie's brother, but at least Ezekiel was a man, a boy in mind, perhaps, but a man. Cunningham's self-named legionnaires waged war on women.

Pinckert jumped down from the loft, landing with a *thud* that shook the cabin.

"Nothing there, Lieutenant," he said. "No firelocks, no molds, not even much in the way of plunder, sir." The disrespect in Pinckert's voice surprised Brodie.

"She's a rebel, though," Abel Hart said. "I can smell the stench on this trollop."

The woman, her hair brown with streaks of silver, stood erect, said nothing. A proud woman, refusing to give her tormenters any satisfaction. Her hands were calloused, her dress made of rough muslin, and her home contained not enough meal to feed a rat. There would be even less when Cunningham left.

"Where is your husband?" Hart demanded.

The woman pushed bangs off her forehead and answered easily, as if she were speaking to her preacher. "In the army of Francis Marion."

Brodie blinked back his surprise. Lieutenant Hart could scarcely believe it himself. Women did not admit that their husbands rode with rebels.

"And where is that damned Swamp Fox?" Hart shouted.

"I do not know."

Now Brodie caught himself grinning. He admired this woman, but the smile vanished when Hart overturned the table, lunging at her.

"Where is he?" Hart shook with rage.

She repeated her answer.

Hart snatched a reaping hook off the wall, waving the blade under the woman's nose. "You will tell me," Hart said icily, "or you will bathe in your own blood."

"I spoke the truth." She did not even flinch. "I do not know, and would not tell you if I could."

Hart pushed her back, his face enraged, and raised the hook over his head. He had just started to bring the blade down toward her breast when Brodie smashed his nose with the rifle butt. Hart reeled backward, mangled nose pouring blood, his lips busted. Spitting out broken bits of teeth, he reached for a belted pistol. Brodie dropped the rifle and lunged at the officer, wrapping both arms around Hart, the impact carrying both men through the door, off the porch, and into the mud.

The pistol had fallen somewhere inside. Brodie heard the snorts of nervous horses, hoofs dancing all around him, shouts, curses, and Abel Hart's groans. He pulled himself to his knees, pounding fists against the lieutenant's head, chest, stomach.

Hands and arms grabbed at him—not those of Hart, though, who lay unconscious on the ground—and he felt himself being lifted off the half-dead officer, but he kicked at Hart, kicked and screamed until he felt himself being hurled backward. He landed so hard, the breath left his lungs, and he blinked back the pain, the rage, as Cunningham's men lifted him off the ground and pinned him against the cabin's walls.

"Striking an officer is a hanging offense," Bloody Bill Cunningham spoke from his black stallion.

"Bugger your orders," Brodie said hoarsely. "I joined Major Ferguson to fight men, not defenseless women."

"Indeed," Cunningham said. "Kill him."

The nearest man drew a knife, but stopped when Pinckert stepped through the door, holding Brodie's Ferguson rifle, aimed at Bloody Bill Cunningham.

"Have you sided with the darky?" Cunningham asked coolly.

"I guess ye methods do not suit me, either, Captain."

"Eighty against one, Pinckert," someone said.

"Only"—Pinckert smiled—"this here be a Ferguson rifle." He stated this as if he said he held Excalibur. "And that yonder . . ." —Pinckert's chin jutted toward the road—"be Major Ferguson himself."

Chapter Seven

That old reprobate, Stuart Brodie thought. *I thought Pinckert was bluffing.*

Yet there rode Major Patrick Ferguson, with at least ten score men behind him, bayonets glistening in the sun. They marched like soldiers, not the ribaldry that followed Bloody Bill Cunningham. Slowly the legionnaires looked toward the jingling harnesses and squeaking leather, realizing, as had Brodie, that Pinckert had not been stalling on the cabin's porch. A murmur of voices welled throughout the blackhearts, although Cunningham stared in malevolent silence. With a snort, Pinckert shot Brodie a grin, although he kept the rifle aimed at Cunningham until Ferguson ordered the weapon lowered. The Bulldog also commanded Bloody Bill's men to release Brodie.

So close had he been to death—again. It took two minutes before Brodie could catch his breath, before he realized what had just taken place. He had turned rabid, into some wild animal, had almost beaten to death an officer with Cunningham's Legionnaires. If Pinckert hadn't sided with Brodie, if the Bulldog and his Loyalists had not arrived at that moment, Brodie's life blood would now be staining the porch. Blinking, he wet his lips and took the Ferguson rifle Pinckert was offering him, then stepped unsteadily to the ground, barely remembering to salute the major.

He didn't feel total relief, not yet, anyway, for, while he considered Cunningham and his men to be nothing more than mercenaries, *banditti*, vermin, Major Ferguson might think otherwise. After all, the Bulldog had addressed Cunningham as captain after reining in his horse, even offered that butcher his compliments. Brodie could face a court-martial, after all, and, at least be hanged from an oak rather than hacked to death with tomahawks, knives, and broad swords.

"Your darky," Cunningham said after an exaggerated bow to Ferguson, "disobeyed my lieutenant, then savagely attacked him."

"The order, I deem, was immoral, Captain Cunningham," Ferguson said in sharp rebuke, and relief flooded Brodie, relief and pride. There would be no court-martial, not for Brodie. Major Ferguson would not even bother with an inquiry. He knew without any interviews that Brodie had been in the right. *God*, Brodie thought, *I love that Bulldog*.

"I have seen the results of your orders all over the Carolinas," Ferguson said stiffly.

Cunningham straightened in the saddle. "Orders given me by Colonel Tarleton and Major Weymss."

"Immoral men," Ferguson said. "Your trail was easily followed, Captain. You leave weeping widows, smoke and ash behind you. I dislike your methods, sir, and this policy of a scorched earth."

The captain let out a laugh full of mock derision. "Indeed, Major. Was it not you who sent word to the Watauga settlements that you would put men to the sword or cord and lay waste to the country over the mountains?"

"*Men*, Captain. Not women." He turned in the saddle. "Captain DePeyster, you will relieve our men on detached service with Captain Cunningham with our thanks, and have them rejoin us immediately." As the New Yorker bolted into the legionnaires, barking out orders to his soldiers, Ferguson faced

Cunningham again. "Captain, you will find Colonel Tarleton in Charlotte Town. I suggest you conduct your raids nearer him, and farther from me."

There was no false pleasantness in Cunningham's voice or eyes as he jerked the stallion's reins. "When you meet Isaac Shelby, Major, and feel the sting of that rebel hornet, you will beg for my aid. Remember that!" He galloped away, leaving his men confused, unsure if they should follow. A few stared at the dust, others just looked at their feet, and a couple tried to rouse Lieutenant Abel Hart.

Brodie stared at the half-dead man. He couldn't even recognize the lieutenant's face, yet he didn't feel ashamed of what he had done, even if Ferguson wound up flogging him, although he remained fairly certain he would not be punished. That louse had been about to murder a woman, carve her up with a reaping hook. Brodie had done what any honorable man would have done, should have done. For the first time in weeks, he no longer tasted bile.

The proud woman had ventured outside the cabin, and Ferguson swept his hat off his head and bowed. "Madam, please accept my apologies from this humble servant of our King."

"This woman's . . . husband," muttered Lieutenant Hart, who had regained consciousness, "rides with . . . the Swamp Fox. She told me . . . as much." When his eyes found Brodie, he tried to stand, only to pass out.

"Then, perchance we meet on the field of battle," Ferguson said, speaking to the rebel's wife. "I will kill him, though I may detest the deed."

The woman curtsied and, with a nod toward the bloodied Hart, said: "I have snake root and hemlock inside, Major. If you bring that *gentleman* in, I will kindly patch him up before you are on your way." The last part seemed more of an order, and Brodie beamed at the sassy lady. She, in turn, gave him a knowing look, mouthing a silent thank you.

Slowly Ferguson shook his head. "Your generosity is appreciated, madam, but I am not one who believes swine should enter a Christian lady's home. Thank you, but, no, our surgeon will attend to this . . . gentleman." He barked an order to have the bloodied lieutenant carried to Dr. Johnson's wagon, then asked DePeyster, who had assembled the rest of the Carolina Loyalists the major had sent with the legionnaires, if he could not do something about this stench. The captain took the hint.

"You men with Captain Cunningham are dismissed!" shouted DePeyster.

With the sudden movement around him, Brodie found his voice. "Major," he said, "there's a woman with us, sir. A widow we found making her way to Gilbert Town. Rebels killed her husband this summer. We should take her with us, sir."

Ferguson's eyes widened and he smiled. "Fetch this creature, Pinckert," he ordered.

Pinckert! Brodie understood, not that he liked it any. *Send the white man, not the darky, to escort a white woman*—Ferguson had to assume the widow was white. Black men, freedmen, even men serving in Ferguson's militia had their place.

* * * * *

The Two Virginias. That's what they called them, back in Gilbert Town. Virginia Sal, rescued (or, perhaps, *captured*) near the summit of the bald knob by Brodie and Pinckert, and Virginia Paul, who Major Ferguson had plucked from the cut-throat command of Captain Zachariah Gibbs, a Loyalist commander who murdered and ravaged the Carolinas as relentlessly as did Bloody Bill Cunningham.

The brown-haired Miss Paul had a darker complexion, stood a little heavier than Virginia Sal, with eyes blacker than coal. She wore calico and muslin, and never dared look at anyone, not even Major Ferguson, in the eye. In the week since they had been back at Gilbert Town, Brodie had not heard the woman utter five words. Virginia Sal, on the other hand, would sing, dance, and chat while she washed clothes and darned socks for the officers. Outfitted in a fine caraco dress—more befitting than the shabby homespun clothes she had donned up on King's Mountain—she had even walked up to Brodie, walked up to him in front of Pinckert and others, looked him in the eye, brazenly placed her hand on his shoulder, and said: "I want to thank you for saving my life, Mister Brodie."

Uncomfortable, Brodie just stood there mute, not breathing until Mrs. Sal had removed her hand and headed toward the well. Stuart Brodie might have been born a freedman, but, even in Ferguson's army, black men did not socialize with white women, especially not in the presence of white men.

He felt the burning stares, could taste the contempt as volunteers from the Carolinas, New York, and New Jersey walked past him. One spit on the ground near Brodie's feet. Only Pinckert seemed not to mind. After the others were out of earshot, Pinckert put his hand on Brodie's shoulder, the same spot where Mrs. Sal had touched him, and said: "Ye might want to thank me sometime, Preacher Darky, for saving ye worthless life back on Brush Creek."

Virginia Sal kept her distance afterward, which brought Brodie a measure of relief. Besides, other things bothered him, worried him.

Often, Mrs. Sal dined with the major, dined at unrespectable hours that gave the righteous ladies of Gilbert Town and several pious officers in the militia reason to gossip.

Then again, Brodie had seen Virginia Paul slip into the major's cabin, too. *Does she look the major in the eye then?* he wondered.

"He's a bulldog, for sure," Pinckert said one night while Brodie stared at the dark cabin.

Brodie lay down, wrapping himself in his bedroll, without responding.

"Ye be worried for the souls of those lasses, or the major's, Preacher Darky?"

He answered with silence, and Pinckert laughed.

"Or be ye thoughts more prurient?"

"Go to sleep," Brodie said.

He should have kept silent, because Pinckert cackled again, and lit his pipe. "Careful, preacher. A word of warning to ye. The two Virginias be white women, and, well, if ye cast a look too long, ye may face unpleasant deserts, no matter how fond Ferguson be of you."

"We should not have women in camp," Brodie said reluctantly.

"Well, officers need the services of laundresses. And they do be a pleasant distraction."

"Indeed. Distractions are not what we need." He sat up, reaching for the canteen that carried rum, instead of water, and took a long pull. "I do not comprehend Major Ferguson's actions. He practices military order, yet he allows these two . . . laundresses . . . in camp. He skewers the actions of men like Bloody Bill and Gibbs, with just reason, yet he vows to burn, hang, and pillage in the Watauga. He beckons those over-mountain men to come and fight us. And then he waits. Waits and . . . ."

Pinckert chuckled. "Aye, what a bulldog."

He offered Pinckert the canteen, but the red-headed giant shook his head and tapped his pipe on a stone. After a final pull, Brodie capped the canteen and dropped wearily to the ground. Pinckert puffed on his pipe for a few minutes, then let out a sigh.

"Here be me concern, Preacher Darky," the big man said. "And it has nary a thing to do with women or our Bulldog's threats. We drill with our bayonets in close order from dawn till dusk. Me ears are numb from the major's whistles. Captain DePeyster, he uses words like discipline."

Brodie waited.

"Now, tell me this, Preacher Darky. Ye been over the Bald of the Yellow, right?"

"Yes."

"Ye have fought renegades and Indians?"

"Yes."

"Ye know them folks along the Nolichucky, not by name, but ye know them as well as do I." Pinckert sucked on the pipe stem before continuing. "Now, tell me this, preacher . . . ye ever known one of those backwater boys to use either whistle or bayonet?" He didn't wait for Brodie's answer, didn't need to. "All this drill be a bloody waste of time. It's the drill that will kill us all . . . them two Virginias."

Chapter Eight

"Help us!" the Reverend Samuel Doak shouted, his voice rising to a crescendo as he concluded his prayer at Sycamore Shoals. "Help us, oh, God of Battle, help us as good soldiers to wield the sword of the Lord and Gideon!"

Musket shots drowned out the preacher's amen, and all around Marty McKidrict voices boomed: "The sword of the Lord and of our Gideons!"

"The sword of the Lord and of our Gideons!"

"The sword of the Lord and of our Gideons!"

"The sword of the Lord and of our Gideons!"

It took a moment before Marty McKidrict realized she was yelling, too. Then she moved, had to or get trampled, as the volunteers swarmed away from the meadow, breaking into groups, stopping briefly to bid good byes to wives, sons, daughters, mothers. A toothless woman, her Cherokee-black hair streaked with silver, placed the end of a finely braided hackamore in Marty's left hand.

"Take Abimelech," the woman said with a lisp. "Nigh twenty-two years old, but he don't know it. Ride him with my blessings, ride down those English tyrants."

Marty was past her, slowly fathoming that the hackamore she clenched pulled a barrel-chested buckskin behind her. She veered from the horde, stopping long enough to bring the stallion closer. It eyed her without much interest, and she rubbed its neck in a circular pattern, its hair uneven with the beginnings of a winter coat. The horse had been saddled, with a bedroll tethered behind the cantle and a sack thrown over the horn, leaking a syrupy substance and grease from food the woman had prepared.

Marty looked up, finding her voice now, wanting to thank the stranger, but she had vanished in the crowd.

"Abimelech," she said softly, and the horse snorted. "Is that Cherokee?"

"Old Testament." She recognized Flint O'Keeffe's voice, saw him smiling at her over the buckskin's back. The Irishman patted the old stallion's haunches. "Abimelech was the Philistine king of Gerar who entered a covenant with Abraham. Genesis."

He waited for a reply, but Marty wasn't sure what he wanted. A compliment? Was he strutting around like some cock of the walk, wanting to be stroked? Talking just to be heard? Showing off his superior intellect, trying to make Marty feel like some uneducated, backwater dunce?

"Mayhap you should have given the sermon today instead of the Reverend Doak," she offered.

O'Keeffe laughed. "Not hardly. I thought Mister Doak did a rousing job and picked the appropriate text. In Judges, Gideon's people rise up against the Midianites, just as we are rising up against oppression." He stared at her for several uncomfortable moments. "Well, your horse looks strong enough, surprising for a nag as old as Methuselah."

The multitude had passed, and 100 yards away officers began forming their men. She could make out the curses of Colonel Sevier.

"You must hate me, Marty McKidrict," O'Keeffe said.

Again, she struggled to find the right answer. Hate him? Not really, but she did suspicion him. After all, he was a man, and she hadn't had much luck with men of late, or ever. She did fear him, though, feared he would find out who she really was.

When she hadn't answered, and when Colonel Shelby had finished booming out stern instructions to his troops, and Colonel Sevier had finished swearing, O'Keeffe shrugged. "Well, you shall hate me now if you haven't already."

Marty's stomach turned. *He knows . . . .*

"I desire you to herd the cattle," O'Keeffe said. "The going will be hard, the cattle skittish. You will find Sergeant Gillespie there, with some of Colonel Shelby's men. Tell the sergeant that I sent you."

She let out a long sigh.

"A cumbersome job, irksome, detestable," O'Keeffe said. "I know. Have you a problem with my order, McKidrict?"

"None whatsoever." Holding the Deckard rifle, she swung into the saddle and kicked Abimelech into a trot toward the cattle grazing by the Sycamore.

* * * * *

The cattle bawled and bunched up, did anything and everything they could to keep from walking up the mountain path in that driving rain that had started almost immediately after the army broke camp. Marty shivered in the saddle, trying to keep her head down, muttering oaths at the stupid animals that trailed Shelby's and Sevier's men. Water streamed down the barrel of the Deckard, which Marty held across the pommel, and poured off the brim of her water-soaked hat. Her teeth chattered, and she figured she would likely catch a cough and fever and die before they ever reached camp that night.

A low tree branch slapped her head, and she almost dropped her rifle trying to save her hat, somehow managing to hold onto both as she cursed. Now she knew what Flint O'Keeffe had meant.

Well, you shall hate me now if you haven't already.

She didn't hate O'Keeffe, though. She didn't understand, however, John Sevier or Isaac Shelby. Here were two pretty smart soldiers. They had sent a colonel named McDowell riding ahead of the legion to let other Patriots know they were crossing the mountains, heading over Roan Mountain on their way to find this Ferguson, and if anyone wanted to join them, so be it. Marty had seen armies before, and heard the stories her father had told of the great Cherokee war, the expeditions against the French and Indians. Armies plodded along, troubled by wagons and cannon, but not Sevier's command. His men carried a woolen blanket and tin or pewter cup, maybe a bag of cornmeal, or, in Marty's case, bear meat and maple sugar. A few had cast-iron skillets, others, gourds, canteens, wooden mugs, pot hooks, tongs, and barrel-hoop broilers—anything they could carry themselves, and nothing overly cumbersome or heavy.

Even in this weather, they would have moved fast if not for the beeves.

By noon, they stopped at Matthew Talbot's mill on Gap Creek to eat in the rain. They had traveled no more, she guessed, than three miles.

"At this rate," Colonel Sevier's voice thundered, "we shall meet up with Major Ferguson when he is one hundred and seventeen years old!" He rode a prancing dun horse through the mud, slapping the horse's side with his hat, cursing the weary men all around him.

"It's the cattle," someone complained.

"Beef be damned!" Sevier roared. "You can eat the haslet of Tories and drink their blood if you're hungry. Now who will follow me? Follow me, and we shall sup on victory!"

Marty chewed on a piece of bear gristle and decided that she was a better cook than Abimelech's owner, and she wasn't much of a cook. She watched as the men emptied their plates and sloshed through the mud toward their horses. Sergeant Gillespie muttered an oath beneath his breath, but Marty didn't mind Sevier's order. She would rather keep moving than sit here and try to stay warm. Besides, moving took her farther and farther from Seb McKidrict.

As soon as she spit out the gristle and climbed onto Abimelech, Flint O'Keeffe galloped to them, spewing orders at the sergeant.

"We sha'n't tarry, Sergeant," O'Keeffe said. "So you must catch up with us. We shall cross the Little Doe just up the trail, and camp at the Resting Place. Meet us there tonight."

"Lord Jehovah," Gillespie stuttered. "That's nigh fifteen miles from here."

"Nearer seventeen, Sergeant. I shall see you tonight!" He spurred his horse toward the head of the column.

* * * * *

Sleet and snow had mixed in with the rain when the herd reached the camp long after sunset. They bedded down the cattle, too exhausted to run off, Sergeant Gillespie said, although Marty figured it was the sergeant who was tuckered out. The man didn't even bother to hobble his horse before heading underneath the rock shelf that sheltered the bone-tired, straggling army of Patriots.

No one sang songs tonight. Marty pulled saddle, blanket, and reins off the buckskin, and picketed him near a patch of snow. She heard the ringing of hammer on iron, and guessed that the smithy named Miller was shoeing horses. She checked Abimelech's shoes, but in the darkness they looked almost brand new, although she would use a pick to pry out rocks and mud before riding the stallion tomorrow.

After pouring grain onto the snow, Marty patted her horse and walked to the rocky ledge to escape the weather. The Big Doe roared nearby, but the sound was soon lost to the crackling of wood. The aroma of hoecakes and fried bacon sharpened her hunger.

"I thought you would have quit by now, Marty McKidrict," Flint O'Keeffe said. He stood to her right, warming his hands over a fire.

"Is that why you had me nursing your cattle?" she asked. This time, she did not hesitate. Her backside ached, her thighs were chaffed, and she was in no mood for the Irishman's preaching or picking.

"Heavens, no. In fact, 'twas not my idea to order you to such a detail. It was Mary McKeehan Patton's, and you may have guessed that no one in Washington County belays Missus Patton's orders. She said to give you the worst job on the first day, and, if you ran back home, to let you go, but if you proved your worth, then you might make a soldier, after all."

"Do I herd your beeves tomorrow?" she asked.

O'Keeffe laughed, then lifted a flask to his lips and drank. When he lowered the container, he whispered: "I doubt if we will trouble ourselves with those bovines on the morrow. You shall find your mess in the far corner near the Doe, last fire by the Shelving Rock." He grinned like a mischievous boy. "Tell Duncan that you made it, that he cannot have your noggin of rum tonight."

"Thanks." Marty turned away.

"Personally," O'Keeffe said, "I never doubted your tenaciousness, McKidrict, and I am glad Missus Patton underestimated your wherewithal."

Marty grunted some reply and moved away from the fire, although she longed to dry her clothes and warm her bones. She moved stiffly, although she knew she would be even sorer at dawn when they marched out. Moving past the fires, she suddenly realized she needed to relieve herself. She should have done it by the cattle herd, or when she was picketing her horse, when she was alone. O'Keeffe had said she would mess with Duncan, only she couldn't remember meeting any Duncan at Sycamore Shoals. She saw the glow of the last campfire, realized that was her camp, and heard a few snores. She walked on, into the shadows, as far into the darkness as she could go. Sleet pelted her as she dropped her britches and squatted, and, afterward, she needed to use the Deckard to pull herself to her feet. Marty buttoned her pants, exhaustion hitting her harder with each step, as she walked to the fire. The man poking the red coals looked at her and grinned, and Marty gasped.

"Willie Duncan . . . ," she began, but never finished. The blow took her in the small of her back, and she collapsed, rolled over, and looked up at her husband.

"Shameless hussy," Seb McKidrict said. "Dressing up like a man. Why, woman, I'll leave welts on your gammons so thick you sha'n't sit down for a week before I send you home."

Marty backed up, dragging the rifle with her, as her husband spoke. She retreated on her backside, ignominiously, in trembling fear until she reached the cavern's stone wall. Seb McKidrict towered over her, and Willie Duncan had picked up a limb from the fire, using it as a torch. The light almost blinded her. Other men in the mess lay asleep, snoring loudly, wearied after the grueling journey from Sycamore Shoals.

"W-w-what are . . . y-you do-doing . . . h-h-here?" Marty asked. "You care not . . . for the . . . Whigs."

"Do not question me, woman!" McKidrict spit on her. "You do not care for Whigs, neither. You do nothing without my say. I come to Sycamore Shoals this morn, and, lo, to my surprise, I find I have a brother already volunteered in Colonel Sevier's militia. An exemplary marksman, I am told. I would have been most unwelcome in Sevier's army if not for my brother, but, because of this Martin McKidrict . . . *hah* . . . the righteous colonel says we can take a chance on Seb McKidrict." He kicked the flat of her soaked moccasin, sending pain to Marty's knee. "You shall pay for embarrassing your husband," he said through clenched teeth, "before I send you home or hell."

"I don't know, Seb." Willie Duncan lowered the torch and grinned. "She might have a use. Remember?"

McKidrict didn't respond, just stared, shaking in rage, then bent his massive frame, reaching for her with his ham-size hands.

The Deckard barrel stopped him, and he straightened.

Marty cocked the rifle, as McKidrict took a few steps back. Willie Duncan just blinked like a simpleton.

"Y-y-you w-w-ouldn't . . . w-wouldn't dare," Duncan stuttered.

"Wouldn't I?" Marty kept the barrel moving from Duncan's stomach to her husband's head.

"You have no right," McKidrict said. "By thunder, I am your husband. I have rights . . . ."

"You lost your rights, Seb McKidrict. Months ago." She shot Willie Duncan a vicious look. "Remember?"

She stood unsteadily, but kept the rifle at the ready. "If you come close to me, either of you . . . I will kill you, the both of you . . . by the sword of the Lord and our Gideon." She couldn't, of course, not now. She hadn't bothered to reload the Deckard tonight, too haggard, and certainly had not expected to see Seb or Duncan in Sevier's camp. She knew the powder had been wet, ruined from the soaking rain all that day. Yet that craven Duncan and the brute she had married didn't know this. At least, Marty hoped that was the case. If they called her bluff, though, Marty would die tonight.

McKidrict stood a little straighter. "I think not," he said, but he didn't sound convinced. "All I have to do is tell Sevier or that fool Irish Virginian who you really are. Then, by Jupiter, they will lay stripes on your back themselves for deceiving them so."

Marty's head shook. "Go ahead, Seb," she said. "Tell them I am your wife." She howled, laughing so hard one of the men in her mess rolled over in his blankets, and muttered a curse and admonition for them to shut up before resuming his snores. "Tell them, Seb. They shall be laughing at you all across the Carolinas and Virginia. Tell them!"

He took one step, raising his fist, but again the rifle stopped him. Marty's eyes hardened. "I will kill you, Seb. Kill you for the beast you are."

"Seb?" Willie Duncan said weakly.

Her husband pivoted sharply, barked out an order for his friend to follow him, that there had to be kill devil to be found in this camp. Duncan dropped the torch, and the two disappeared in the darkness.

Marty exhaled slowly. *I'm glad I went to the toilet first,* she thought, and giggled childishly. She picked up the limb Duncan had dropped, and returned to the campfire, tossing the wood on the coals before squatting and hurriedly began cleaning and reloading the rifle. She spied a plate full of hoecakes on a rock to her left.

Once the Deckard was ready, she laid it across her lap, picked up the food, and ate ravenously.

Suddenly Marty laughed again. "That's the first time I've ever been sure of myself around men," she said.

"Damn you, squire!" The nearest man rolled over in his blanket again. "Can't a body get a wink of sleep in the miserable cave? If you do not shut your trap, I shall whip your bloody arse!"

Chapter Nine

She woke cold, stiff, exhausted, and scared, jerking upright and scanning the granite shelf for her husband or Duncan, but found neither. The man who had briefly stirred while she fought off Seb and his simpleton friend last night squatted over gray coals, his breath frosty in the frigid morning, trying to bring the fire back to life. He glanced at her, rolled his eyes, and muttered: "You don't sleep worth a damn."

It had been a troubled sleep. Marty offered a hoarse apology, and crawled from underneath the covers, rolling up the bedroll and checking her rifle.

"I'd druther you snore, McKidrict, than be tormented all night by hobgoblins and bugaboos." The man bent over the pit, blew on a smoking coal, and lifted his head. "Gather some faggots for this fire. Your brother and Duncan will miss their breakfast if they tarry much longer." He turned to the other sleeping figure and bellowed: "Rise, Bickley, and earn your keep!"

The rain had stopped, but gray clouds obscured most of the sunlight, and a heavy fog covered the ground. Branches hung low, heavy with ice, and Marty felt as if she would never warm herself, even after her messmates had gotten the fire roaring again and she had finished two cups of scalding coffee.

"I am Ryan Folson," the big man said, "and this is Edisto Bickley."

Bickley lifted his gaze from his long rifle's flintlock and offered a beaming smile. His hair was dark, braided into a queue, and he wore grease-stained buckskins and a wolf-skin hat. A wiry man, face covered with beard stubble, he replaced his grin with an intense grimace and went back to working on his rifle.

"He don't say much," Folson said, as if Ryan Folson could outtalk John Sevier or Flint O'Keeffe. Folson might have been the tallest person Marty had ever seen. Even in his water-soaked moccasins, he would have towered over Seb McKidrict, although her husband bested him by ten or fifteen pounds. Folson's hair was stark white, but he didn't look much older than Bickley or Duncan. He wore a tan-colored hunting frock and black breeches, with a hawk feather stuck in his wide-brimmed hat and a pewter Cross of Lorraine hanging from his neck.

"Teever Barnes pulled sentry duty," Folson instructed Marty. "Save him some coffee and hoecakes."

His gaze lifted, and Marty heard the footfalls as Seb and Duncan stumbled into the camp, their eyes rimmed with red, faces pale. Both men avoided any eye contact with Marty, and said little as they rooted in their possible bags for tin plates and cups.

Marty stuffed her own cup into a bag, gathered the Deckard and bedroll, and bid good byes to Bickley and Folson. "Best get to the cattle," she told Folson. "See you when we noon, I guess."

* * * * *

After tending to Abimelech, she walked along the banks of the roaring Big Doe until she reached the herd, finding O'Keeffe, Gillespie, Sevier, and Colonel Isaac Shelby arguing on a rock underneath a pine.

"The citizens of the Watauga settlements gave us this beef," said Shelby, a pious man whose chiseled face lacked any gaiety. Although five years younger than John Sevier, he looked ten years older. He stood taller than Sevier, not to mention fatter and grayer, and, while Chucky Jack might have been the best rifle shot, best horseman, and best cusser over the mountains, Marty felt certain he could not match Colonel Shelby's icy stare.

"I am not, however, resolute in herding cattle if it slows our progress."

"It *is* slowing our progress, Colonel," Sevier said. "Sergeant Gillespie has suggested that we slaughter what our boys can carry."

"I detest waste," Shelby said.

"Won't be waste. We kill just enough for the boys, drive the rest back toward Sycamore Shoals."

"Which will cost us men."

Sevier shook his head. "Cattle are smarter than men, oftener than not. I think once the beeves get the general idea that they are walking home, downhill, they shall not need chaperones."

"Very well," Shelby said. "But let us not waste time. We have tarried too long, and this butchery will cost us even more daylight."

He saluted stiffly, pivoted after a click of his heels, and almost barreled over Marty, who slipped on the slick grass. She found herself sitting on her gammons, staring up at Shelby's unfriendly face. The colonel did not offer his hand.

"You are . . . ?"

"Marty McKidrict." Unable to match his glare, she focused on her feet instead.

"McKidrict's the one who bested Colonel Sevier in a go at shooting the other day," Flint O'Keeffe chimed in.

Shelby snorted. "I hope he fights better than he walks," he said before storming away.

* * * * *

It took most of the morning to slaughter and butcher the beef. The cattle stampeded, and Marty spent at least an hour guiding Abimelech through the brambles, chasing scared beeves out of the thick forest, and then pushing them down the icy trail. The job was, however, better than slamming axes into the heads of the animals and carving the meat into steaks. By the time Marty returned to camp, she found Sergeant Gillespie, Bickley, Folson, and a few others she did not recognize covered with blood and grime. Abimelech faltered at the smell of death, and Marty needed a wide arc to steer the old stallion around the scene before gathering the rest of the living beeves and driving them down the mountain.

Butchery complete, the army pushed on, following Bright's Trace through a gap, Yellow Mountain to the south, Roan Mountain to the north, a heavy snow falling all around them. They stopped four miles later at the Bald of the Yellow to chew practically raw beef, which they washed down with water, providing the contents of their canteens hadn't frozen. Marty stood in ankle-deep snow, blood dribbling from the corners of her mouth as she ate the lukewarm steak Bickley had handed her.

"Fire your weapons!" Flint O'Keeffe ordered as he marched past, churning up snow. "Fire your weapons! Test the powder."

Marty dropped the reins, figuring Abimelech wouldn't go anywhere, aimed at the clouds, and pulled the trigger. Snowflakes stung her face, and, if she hadn't felt the rifle's kick or caught the flash of white smoke, almost lost in the wind and gray skies, she would have thought her trusty Deckard had misfired. She barely heard the reports of other rifles.

"Reload!" O'Keeffe ordered.

By the time Marty had finished, O'Keeffe had returned, now trailed by Sergeant Gillespie, their heads bent low in the blustery wind. "Roll call!" O'Keeffe called out, and Marty listened for the names.

"Barnes . . . Duncan . . . McKidrict . . . Folson . . . Bickley . . . !"

"McKidrict, Marty!" she answered, and listened as Gillespie and O'Keeffe walked by.

"Dryden . . . England . . . Bullen . . . Golf . . . Waldrin . . . Lewis . . . Vance . . . Jamison . . . !"

The voices faded.

"What was that about?" Bickley asked.

"Parade," Folson replied, and spit out a hunk of meat too tough for him to chew. "And drill."

Yet Gillespie and O'Keeffe, or rather Shelby and Sevier, had not finished. The sergeant and lieutenant returned, barking orders to fall in, leaving their horses ground reined, and for the next hour they drilled in the snow and ice, coming to attention, shouldering their rifles, trying to make sense of the strange orders Sergeant Gillespie kept screaming: "To the left, dress! . . . To the right, face! . . . Common step! . . . Quick step."

They even made the soldiers practice shooting, something Marty figured she knew better than Gillespie or O'Keeffe.

"Poise firelock!" Gillespie ordered.

"In two motions, you blubbering idiot!" Marty looked up, saw the sergeant screaming at Teever Barnes. Gillespie ripped the rifle from the farmer's grasp, and moved quickly, keeping the rifle perpendicular, bringing it from his shoulder to in front of his face.

"Two motions!" Gillespie yelled. "You will cock your rifle in two motions, you will take aim in one motion, and you will fire in one motion . . . at my command."

Orders resumed. They fired into a snowbank, and Gillespie spat his contempt. More commands. More criticism and curses. "Half cock . . . firelock! . . . Grip that rifle like a man, Willie Duncan, not a damned harlot! . . . Handle . . . cartridge! One motion! Do it in one motion, damn you! . . . Prime firelock! . . . Shut . . . pan!"

She felt like a child, quite certain Folson, Bickley, and the others had similar emotions. They knew better than most how to fire a gun, but the army obviously saw things differently.

When they finished following the sergeant's commands and had fired again, Gillespie turned to the surprisingly silent Flint O'Keeffe and said: "It's hopeless, sir."

The Irishman nodded his agreement, and the two walked away, leaving Folson, Seb, and Duncan mumbling curses.

"Mount up!" Sergeant Gillespie yelled from somewhere up ahead, and Marty pulled herself into the saddle, her leg muscles screaming in rebellion.

As they left the table top and headed down, the rider in front of her, Dryden, craned his neck and whispered: "Crawford and Chambers have deserted. Pass it on."

She turned in the saddle, glad to be out of the wind for just a few seconds, and thankful that Edisto Bickley rode behind her and not her husband or Willie Duncan, and repeated Dryden's report. That, she assumed, explained the reason for the roll call.

"Aye," Bickley acknowledged. "Samuel Chambers talked more like a Tory than a Whig." He grinned. "I gage we'll scourge him and his friend along with Ferguson's lot, the traitorous swine."

Marty made her teeth stop chattering. "You mean, you think those two quit to tell the British?"

"Me thinks that is so, for I warrant Major Ferguson will pay a tidy sum of gold to know of us." It was the most she had ever heard Bickley say. He turned toward Ryan Folson and said: "Sammy Chambers and Jimmy Crawford have flown the coop."

* * * * *

The snow had stopped by the time they left Elk Hollow, and they halted a few hours later at Roaring Creek, making camp quickly, roasting beef over small fires, devouring the meat before they could even taste it.

Haggard, fighting off sleep, Marty braced her back against a fallen tree, keeping the Deckard within reach, and her eyes on Seb and Duncan while she ate. Neither gave her the slightest bit of attention, but she knew better than to relax.

She slept that night with the rifle in her arms.

* * * * *

After breakfast, Sergeant Gillespie and Lieutenant O'Keeffe arrived to drill the beleaguered company again. Marty lifted, lowered, and dry-fired—O'Keeffe intent on saving powder and lead, but also to keep the whereabouts of the legion harder to locate after the defection of Chambers and Crawford—until the rifle felt heavier than a blacksmith's anvil, until the piercing pain in her arms equaled the agony in her legs and back.

"Do you wish you were back on that creek with your brother?" Sergeant Gillespie's breath stank of sot weed as he shouted in her face. She hadn't shouldered her rifle briskly enough to suit him.

"No," she answered, honestly enough.

"You're a girl!" Gillespie's voice boomed, and blood drained from Marty's face as the sergeant's saliva peppered her nose and cheeks. She almost broke into tears. "I bet you have an oyster basket rather than balls, McKidrict!" He spun away from her, almost lunging at Teever Barnes, ripping the heavy rifle from his arms.

"Do not laugh, Teever Barnes, for you are a woman, too!"

Marty checked herself, shuddering as she realized Gillespie hadn't noticed anything, had meant only to insult her. She made the mistake of wiping the spit from her face, which brought Gillespie back, bellowing at her with his stinking breath, until he finally raised his arms in despair and again lamented to Flint O'Keeffe: "They are a hopeless lot, sir."

* * * * *

Worn out after the discipline, they descended Bright's Trace, nothing more than a foot path, really, and so stony, so rough, Marty knew the blacksmith would be busy when they camped tonight. Following Roaring Creek and then the North Toe River, the army—after nooning and drilling for another hour at a place called Davenport's—left the cold of the mountains for the meadows below, moving, miraculously it seemed, from the dead of winter to a false spring, leaving the cold of the mountains for the meadows below.

Behind them stood the blue ridges that climbed some 6,000 feet into the horizon. Ahead of them lay crab-apple orchards, forests bright with the colors of fall. In the mountains, up along the Tiger, autumn had passed, but here it seemed as if God had thrown a patchwork quilt over the country. It looked so peaceful, Marty almost forgot how tired she felt.

They camped at Cathey's Plantation along Grassy Creek, having traveled twenty of the hardest miles imaginable. Marty led Abimelech to the blacksmith, asked if he would shoe the old stallion, receiving a sour grunt of affirmation, and left the horse with a handful of parched corn and the last of the oats. She pulled off her moccasins and soaked her feet in the cold but refreshing waters of the creek, staring at the elm-dotted plantation.

"'Tis quite inspiring, is it not, Marty McKidrict?"

Marty shot a quick glance at Flint O'Keeffe, waiting to see if he would order her to fall into formation for more exercise, but the lieutenant simply fingered the brim of his hat, which he held at his waist, soaking his own bare feet in the creek—she hadn't even heard him approach—and marveled at the serenity.

"Reminds me of . . . ." O'Keeffe laughed. "There's a place where the meadow is green in the summer, the creek bubbles to life. Not too big, not too small, and the mountains are blue in the distance, not too close, not too far. It's a place where you respect the land, and the land respects what you offer. It's not an easy place to live, but it's not impossible to make a living. I can't think of a place better to see one's sons and daughters grow."

Marty smiled painfully. Once, she thought the cabin on the Tiger might be such a place, but Seb McKidrict had ruined any illusion.

"Your home?" she asked.

"Aye," O'Keeffe replied, "only I'm still looking for it."

"So am I." She hadn't meant to answer, but the words came out automatically.

"Then we have something in common," O'Keeffe said. "Fathom that."

She looked at her dirty fingernails just to keep herself from seeing him. Fear prevented her from looking at O'Keeffe, although she wanted to. How long could she avoid him? His eyes, she could feel bore into her soul, and she shivered, about to give in, but Ryan Folson rescued her. His booming voice and heavy feet interrupted her thoughts moments before his crushing hand pounded her back.

"McKidrict, you got some dainty feet, boy."

The big man passed her, and Marty blushed, for white-haired Folson and Edisto Bickley stood beside her—stark naked. The big man let out a rippling fart, spun around, spread out his arms, and toppled backward into the deepest pool of cold water. Bickley entered with more trepidation, grimacing at the creek's bite, before lowering himself a few rods from his friend.

Sitting up, Folson wiped his face and bellowed: "Come on in, boys! Water will relieve your aches."

"B-best j-j-join . . . us, Lieu-t-t-tenant," Bickley added. "W-w-eather won't . . . w-won't stay . . . w-warm."

"Aye," said Folson, unaffected by the cold. "You, too, Lieutenant."

"Alas," O'Keeffe said, "the army does not tolerate fraternization."

"You're not a Continental, Lieutenant," Folson said. "Nor are we. We're just a legion of over-mountain men, neighbors, farmers, hunters, and innkeepers. Wash the stink off you. Get your blood flowing again. You can drill us like demons come morn."

"Indeed," O'Keeffe said, and, to Marty's horror, she found the Irishman unbuttoning his breeches. Marty swallowed uncomfortably, almost frozen, but a wild cry shook her to move. Running toward the creek, howling like demons, raced Barnes, Dryden, Golf, and Vance, every one of them naked. Young Golf even stopped beside an elm and began urinating on the trunk.

Quickly Marty gathered her moccasins, embarrassed at the sight of Flint O'Keeffe's buttocks as he tested the water, and sprinted from the creek.

Chapter Ten

She woke with a gasp, and sat bolt upright, pulling the bedroll up over her chest, trying to collect her thoughts, find her bearings. The dream had been so vivid, yet it had only been a dream, and Flint O'Keeffe was nowhere around.

"Another bloody-bone chasing you in your sleep, McKidrict?" Bickley asked good-naturedly from underneath his blankets.

Before she could answer, Ryan Folson, stoking the burning fire with a long piece of blackened beech, swore vilely. "How long have you been awake, Edisto?"

"I am slow to percolate, Ryan."

"Aye. You just lay in bed and wait for me to get the fire going, every bloody morning. Move your arse, you lazy King lover. And that goes for you as well, McKidrict. I'm tired of being a house slave for the both of you."

Laughing, Bickley tossed off his covers and rose. Marty stretched her stiff leg muscles, and arced her back before she stood, still remembering the dream. It had been no nightmare, though, no ghosts, no Willie Duncan, no Seb McKidrict, just her and Flint O'Keeffe and the creek. She might have preferred bloody-bones and raw-heads.

She shook out her bedding before rolling and lashing it, then checked the Deckard rifle and followed Folson's orders to gather more firewood. The morning had dawned clear, not even a hint of frost on the ground—far more inviting than the nights they had spent in the mountains. It was Friday, somebody in the neighboring mess announced, September 29th. Only a few days had passed since she had arrived at Sycamore Shoals, since she had taken charge of her own life. Seemed more like years.

Back at the campfire, she handed Folson a few pieces of dried wood, dropped the rest on the ground, and returned to clean her long rifle.

"Your brother and that weasel Willie Duncan will get no breakfast today, either," Folson grumbled as he tossed the last of the butchered beef in a skillet. "I am tired of serving as a slave to those rogues, as well. Teever Barnes is the only one in this mess worth a salt lick."

Marty scanned the camp, finding no sign of Seb or Duncan, which didn't surprise her. Those two had kept their distance from her since that fateful night at the Resting Place, had been sneaking off to find rum or a game of chance in some other mess. Nor did she see Barnes, but he often pulled the last sentry duty, or went to tend their livestock long before anyone else—even Folson—had risen. Barnes kept busy, probably to keep his mind occupied, to stop thinking about the battle soon to come. Marty didn't blame him at all. Just the other night, Ryan Folson had told her about Barnes's brothers, a pair of Tories from the family farm south of Gilbert Town.

A sloshing water pail told her that Bickley had returned from the creek. He hooked the pail over the coals to heat the water for coffee while Folson fried the last of the beef, already turning rancid.

"We have company," said Bickley, jutting his chin eastward. Marty lifted her head, but Folson leaped to his feet, obscuring her view.

As the big man muttered several oaths underneath his breath, Marty peered over his tall frame, and swallowed down fear. Here came Sergeant Gillespie and Lieutenant O'Keeffe, a little early to begin those numbing drills. Usually they let breakfast settle before barking out orders for formation. When the dream began to etch itself back in Marty's memories, she tried desperately to block it out, and began toying with the Deckard's frizzen. She started to sit back down, but Bickley spoke.

"I reckon all the colonels want to view our parade this fine morn."

Marty looked again. Sure enough, Colonel John Sevier strode purposefully behind Gillespie and O'Keeffe, moving at such a gait he soon overtook them. A short distance beyond that walked Isaac Shelby and the Virginian, Colonel William Campbell.

She had only seen Campbell from afar, a busy Scot in buckskins who, Marty realized now, matched Ryan Folson in height. At first, Campbell had turned down Isaac Shelby's request to send troops to squash Major Ferguson, explaining that his duty was with Virginia and arguing that, if Ferguson brought his troops there, he would be farther from Cornwallis, bettering the chances of a Patriot victory.

Shelby had written again, more urgently, stressing the fact, Marty had learned, that without William Campbell and his Whigs, the over-mountain men had no chance of victory. So Colonel Campbell had arrived at Sycamore Shoals, with 400 Virginians and a nasty temper.

A veritable giant, standing six foot six, he was in his middle thirties with dark hair braided and plaited in a long queue. Campbell soon left the pudgy Shelby puffing in the rear, passed O'Keeffe and Gillespie, moved around the hard-charging Sevier and stormed into the camp, angry eyes taking everything and everyone in sight.

They let the meat burn on the skillet and the water boil over.

"Where is McKidrict?" Campbell bellowed.

Marty's mouth turned dry. "I am . . . ."

"Not you! Your brother! And that dunce who follows him like a pup."

O'Keeffe's eyes locked on Marty as the others reached camp, and he let out a long sigh of relief. Folson tugged on his ear and answered Campbell's question. No one had seen Seb McKidrict or Willie Duncan since last night.

"Why didn't you report this?" Sergeant Gillespie thundered.

"Report what? Those two louses are never around when you need them. Out looking for a game of hussle-cap or cross-and-pile."

Colonel Campbell exploded: "General Washington has forbidden such gambling in the ranks!"

"Well, sir." Folson grinned; Marty could read his mind: *This is not the Continental Army, you idiot.* Folson possessed enough common sense not to say that, however. Instead he addressed the subject of the two missing men. "McKidrict and Duncan show up for supper and show up for breakfast and drill, Sergeant. I . . . ."

"I do not see them now," Campbell said. "Do you see them, Folson? You are cooking breakfast. So where are they? McKidrict!" The goliath towered over Marty, thrusting a long, gloved finger in her face. "He is your brother. Where is he?"

Marty stuttered, trying to find the right answer.

Flint O'Keeffe came to her rescue. "Colonel," he said softly, stepping between the furious Virginian and Marty, "mayhap we should explain our concern." The finger lowered, but Campbell's face remained a brilliant crimson. He owned a temper worse than Seb McKidrict. "McKidrict and Duncan are gone," O'Keeffe said. "Teever Barnes found their horses missing this morning, and reported the disappearance to me . . . ."

"'Tis what you should have done, Folson," Gillespie interjected.

"We were not sure if Duncan and McKidrict had deserted, or if someone had stolen their horses," O'Keeffe continued, ignoring the interruption. "Were not sure, till now. They left sometime last night, it appears. Eugene Vance found their trail heading over Grassy Creek. Now, if they had turned back, that would be one thing. But they appear bound for Gilbert Town, and Ferguson."

"He's your brother," Isaac Shelby stated.

"Sir," Marty said, "I have not spoken a word to my . . . my brother in days. We have . . . different views."

Sevier cleared his throat. "Is his view Tory?"

Folson answered. "Seb McKidrict's view is greed. Greed and murder. Ask anyone in the settlements, and they shall affirm my belief. By Jupiter, we never even knew Seb had a brother till Marty showed up at the Shoals. I say to the devil with both of them. Better off we are, gentlemen, without those two."

Yet everyone still stared at Marty, who shuffled her feet, gripping the rifle barrel tightly. She had to answer.

"That Seb and Duncan deserted . . . that does not surprise me," she said. "All this drill left a strong distaste in their mouths. And Ryan speaks the truth. If Seb thinks Ferguson will pay even a shilling to know about us . . . well, he is neither Whig nor Tory, me thinks. Merely a brigand."

"And blood is thicker . . . ." Campbell whirled, kicked the handle of the skillet, spilling burned meat and the pail of water into the sizzling coals. "First Chambers and Crawford, now these two cowards. Four desertions in two days. And your men, Colonel Sevier. *Your men!*"

"There will be no more, Colonel," Sevier spoke mildly, although he clenched both fists until his knuckled whitened. "I promise you that. Lieutenant O'Keeffe!"

The Irishman snapped to attention.

"This is an army, Mister O'Keeffe, not a gang of rogues. If we desire to win a battle against Major Ferguson, we must have discipline."

"I agree, sir."

"Very well, then we must make an example. We let Crawford and Chambers go, but we cannot let these two men go unpunished. You will strike out with Sergeant Gillespie and four men of your own choosing. You will bring back these two moral-less fiends, alive if at all possible, dead if they resist. Your discretion."

"Yes, sir."

Campbell spoke next. "You will take McKidrict's brother with you, Mister O'Keeffe. We shall learn if this runt is loyal to our cause, or loyal only to his perfidious brother."

* * * * *

They rode hard through the valley, had to in order to catch up with Seb and Duncan, resting and watering their horses briefly before disappearing in the gap of the Blue Ridge. She feared old Abimelech would falter at this pace, but the stallion seemed determined to match the stride of the younger mounts, much the same way Marty had pushed herself not to be bested by any man.

Flint O'Keeffe had chosen three others to accompany them on this manhunt: Eugene Vance, the best tracker, plus Folson and Bickley, the most seasoned and best shots in O'Keeffe's company.

Shortly before they departed, the commanders had agreed that it would be in the army's best interest to divide, lest the British be closer than they thought and ambushed the Patriot forces. Along the Blue Ridge, Colonel Campbell would lead his Virginians through Turkey Cove and on past Wofford's Fort.

Shelby and Sevier would follow the North Cove of Catawba Creek. With luck, Flint O'Keeffe and his small command would rejoin Colonel Sevier that night at Honeycutt's Creek. If not, they would meet the next day at Quaker Meadows.

As they entered the granite pass, O'Keeffe sent Vance and Sergeant Gillespie on ahead, to scout for ambush. One man with a good eye and long rifle could easily hold off an army through this narrow trail.

Marty wasn't worried, though. Neither Seb nor Duncan had ever been much of a marksman, hadn't even considered the possibility of pursuit. After all, no one had gone after Crawford and Chambers. They hadn't bothered to hide their tracks, and had slowed down. Vance guessed the two men were only a couple of hours ahead of them now.

"It could be a trap," Vance suggested.

"Could be." O'Keeffe nodded, and sent Vance and Gillespie on a scout.

Marty knew better. Seb and Duncan had been forced to slow down, not because they planned some ambuscade, but because they had never taken care of their mounts.

She rode at the point of the column through the rock-lined path, long rifle cradled in her arms. When the trail became wide enough for two horses, O'Keeffe pulled up alongside her.

"I desire you to know that I never thought you would have fled with your brother," he said huskily. "Colonel Campbell's suspicions of you are unfounded."

Is that why you looked so relieved when you found me at camp this morning? Marty wondered.

O'Keeffe was not a fool, and he sported an excellent memory. He would not have forgotten their debate back when he had surprised her at the cabin on Tiger Creek. "Nary a whit I care about taxes," she had told him then. "About representation, about the rights of Whigs or Tories. . . . This war is not mine."

Only now it was hers, and she no longer considered this rebellion to be an act of arrogant men. She had grown to enjoy the pleasant banter between Ryan Folson and Edisto Bickley. She even liked John Sevier, although she couldn't say the same of Isaac Shelby and certainly not William Campbell. Didn't like them, maybe, but she did respect them. Thunderation, she no longer even minded those incessant drills, or Gillespie's tirades. All the sergeant wanted to do was make them better soldiers, make them a match for Major Ferguson's Tories by the time they met in battle. Sergeant Gillespie just wanted to keep Marty—and the others—alive.

And as much as she kept telling herself that she did not like O'Keeffe, she found herself attracted to him, enjoyed his company, and, when he finally pulled his horse alongside her and spoke his reassurance, it pleased her.

"When we overtake your brother," O'Keeffe said softly, "I desire you to stay behind. Hold our horses. He will fight, most likely, and I do not wish his blood on your hands."

Marty spat out her contempt. "My blood has been on his hands many times."

The silence lasted only a few minutes. O'Keeffe hadn't expected this outburst, the unbridled hatred. Truthfully it had surprised Marty, too.

"Be that as it may," O'Keeffe said, "this war is not brother against brother."

She let out a mirthless chuckle as she shifted the weight of the Deckard. "It most certainly is, Lieutenant, or haven't you been listening to the men back in camp? Teever Barnes's brothers are Tories from Rutherford County. Most likely they shall ride with

Ferguson. Others back at Sycamore Shoals spoke of their way-ward brothers and uncles and fathers. They damned their own kin as traitors, and their own kin damned them. It most certainly is a war of brother against brother. Me and Seb, we're no different than Teever Barnes and his brothers." That stopped her. She almost laughed. *Oh, I dare say me and Seb are much different than the Barnes boys.*

All this time she had kept her eyes forward, trained on the trail, but now she shot O'Keeffe a glance, glad to find him staring at her. For a moment, Marty thought the Irish Virginian did not trust her, no matter what he had said. She would not have blamed him, either. After all, she was a McKidrict, and folks across the mountains didn't think much of that name. Yet the look in O'Keeffe's eyes said something else. He just wanted to keep her out of harm's way.

Well, Marty thought, *I like you, too, Flint.* As much as she had tried not to.

"You ever killed a man, Marty McKidrict?" O'Keeffe asked bluntly.

When she didn't answer, he said: "You shall see enough death soon. Leave your brother to . . . ."

A rifle shot cut him off.

Chapter Eleven

The shot echoed off the pine-lined granite walls in the distance, coming from where the canyon widened and began flattening into a meadow. Flint O'Keeffe hesitated for just a second, then spurred his horse into a gallop, calling out for Marty to stay put. She bit her lip, wondering, then had to pull hard on the reins to keep from being bowled over as Ryan Folson and Edisto Bickley charged past her. She almost lost her seat in the saddle as Abimelech bolted, following the others.

For a moment, Marty tried to regain control of the stallion. She had never believed in runaways. Her father had taught her that much. "Easiest thing to do is to stop a horse," he had told her time and again. "Pull the rein hard, one-handed, child, turn that cuss's head till it's practically staring you in the eye. He won't have nowhere to go then, but in a circle." She remembered that now. Still, she leaned forward, grinding her teeth, clutching the Deckard, giving Abimelech plenty of rein.

In the meadow, she took in everything, galloping after Folson and Bickley to a grove of crab-apple trees. O'Keeffe was already there, with Eugene Vance and Sergeant Gillespie, pointing at the hill beyond them, Vance's horse on its side in the clearing, lifting its head, legs flailing, trying desperately to stand, flakes of blood spewing from its nostrils. She heard another shot, felt a ball *buzz* past her ear, heard O'Keeffe screaming at her, and then she made the trees, pulling the old stallion to a stop as Folson and Bickley dismounted, Folson firing his flintlock the second his feet touched the ground.

"Don't fire till you see your target!" O'Keeffe yelled, then turned his rage back at Marty, who remained mounted.

"I told you to stay in the canyon!"

"Horse . . . ." She tried to catch her breath, not from fear, but exhilaration. "Spooked. Couldn't stop him."

A grin almost replaced his grimace, but somehow O'Keeffe managed to control this façade.

"There's only two of them," Eugene Vance reported. "In those rocks."

"Might as well be a fortress," Edisto Bickley said.

Folson had reloaded. Shaking his head, he pointed the rifle barrel at the beginnings of a deer trail through the trees. "We can flush them out," he said, "if we make it to the forest before they shoot us dead."

Seventy rods, maybe, Marty figured, trying to make out the distance. But over open ground. Nor would it be easy to flush out anyone in that mess of trees, rocks, and brambles. Plus, it would turn dark soon, easy for these assassins to sneak away and plan an ambush farther up the trace.

Marty stopped, realizing for the first time who these assassins were. Seb McKidrict and Willie Duncan. It had to be them. She had underestimated that old louse of a husband, should have known better. Seb hadn't survived all these years as a thief and murderer with dull wits. He had escaped pursuit from Regulators many times. Marty had thought he would ride his horse to the ground, trying to reach Major Ferguson to collect a bounty of Judas money, but he had stopped, anticipating pursuit, and set up an ambush.

"Sergeant," O'Keeffe was saying, "if we wait till dark, we could sneak in . . . ."

"They'll be gone by dark," Gillespie said. "Folson has the right idea. Charge across there, all of us, and try to flank them."

"Aye," said Folson, always game for a fight. "Let them go now, and they will torment us again. Besides, we have already lost Gene's horse."

While the lieutenant pondered this, Gillespie continued to state his case. "They have shown themselves poor marksmen, Lieutenant. A good rifleman would have killed Vance or me, not mortally wound a horse. The distance is less than one hundred rods. They would not be able to kill more than two of us, me thinks, if luck favors them, and luck has not, so far. Besides, Vance can provide us with some cover from here."

O'Keeffe stared at Marty, and she anticipated what he would suggest. He would have her stay in the trees, let Vance ride her horse across that ground. It made sense, too. Marty knew that. She was a better shot than Eugene Vance, had a better rifle. So, she waited, understanding and accepting the fact that she could not disobey O'Keeffe's orders twice.

"They have not fired upon us in a while," Gillespie said. "We should not tarry, give them a chance to flee."

"Indeed, Sergeant," O'Keeffe said, and ordered Marty to dismount, to relinquish her horse for Eugene Vance, praising her ability as a marksman, that she would be of utmost service by staying in the grove and firing at the deserters.

With a nod, she dropped from the saddle and handed the reins to Eugene Vance. Gillespie pointed to a dark spot in the trees. "Spotted their smoke up yonder," he said. "Does not mean they are still there, though. You will have to detect their muzzle flash when we gallop across. Mayhap you shall hit one, save us the trouble."

"Aye." Her throat had turned dry. She braced the rifle barrel against a tree trunk, not daring to look over at the men as they

tightened cinches and checked rifles. O'Keeffe's piercing—
"Charge!"—caused her to tremble, and hoofs thundered over
the ground. Marty waited for the gunshot, tried to predict
where she would see the flash, but nothing moved, and she
groaned.

They had underestimated Seb McKidrict again, thinking he
would fire quickly, but the sorry swine had held his fire, waiting,
he and Duncan, for the riders to get closer. Fearfully she turned
to find O'Keeffe, realized her mistake, and looked back at the
woods. Still no shot. She felt a measure of relief. They were halfway
across, and still no one fired. Maybe they had fled already, found
some back trail to sneak away. That seemed most likely.

She chanced another glance. Vance had reached the woods
first, causing Marty to grin. Good old Abimelech, thinking
he was a young stallion in a race. O'Keeffe disappeared in the
thicket, then Bickley, finally Folson. They had made it. Seb and
Duncan must have left. She stood up, keeping the Deckard
pointed at the spot, but no longer anticipating any danger. A
minute passed, and she listened for the sound of gunfire, not
surprised that she heard nothing more than the wind and the
clattering of hoofs on stone. Two minutes. More silence. Three
minutes—an eternity.

Then a figure exploded from the forest, about twenty rods
from the animal trail. After a gasp, Marty recovered, tightened
the stock against her shoulder, swung the barrel. A thin man
mounted on a chestnut horse, pulling another horse, its saddle
empty. The rider saw her, lifted his own musket, fired first. There
was a flash in his pan, but nothing more. He cursed as her finger
tightened on the trigger.

Suddenly she screamed, collapsing to the ground, the unfired
Deckard falling beside her. She writhed on the ground, her right

side burning as if on fire. Warm blood streamed across her flesh about halfway between her armpit and hips, drenching her shirt, the linens she had used to conceal her breasts, and the hunting frock. She hadn't even heard the shot.

"Seb," she said through a tight jaw, and cursed her husband, cursed herself for being fooled again.

They had waited, anticipating the charge, and let the riders go unchecked until they had to be deep in the woods. Meanwhile, Seb and Willie Duncan remained at the edge of the forest, hidden in the shadows and pines. Duncan rode out, leading Seb's horse, to draw the fire of the sentry sure to have been left behind, especially since one had no horse. Patiently Seb had waited, and, for once, his shot proved true.

Through the agony, she remembered a conversation they had had, back when she and Seb had first arrived on the Tiger, and Marty had won a shooting match against Willie Duncan. "She shoots better than you, Seb," Duncan had said. Her husband had grunted and grinned. "Only when I don't have to, and only when no one is shooting at me."

Horses. Coming closer. Too soon to be O'Keeffe. Marty lifted her head, couldn't believe it. Duncan was charging toward her, and Seb running behind, shucking his musket and lifting a hatchet. Coming to kill her. Idiots. They should ride off, put distance between them and O'Keeffe, but Seb's blood must be boiling. He had recognized Marty, and wanted to make sure she was dead.

She lunged for the rifle, grabbed the stock, pulled it closer, then rolled over. She slid against a tree, rose to a sitting position, and, fighting the pain in her side, raised the rifle. Only she couldn't steady it. It seemed as heavy as a singletree, the barrel waving crazily, and she felt sick, dizzy.

Duncan let the trailing horse go, drew a pistol as he got closer, but Vance's mare continued its death throes, and the smell of blood frightened the chestnut. The horse reared. Duncan cursed.

Marty fired. She didn't know if she hit Duncan, because Seb was upon her.

Marty rolled over, tightly gripping the stock and the hot barrel, using the Deckard to fend off Seb's awful swing of the hatchet. The metal blade sang against the long rifle's barrel, and the force of Seb's swing, his clumsy running and his massive bulk catapulted him over Marty. He crashed with a *thud*.

Marty's arms trembled, and she clawed her way to her feet. She raised the rifle like a club, shouted out some primal scream, and swung at her husband. Missed. Then her own momentum carried her over, and she fell into a boulder-lined pit, sharp stones stinging her back, her head, her arms. She tasted blood in her mouth, realized she had bitten her tongue. Her rifle lay at her side.

Seb leaped in after her, cursing, swinging the hatchet again. Willie Duncan shouted something. Her rifle ball must have missed him. The hatchet blade hammered the earth, barely missing Marty's head. Seb jerked it free. Raged filled his eyes, like he was some demon. He raised the weapon again, shouting something incoherent, something inhuman. Summoning all her strength, Marty jerked up the rifle, slamming the barrel into the big man's groin. He let out a grunt, staggered backward, and tripped. Another *thud*.

Marty spit out blood, tried to stand, but the world spun out of control. She glimpsed Duncan standing above her, wielding a giant knife.

"My God!" Duncan said, but the words seemed so far away, and he was looking beyond Marty. "Seb!" Duncan said.

The spinning slowed. Duncan's right ear was a bloody mess—her shot had done some damage, after all—and his eyes fell back on Marty. He started down, suddenly stiffened, and toppled to his side, rolling into the pit, groaning, resting against Marty.

She kicked herself away from him, backed up till she could sit. That's when she saw Seb, lying just a yard or so away, looking so peaceful, eyes closed, like a sleeping child. Well, at least his face looked relaxed. Just above where his head rested, propped up, the ragged boulder had been stained by Seb McKidrict's blood and brains.

* * * * *

She must have passed out for a minute or two, because, when her eyes fluttered open, she found Flint O'Keeffe close to her, pressing both hands against her side to stanch the flow of blood, biting his lower lip, his brow furrowed.

"How bad are you hit?" he asked, once he noticed she was conscious.

Instead of answering, Marty sucked in air.

"Vance!" O'Keeffe shouted. "Get a fire started, and make it hot. I need boiling water, strips of cloth to use as bandages, and your knife, white hot, to cauterize McKidrict's wound."

"Cloth might be a problem . . . ."

"Just do it!"

The dying mare snorted.

"And somebody put that animal out of its misery!"

O'Keeffe looked back at Marty, only briefly, avoiding eyes, and started fumbling with her hunting frock. Blood dr from her lips, and she felt dizzy again, not from pain,

She reached out for him, awkwardly, and put her hand atop his. He stopped, swallowed.

"What about this little traitor?" someone asked. She thought it was Folson, but couldn't be sure.

A muffled gunshot. Marty trembled. Mercifully they had killed Vance's horse. O'Keeffe looked away again, but Marty kept holding his hand, squeezing it.

"How bad is Duncan hurt?" O'Keeffe asked.

"It's mortal, Lieutenant." Sergeant Gillespie was speaking. "He won't see Quaker Meadows. I doubt if he'd live to see Honeycutt's Creek if we have to pack him out. You hit him high, but it might take him a while to die."

O'Keeffe's face hardened. "Hang him."

Marty tried to squeeze his hand tighter. She wanted to tell him no, not to do it, but he pulled away, standing now.

"Sir?" Gillespie asked.

"Hang him. I shall not sit here for a day or two waiting for this hydra to breathe his last so we can be gravediggers. Nor will I load him on his horse and have him suffer before we bury him. He is a deserter, an assassin, a Tory traitor. You men take him to the trees and hang him from that oak. It has a good sturdy limb. I shall tend to McKidrict. How's that fire coming, Vance?"

A stutter was the only reply. Wild stares trained on Flint O'Keeffe. Even Ryan Folson could not comprehend the order.

"Hang that son-of-a-bitch!" O'Keeffe barked. "You have your orders. I take full responsibility and will tell Colonel Sevier."

* * * * *

Again, she must have blacked out.

She opened her eyes, gasped, but found herself fully clothed, although Flint O'Keeffe moved over her, fumbling again with her frock. Too weak to resist. He'd learn her secret, thanks to Seb McKidrict, and that lucky shot. He'd see her breasts wrapped tight with linen. He'd . . . .

He stared at her, shaking his head. They were alone in the pit. She tried not to think about what Gillespie and the others were doing at that moment.

"You're one stubborn girl."

Marty shivered, uncertain. "How . . . ?" she said at last.

"I am a man, McKidrict. The way you look at your fingernails. The way . . ."—his head bowed; his voice lowered—"the way you ride your horse."

"Did you know at the cabin on the Tiger?"

His head shook. "Not until the creek when we bathed. You blushed, bolted like a frightened filly." He laughed, and opened her frock, checking over his shoulder to make sure his men were not around. "Ryan Folson thought you just had a bowel complaint, but I had other suspicions." Another chuckle. "Back at your cabin, I called you the most singular individual I have met since leaving Williamsburg. My opinion has not changed."

She closed her eyes, felt his fingers moving gently. "It's not too bad, though it must hurt like blazes."

"Are you going to . . . ?" *That hurt.*

"Sorry," he said. "They'd send you back home. Part of me desires that. But . . . no . . . I enjoy your company. What is your name?"

"My mother wrote Martha Anne in our Bible, but it's always been Marty. I . . . ." She sucked in air again.

She no longer felt his touch, realized he was gone, and opened her eyes, anxious, tired, hurting, although some of Seb's beatings had caused more pain. She felt a measure of relief when she spotted O'Keeffe again, coming back down the pit, gripping Eugene Vance's knife in his hand.

"It does hurt like blazes." Marty tried to smile.

O'Keeffe grunted something, and then he said: "I fear this will hurt worse."

Chapter Twelve

Months had passed since Stuart Brodie felt such a pang in his heart, but, when he tethered his mule at the farm near Bedford's Hill, he remembered the good times he had shared with his brother on the Long Canes. Laughing—singing—trading—telling lies. It had been a fine life, before the war, the butchery. He tried to block out the sudden image of Ezekiel's bloated, bloodied body swinging from the hangman's rope, but couldn't, not even when Saul Pinckert—Brodie had only learned the big man's given name a week earlier—swallowed a tiny, fair-skinned woman with his massive arms, and lifted her off her feet, spinning her around on the porch.

The woman squealed for Pinckert to let her down, but her small feet didn't touch the wooden planks until screams sounded inside the cabin.

"Papa! Papa!"

Suddenly Brodie felt alone. No, more than that. He felt lonely and out of place at this rugged farm, as if he were spying on Saul Pinckert and his family. Four children, the oldest not more than nine, raced through the doorway and leaped upon Pinckert, knocking him to the ground, showering him with kisses, as the tiny woman stepped back, caught her breath, and let out a girlish giggle.

"God bless Major Bulldog," Pinckert said with delight.

"Are you free, Saul?" the woman asked.

"Furloughed," Pinckert managed to answer between hugs and kisses.

Furloughed, Brodie thought. He didn't understand that, either. Major Ferguson had given hundreds of volunteers furloughs, told them to go home, see their families, enjoy a respite but be prepared to return to Gilbert Town at a moment's notice. Why would an educated military officer, a regular in His Majesty's 71st Highland Regiment of Foot, not some volunteer militiaman or brigand like Zachariah Gibbs or Bill Cunningham, decrease the size of his force? It was just another of the many questions—questions that kept multiplying—that Brodie wanted to ask his commander.

Why threaten these over-mountain men?

Why drill with the bayonet?

Why cut your force by hundreds?

Why . . . why give me this Ferguson rifle?

"Who is this man, Saul?"

The woman's question interrupted Brodie's thoughts, and he removed his cocked hat, and bowed. Pinckert pulled himself to his feet, the youngest child, a red-headed girl maybe two years old, clutching his neck, burying her beautiful face into his greasy, smelly clothes.

"This be Preacher Dar . . . this here be Stuart Brodie, me friend. Mister Brodie, this be me wife, Matilda. And these be our brood . . . Caleb, Isabella, Joachim, and Nellie. The major furloughed Brodie, too, Matilda. He got no home . . . rebels burned him out down around Ninety-Six . . . so I brung him home, Matilda, to sup with us."

The invitation had surprised Brodie even more than Ferguson's furlough.

He nodded at the children, donned his hat, and spoke to Mrs. Pinckert. "It is a pleasure to make your acquaintance, madam. You have a lovely family, and a beautiful home."

Unsure of her response, Brodie waited. Matilda Pinckert stared at him, maybe with suspicion, or bigotry. Would she invite him, a man of color, into her home? He steeled himself for the worst, and thought of another question. *Pinckert, you bloody fool, what were you thinking, bringing me here?* Then another: *And why in blazes did you accept, Stuart Brodie?*

Unexpectedly the woman smiled, shook her head, and turned to her husband. "Such manners, Saul, here beneath Pilot Mountain!"

"Educated, Matilda. Hails from Charles Town. Let us eat, woman. We be famished."

* * * * *

They dined on boiled beef, pecans, carrots, and twelfth cake, washing it down with scuppernog. After Pinckert kissed his children good night, he and Brodie retired to the barn, where Matilda had made a comfortable bed for their guest. Pinckert smoked a pipe, while Brodie sipped the last of the wine.

He had never imagined Saul Pinckert as a married man, but the farm was lovely, surrounded by elm and oak, shaded between Pilot Mountain and the South Mountains, spitting distance from Kirksey's Store and South Mountain Gap. A good cabin, barn, lean-to, privy, corral, even abandoned quarters for a few slaves, although Brodie doubted if Saul Pinckert had ever owned another man. Farmland had been cleared, requiring a lot of sweat, a lot of toil. The well water tasted sweet, and deer grazed along the creek in the dusk. Pinckert's children didn't know quite what to make of Brodie. Likely they had never seen a black man, slave or free, before. Yet they were polite, trying their best—except the overly shy two-year-old girl—to make him feel at home. Home.

"You have a lovely family, Pinckert," Brodie said.

"Aye. 'Tis what I be fighting for."

He considered that briefly, wondered if somewhere over the mountains, a couple of Isaac Shelby's men were having a similar conversation. Brodie tried to shake that image. He didn't like it. Men riding with Isaac Shelby and Elijah Cooke had no families. They were nothing more than scavengers, with hearts blacker than ravens, plunderers, murderers. Then again, that's what he had considered Saul Pinckert a few months ago. Besides, Bill Cunningham and his men claimed Loyalist sympathies, riding for the King, and what were they? Scavengers, with hearts blacker than ravens, plunderers, murderers.

War could quickly turn into a complicated matter, and Brodie didn't like thinking about it.

"You surprise me . . . Pinckert." He tried to call the big man by his given name, but it just twisted his tongue. Saul did not fit. Pinckert was, well, Pinckert. That fit.

"Surprise meself at times. Welcome to me home, Preacher Darky. I shall see ye in the morn."

* * * * *

They were splitting firewood after breakfasting on hoecakes and bacon when Pinckert eyed the riders. Blinking away sweat, Brodie followed the big man's finger and saw the dust, then the men, just below Pilot Mountain. Instinctively he sank the axe blade deeply in an oak log and reached for the rifle. Pinckert tucked the stock of his own musket in his armpit, and told his oldest son, Caleb, to hurry to the cabin, pull in the latch string, and stay put.

"But Papa . . . ."

"Mind me, boy." His son obeyed.

The horses were practically done in, and so were the riders, a pair of bearded men in buckskins, eyes bleary, faces scratched, pale, gaunt. They reined up just in front of the woodpile. One man licked his lips; the other just slouched in the saddle, their Adam's apples bobbing as they debated what to say. Neither Pinckert nor Brodie spoke.

Finally the first man cleared his throat. "Your well looks inviting."

"Ye horses be welcome to it," Pinckert replied. "And so be the two of ye, if ye be loyal to His Majesty." Like he was itching for a fight.

The second man sighed heavily, straightening in the saddle. "Indeed. We seek Patrick Ferguson. We bring news, urgent news of the rebels' movement."

They called themselves Samuel Chambers and James Crawford, from Washington County, and they had just deserted Colonel John Sevier's army. They let their horses drink before slaking their own thirst. Brodie would give them that much; otherwise, he would not have paid one halfpence for either of the two. A pair of deserters, rogues with information for the Bulldog. Only, Brodie surmised, this information came with a price.

"How many men does Sevier have?" Pinckert asked.

"More than two hundred," the man called Crawford replied, "but there's more with him."

"How many?"

"I reckon that we should tell this Ferguson chap directly," Chambers said.

Brodie and Pinckert exchanged glances, and the big man, looking over his shoulder at the cabin, slumped.

"I can take them to the major," said Brodie, reading Pinckert's mind. "You stay here with your family. You are on furlough."

"So be ye."

"Aye, but I have no family." Neither one had to leave. Chambers and Crawford could simply follow Cane Creek down to Gilbert Town and find the major themselves, but Brodie figured it was his duty, and, if these men were telling the truth, then the Bulldog would not wait for his furloughed men to return. The army would move out, and Brodie wanted to be with them. He would not miss this fight. That much he owed Ezekiel.

* * * * *

Matilda Pinckert fed the two deserters, then filled a homespun sack with raw potatoes and bread. This she gave to Brodie, who tied it behind his saddle, and doffed his hat.

"Your generosity knows no bounds, Missus Pinckert," he said.

"Nor do your manners," she said. "A small part of me wishes Saul was leaving with you. Mayhap some of your education rub off on him."

"Unlikely, madam," he said, and she covered her mouth, trying not to laugh, but failed.

He shook Saul Pinckert's hand, then kicked his mount into a trot down the path toward the creek, riding behind Chambers and Crawford, letting them lead the way. Brodie didn't trust them enough to show them his back.

* * * * *

Patrick Ferguson guffawed. He rose from his seat behind the desk in William Gilbert's cabin, put his crippled arm in the sling, and shook his head after hearing the report from Chambers and Crawford.

"How many men did you say?"

Crawford answered: "Sevier has about two hundred and fifty. Colonel Shelby, the same number. But Colonel Campbell had nigh four hundred, and McDowell brought better than a hundred from Burke County. You got your hands full, General."

"Major," Ferguson corrected, and poured himself a cordial. Virginia Sal had brought in a tray of glasses and a decanter of liquor. Brodie didn't like seeing her here, a beautiful woman, a distraction, the five officers and two deserters, and even Brodie, in the cabin staring at her stunning red hair, her shapely figure, those mesmerizing eyes. Evidently Ferguson enjoyed their reaction, their envy, as if he were telling them: *She's my woman, boys.* Brodie didn't like that. Even less did he like the Bulldog's reaction to the report from the two over-mountain men.

"You would have me believe these backwater brigands have mustered an army of a thousand?"

"They'll be more," Chambers said. "Cleveland, Williams, Winston, Clarke. They're all bound to come together before they meet you in battle."

The major drank the persico. "A ghost legion," he said, chuckling and motioning for Virginia Sal to return with the liquor and refill his glass. "These phantoms just appear, crawling out of the woodwork like cockroaches."

The woman put the tray on the desk, and looked relieved. It had to be heavy.

Ferguson refilled his glass and smiled at Virginia Sal. Leaving his drink untouched, he called out: "Captain DePeyster!"

Abraham DePeyster snapped to attention. "Yes, Major?"

"Where is William Campbell?"

"Per last report, Washington County, Virginia."

Ferguson nodded. "Not North Carolina."

"No, sir, but . . . ."

A raised hand cut off the captain, and Major Ferguson tilted his head at Stuart Brodie, standing in the doorway.

"Do you believe, Mister Brodie, in this ghost legion?"

"They would have a tough go crossing the mountains at this time of year, and there's more bad weather moving in, it appears, but I put nothing past Shelby or Sevier, sir. I am not familiar with this Virginian, though."

"He's there!" Crawford exclaimed. "I tell you, Campbell's there . . . he and four hundred militia!"

"Your services are appreciated," Ferguson said. "Ensign Yarbrough, would you and Miss Sal be so kind as to escort these fine men to the tavern? Pay them a pound of sterling each and a firkin of ale."

A chubby yellow-haired officer saluted and hurried the two deserters out of the cabin, Virginia Sal leading the way, Chambers protesting loudly that they were telling the truth, that they deserved more payment. Brodie closed the door.

"I am not sure but their story is all puffs, flam, and gasconade," DePeyster said flatly.

"Nor am I." Ferguson smiled. "But I dare say their mathematics are not to be trusted. A thousand men? My guess is half that." He was looking at Brodie again.

Brodie only shrugged.

"Well, gentlemen, we have lured the mouse from the mountains." Ferguson filled glasses with the peach liquor for everyone in the cabin, passing the cordials with his one good hand, moving like an experienced innkeeper, even reminding Brodie of Ezekiel back at Brodie's Inn. Ferguson raised his glass in toast. "To victory."

Brodie lifted his glass, puzzled.

"I knew those backwater fiends would not take my directive lying down," Ferguson said. "It would bring them out of their mountain hide-outs. Pride is the ruin of men, and Isaac Shelby is a proud rebel. Now I will fight him on a field of my own choosing." He downed the persico and threw the glass into the fireplace, smashing it to pieces.

To Brodie's surprise, the other officers did the same. "To victory!" they said, and flung the cordials. Brodie quickly finished his drink, not liking the taste of the peach concoction, and shattered his glass, wondering what William Gilbert would think, if that happened to be his glassware.

"There is the matter of the men you have furloughed," DePeyster said.

"All part of my plan," Ferguson said. "Send our men home, scattered all about the country, and soon they would detect the movements of our enemy better and quicker than our unsuccessful scouting parties." He nodded at Brodie. "It worked. Mister Brodie saw those two gluttons, and brought them here. Now we have the advantage. They are, most likely, at or near Quaker Meadows. We shall meet them, gentlemen, and give them the taste of bayonets. They are militia, but not trained as are our Loyalists. These men cannot abide cold steel, nor has any rebel militia ever stood more than two volleys. We will crush them. No more ambuscades, not more cowardly tactics. Crush them. Kill them."

"The furloughed men?" DePeyster asked again.

"They will join us. Our men have pride. Send riders out in all directions, Captain. Have them gather our brothers, tell them to meet us before we take the field of battle. We ride at dawn."

Brodie opened the door, letting the officers file through first before stepping through the doorway himself.

"Mister Brodie!" Ferguson called.

He turned.

"Do you still doubt me?" The Bulldog's eyes twinkled.

"I never doubted you, Major," Brodie lied, and walked outside.

Chapter Thirteen

She sat upright, instantly wide awake, and clutched her side, groaning at the pain the movement caused. Slowly Marty's eyes adjusted to the darkness, and the soreness subsided as she remembered where she was: in a cabin at South Mountain Gap, nursing the wound from Seb's rifle ball. Gingerly she tossed off the patchwork quilt and swung her feet over the side of the bed. Marty pushed herself to her feet and stumbled to the basin, filled a wooden mug with water, and drank.

Next, she ran her fingers through disheveled hair before reaching inside her hunting frock and shirt, testing the bandages wrapped around her side; at least she hadn't reopened the wound. Flint O'Keeffe had done a good job, although she doubted if that stench of burned flesh would ever leave her nostrils, or if she could forget the searing agony when he pressed that hot knife against her side.

She didn't remember much of the journey back to Sevier's army. For Marty's sake, they had traveled slowly. Guessing that they would not reach Quaker Meadows in time, O'Keeffe had guided them toward Cane and Silver Creeks. On Sunday afternoon, they had caught up with the command a few minutes after the clouds burst open. Lucky, she figured. Wounded as she was, if she had been forced to ride much longer in that numbing rain, she most likely would have caught her death.

In the grayness before dawn, rain pelted the cabin. Staring outside, Marty made out little movement in the makeshift army camp, although she smelled coffee boiling somewhere, and could almost taste the bacon some mess was broiling. She thought she heard a child crying somewhere. A horse snorted from the corrals, and water sloshed as a shadowy figure made its way through the muck and mud from a privy to a tent. The army would not be moving today, Marty thought, not in this weather.

She made herself walk, standing straight, masking pain, no gasps, no shudders, nothing that would make Flint O'Keeffe or Colonel John Sevier tell her she would have to stay behind. The storm would give her some time, maybe another day, but not more than that. Sevier and Shelby did not believe in delays. Earlier that morning, she had heard John Sevier cursing God for the drenching weather. So, Marty figured she had one day to heal enough to continue the march toward Patrick Ferguson and his Tories. Sitting on the edge of the bed, she groaned.

That little trek to the door and back had worn her out. She started to fall backward, exhausted, when she finally remembered the nightmare.

* * * * *

Sergeant Gillespie helps Marty on the horse, and she nods as he tells her they cannot waste time, that they have to ride back to report to the colonel. "Leave him behind," Eugene Vance suggests, pointing at Marty, but O'Keeffe shakes his head. "Some Tory might come along and kill him, call it retribution. McKidrict rides with us."

Retribution. Marty looks up, tries to look away, but can't, transfixed, hypnotized the way a rattlesnake would stun a rabbit with its glowing eyes, right before striking.

Willie Duncan's limp body sways in the breeze, his head tilted at an awful angle. Below him, on a stake pounded into the ground, rests Seb's bloodied head. Crows kaw in the distance, waiting for the riders to leave so they can begin their feast. She doesn't know what they have done with Seb's body, or who chopped off his head and put it on the post as a warning. She doesn't want to know.

A piece of parchment has been tied onto Duncan's body, and written in blood—Seb's or Duncan's or both—is a message:

> *Tories*
> *This is*
> *Your*
> *Future*

She can summon no remorse for either Duncan or her husband— she's a widow, Marty suddenly realizes, and free—not after all they have done to her. But no one, deserter, Tory, or Patriot, deserves this, to be left for crows, wolves, and worms, to be used as a message. Wasn't this what the Patriots were fighting against?

She kicks Abimelech into a walk, heading toward the canyon, telling herself to look straight ahead, only she cannot stop from turning her head, staring at the swinging body and decapitated head. Duncan's body turns, its back to her, then spins around. It is no longer Willie Duncan hanging there, but Flint O'Keeffe. Nor is it Seb McKidrict's ghastly head, but Flint O'Keeffe's. His eyes open, his mouth opens, and Marty screams herself awake.

* * * * *

She let herself drop onto the quilt.

It had been like that back among the crab apples and meadow. They had hanged the dying Willie Duncan, and cut off Seb's head, putting it on a post near the swinging body. Someone had written a note in blood as a forewarning. The dream bothered her almost as much as had the sight of those depredations. Flint O'Keeffe had ordered Duncan's execution, so what did the nightmare mean? She tried not to dwell upon it.

Closing her eyes, Marty tried to sleep, knowing she could not.

* * * * *

"Fresh beef," Ryan Folson said with a grin. "Well, fresh enough, compliments of the McDowell brothers." Water poured off his hat brim as he handed Marty the plate. Rainwater also covered the barely browned strips of beef, as well as a water-logged piece of cornbread.

Sitting up, Marty picked at the food.

"Want me to take a look at your bandage?" Folson asked.

"No!" she snapped, then forced a smile, muttered an apology, and speared a piece of meat.

"Tempers flaring all over camp." Folson pointed to his black eye. "Even Edisto took a swing at me this morn. Rain, cold, all that marching, all that drilling. Builds up on a man's nerves. How do you feel?"

"Better," she said. "I don't remember much after getting shot." Actually, what she did remember, she wanted to forget. "What has been going on?"

Folson laughed. "Everything." He did his best to fill her in. The divided forces had converged on each other as planned, meeting up before they made Quaker Meadows. The McDowell brothers had driven cattle out of the mountains to be slaughtered, even helped tear down their own fence rails to fuel fires. While Marty had been slumped over in the saddle, more volunteers had joined the growing army. Benjamin Cleveland, a Virginian, had arrived from Wilkes County. A short time later, Major Joseph Winston showed up with his militia from Surry County.

All this had happened before Marty and the others rejoined the force. Now, the rain had stopped them.

"Sixteen miles from Gilbert Town," Folson said. "Never seen such an army, McKidrict. Why, we must have near fifteen hundred souls, wetter than trout. Only sixteen miles from stomping them Tories, and, instead of killing the lot of them, we're practically drowning. Raining so hard, a body cannot even see Pilot Mountain from here. That's why I volunteered to bring you some grub." He pointed at the ceiling, leaking in a few places, but at least not over Marty's bed, or Folson's chair.

"Where's Flin . . . where's Lieutenant O'Keeffe?"

"Big parley going on with the officers. I figured they would have tossed you out, to keep them high-and-mighty boys dry, but it was Colonel Shelby . . . Shelby, that pious son-of- . . . well, cannot curse the man now. Shelby, he insisted that you rest. You're a hero, McKidrict, after killing your brother, the traitor, like you did."

Her appetite vanished, and she set the plate aside. She didn't feel like any hero. Nor had she killed Seb, not really. The big fool had slipped or tripped and cracked open his skull. She tried not to picture him dead, just a few feet from her, but then the vision reappeared: a decapitated head stuck on a bloody post, the eyes opening, the facial features changing into those of Flint O'Keeffe.

She shot out of bed, clutching her side, spilling soggy beef and cornbread onto the floor. She lunged toward the door, but the cabin suddenly started spinning, and she almost toppled onto the porch, would have, if Ryan Folson had not grabbed her arm and pulled her upright.

"By Jupiter, what are you doing, McKidrict?" he said. "Best rest. You're pale as a ghost."

She blinked, recalling the sound of the crying child. "Whose cabin is this?" The question suddenly struck her.

"Belonged to some family of Tories," Folson answered with a sneer. "Colonel Sevier, he confiscated it, kicked the woman and her brood out. Four little Tories and their King-loving mama." He spit.

"Where are they?"

"In the barn, I suspect. If they haven't tried to swim their way to Gilbert Town by now."

Marty spied the Deckard rifle and her traps in the corner. She freed herself from Folson's grasp and gathered her belongings, pulled her hat on her head, cradled the long rifle in her arms.

"Where are you going?" Folson called out.

"To the barn," she answered.

* * * * *

"Noble," Flint O'Keeffe told her.

The rain had slackened to a fading drizzle, but water had turned the farmland into a pond, flooded the banks of the creek. In the barn stall, Marty stopped brushing Abimelech.

"Sending a mother and four children back to their home in a rainstorm is not noble," she said.

His gaze fell to the muddy straw. "I suspect it is not." She could just barely hear him.

"Beheading a dead man, even a piece of trash like Seb, and hanging a weakling dying from your rifle ball, that is not what I would call noble, either!" The brush catapulted out of her hands, barely missing O'Keeffe's bowed head, and splashed in a puddle of water just outside the barn door. Marty hadn't meant to shout at him, hadn't meant to throw the brush at him. It had just happened. Still, she did not feel ashamed. Her side burned, but she ignored the pain. Turning savagely, she let out an oath, balled her fist tightly, and slammed the barn wall. Skinned knuckles began to bleed. A spasm of pain rocked her back and chest. "Men," she said contemptuously, and cursed again.

"I did not order the Pinckerts banished to this barn," O'Keeffe said. "That was Colonel Sevier's decision, though the woman is a Tory and her husband, most likely, rides with Ferguson. I ordered Duncan hanged . . . to . . . ."

She heard him walking toward her, but did not face him, would not look at him until she could dam those tears welling in her eyes. His hand touched her shoulder, her hair, then dropped away. Still, she stared at the wall.

"I was indentured as a cooper in Williamsburg," he said. "Thought I wanted to be a preacher, though, so I fled, a criminal, to North Carolina. Most likely I would have died a wanderer, till I met a lovely woman on the Second Broad Brook. But then came this rebellion, and I, as did Caitrín and her family, sided with the Patriots. Zachariah Gibbs and his vermin swept through one night last spring. I was gone. So were Caitrín's father and brothers, except the youngest, only five. Caitrín and Patrick were tied up and left inside, and the cabin fired. After that, I joined Elijah Clarke, burning and killing. Murder, it was. And then one evening around Ninety-Six, just a week after we had heard of Tarleton's butchery at the Waxhaws, we raided this Negro's tavern. And we killed this innkeeper, only a simpleton. Every time I see one of the freedmen riding with us, I see that poor bloke's face. Left him hanging there, we did, choking to death, left the notes . . . 'Tories, this is your future' . . . 'Tarleton's Quarter' . . . and rode away."

Thunder rolled in the distance.

"That is when I came to realize that I was no better than Zachariah Gibbs. So I crossed the Blue Ridge, found my way to John Sevier, believing he was a true Patriot, a true soldier. And, I guess, I was still searching for that home . . . ."

Now she found the words. Softly Marty said: "Where the meadow is green in the summer, the creek bubbles to life. Not too big, not too small, and the mountains are blue in the distance, not too close, not too far."

"You remembered?"

She nodded, and turned.

"It's a place where you respect the land, and the land respects what you offer," O'Keeffe said. "It's not an easy place to live, but it's not impossible to make a living. I can't think . . . ." Tears streamed down his face. "I saw you lying there, shot, mayhap dying, and I just went mad, Marty," he blurted out. "A craziness took hold, perhaps Lucifer himself. I became the monster I was riding with Colonel Clarke. I became Satan, Zachariah Gibbs . . . God have mercy on my soul, I ordered those men to hang Willie Duncan, and did nothing to stop Eugene Vance when he sawed off your . . . ."

She pressed her fingers to his lips, stepped closer. "This war won't last forever," she said. "I would like to see that place, your home in the meadow, near the creek."

Blinking away tears, he managed to smile. "I have to find that place, first."

"I'd like to look," Marty whispered. "I . . . I can't think of a place better to see one's sons and daughters grow."

He pulled her into his arms, and kissed her. Marty forgot all about the bandaged side. Her lips parted. She felt a hunger, but suddenly she was falling backward, pushed, bouncing off Abimelech's side.

The horse snorted, stomped its hoofs, and Marty's eyes shot open.

"McKidrict!"

Colonel John Sevier had stepped into the barn.

Marty patted the old stallion, came out of the stall, and answered. Flint O'Keeffe stood nearby, wiping his mouth, stuttering.

"What is the meaning of this, McKidrict?"

"Sir?" She prayed Sevier hadn't seen them kissing.

"Sending those Tories to their cabin!"

"I . . . uh . . . ." She stuttered, trying to find an answer. *A woman and four children*, she wanted to say. *A two-year-old girl. I am not one to make war on families.* The words, however, stuck in her mouth, her resolve weakening.

"You insolent . . . ." Sevier sounded much like Isaac Shelby and William Campbell. Maybe the rain, the drill, the tortuous march had gotten to the commanders, too.

"It was my order, Colonel," O'Keeffe said. "I asked McKidrict, if she were feeling better, to go to the barn and send the Pinckerts back to their home."

Sevier shook his head with contempt. "Generosity for Tories! We could have used that cabin for our meeting, O'Keeffe, instead of that old slaves' house."

"Yes, sir, but, well, I thought we are here to fight Major Ferguson and his Tories, not a family of . . . ."

"Enough." His eyes bore into Marty. "How are you, McKidrict? Can you ride? Shoot?"

"Yes, sir."

"Good. We leave for Gilbert Town at dawn. Some say Ferguson has fled, but I am not sure of anything except this . . . we shall find him, and defeat him. One thing came out of our meeting that you both should know. We will no longer act like those backwater fools Ferguson thinks we are, but an army. There have been too many fights among our men, too many disagreements, too much insubordination." On those last words, Sevier glared at O'Keeffe, then focused again on Marty. "Colonel Campbell is taking command of the entire force, fourteen hundred men. He did not want the command, but Isaac persuaded him to accept. I answer to him. Colonels McDowell, Shelby, Cleveland . . . everyone . . . reports to him." He marched until he stood inches from Flint O'Keeffe. "And you, *Private* O'Keeffe, will report to Sergeant Gillespie."

Chapter Fourteen

The weather had cleared the following morning, although the skies remained dreary, typical for October. After breakfast, the legion of Patriots, 1,400 strong, assembled to hear Colonel Benjamin Cleveland speak.

"The enemy is at hand," the Virginian said. "Up and at them." Unlike Shelby or Sevier, Cleveland didn't march up and down the line, probably because the pale cuss weighed better than 250 pounds, little of that muscle. Folks said that he was an old fire-hunter, that, as a boy, he had spent more time chasing deer or selling furs and pelts than he had in church, but those days were 100 pounds and thirty years behind him. He hated Tories, though, with good reason.

"Most of you men know the sacrifice we Clevelands have paid for liberty. John Murray's Tories tried to stop us from reaching you, but they failed. They ambushed us near Lovelady's Shoals on the Catawba, hidden in the cliffs, fired on us while we were fording the river. Like assassins. My brother, Larkin, will limp from that musket ball that found his thigh. But we, gentleman . . ."—he dipped his fingers into a waistcoat pocket and withdrew a flattened lead ball—"we, gentlemen, will send this back to those sons-of-bitches, with better results."

A few men—Cleveland's, no doubt—cheered, and the colonel waited for the noise to subside. "Now is the time for every man of you to do his country a priceless service," he said, "such as shall lead your children to exult in the fact that their fathers were the conquerors of Ferguson." He took off his hat. "When the pinch comes, I shall be with you. But if any of you shrink from sharing in the battle and glory, you can now have the opportunity of backing out, of leaving. You shall have a few minutes to consider this matter."

A smiling Major McDowell stepped up next—"to offer his farthing," Ryan Folson whispered with a sigh. After him, Isaac Shelby took to the stump.

"Speeches," Edisto Bickley grunted, and pulled down his wolf-skin cap. "Talking never killed no Tory."

"You want to back out, Barnes?" Eugene Vance asked, snickering.

Teever Barnes answered with a curse.

Marty could feel Flint O'Keeffe's eyes drilling through her, pleading for her to accept Cleveland's generosity, step back, go home, while she had the chance. She planted her feet deeper in the mud, gripped her long rifle tighter.

"You who desire to incline Colonel Cleveland's offer," Isaac Shelby said, "will, when the word is given, march three steps to the rear, and stand, prior to which a few more minutes will be granted for your consideration."

Shelby seemed to be staring at her, but Marty just looked ahead. Her side didn't hurt so much, not today. Instead, she felt Flint O'Keeffe's pain. John Sevier had shamed him, demoted him, reduced him to the ranks. She should have spoken up. After all, O'Keeffe had not sent the woman and her children back to the cabin. That had been Marty's doing. Yet words had failed her.

She waited for John Sevier to give a speech. Seemed like every officer wanted to talk this morning, but Sevier just sat on his horse and glared at Flint O'Keeffe.

"Give the word," Shelby commanded, and Sergeant Gillespie spun on his heel, facing what had been O'Keeffe's company.

"Any man wishing to accept Colonel Cleveland's offer, take three steps back, now!"

Marty listened for any movement, any sound. A minute passed, and she had not budged. Nor had Flint O'Keeffe. She heard something then, a rising noise coming from her left, some commotion. No. Applause. The men were applauding. No one had backed out.

"I am heartily glad . . . ," Shelby began.

Whispered Flint O'Keeffe: "You bloody fool . . . ."

* * * * *

Sergeant Gillespie dismissed the company, but not before directing the soldiers to put rations for two meals in their sacks, and be ready to move out in three hours. Before marching down Cane Creek, however, most of the men were given a noggin of whiskey, compliments of Cleveland and McDowell. By the time Sergeant Gillespie's company rode past, however, the kegs were empty.

As they headed out, Marty glanced back at the farm. The mother stood on the porch, baby in her arms, the other children gathered around her, crying. Not from relief that her tormenters were leaving, though. No, Marty guessed that she feared for her husband's safety if indeed Mr. Pinckert, whoever he was, rode with Major Ferguson.

Sighing, she turned around, in the corner of her eye catching Edisto Bickley staring at her. She shot him a glare, but he chuckled.

"Want to know my thoughts, McKidrict?" Bickley asked.

"No," she said.

He told her anyway. "War is hypocrisy."

She looked away.

"What do that mean, Edisto?" Teever Barnes asked. "Hypocrisy?"

"Means a body says he has these morals, these values, but he don't, not really. Preaches one thing, but don't do what he preaches. Kind of like that Moravian we chased into the canebrake that time two summers back. Hypocrisy. That's what war is. Best you learn that, McKidrict, and accept it."

"You talk too much," she said.

Bickley cackled. "First time anyone has ever said that about Edisto Bickley."

The others, even Sergeant Gillespie, chuckled at that, but Marty refused to smile. Nor did she hear Flint O'Keeffe laughing.

* * * * *

They didn't make it far that day, making camp along the creek at Marlin's Knob. Flint O'Keeffe volunteered for guard duty—it had to be awkward for him, Marty thought, once giving orders, now taking them. *My fault.*

She fell asleep before he returned, relieved by Ryan Folson, and was gone again when Marty woke up.

They moved the next day, early for once, cautiously. No speeches. Just a nervous silence. Everyone expected a battle today. Colonel Campbell sent riders scouting the trail ahead, and once again Flint O'Keeffe volunteered. This time, Marty tried to volunteer herself, but Sergeant Gillespie told her to bide her time, remember that wound in her side. "You shall get your chance to kill more Tories, McKidrict," he said. "Mayhap before the day is done."

They forded winding, flooding Cane Creek repeatedly, anxiously, with hardly anyone speaking. Once, Teever Barnes reminded his friends that Lieutenant Larkin Cleveland had been shot in the thigh while fording a stream. Tories might attempt that again. "Cane Creek," Ryan Folson reminded him, "is not the Catawba River, even like this."

No fight came, however, even when the army marched into Gilbert Town, although a riot almost broke out when Colonel Campbell ordered the inn off limits to everyone but officers. Teever Barnes swore after unsaddling his horse, cursing his family and Major Patrick Ferguson for running off, like cowards. He had been wanting to fight, to kill, to scourge the earth.

Marty knew better. Barnes had been scared to death.

"The fox has fled." Ryan Folson ran his fingers through his thick hair. "But where?"

Ninety-Six, some said. The British major had taken his Tories south a few days earlier, after receiving word from two deserters that the rebel army had formed and crossed the mountains.

"He didn't believe, however, that you had so many men," a Whig named Jonathan Hampton reported. From the look on Hampton's face, he could scarcely believe it himself. "He called you a ghost legion."

"Ghost Legion." John Sevier chuckled. "I like that. And we shall send him to the Holy Ghost before long."

"Not if he's holed up at Ninety-Six," Edisto Bickley said that night. Ferguson's army could fort up in the garrison, which had 400, maybe 500 Tories. They would never flush them out of Ninety-Six, no matter how many more men kept joining this— this *Ghost Legion*.

And, by scores, more joined. Major William Candler brought thirty Georgians, and others were nearby, the gossip spread.

William Hill's South Carolinians were camped at Flint Hill, and Edward Lacey, another South Carolina Whig, was riding with his men, trying to locate the fleeing Tories.

"Well, as much as I would like to hang them King lovers," Ryan Folson said after swallowing a mouthful of coffee, "he can run all the way back to Ninety-Six. Let him go. We can go find Zachariah Gibbs or Bloody Bill Cunningham or even Colonel Tarleton himself. I know them boys will fight us. Would not have to ride so much, either. Let Ferguson run."

"He isn't running."

Marty looked up, surprised to see Flint O'Keeffe squatting by the fire, filling a mug with Folson's unpalatable Patriot coffee.

"What do you mean, Lieuten . . . by Jupiter, can I call you O'Keeffe now, Lieutenant?"

The Irishman grinned. "You can call me Flint, Ryan."

"Well," Teever Barnes said, "I think the colonel was too hard on you, busting you the way he done. I was half a mind to let that mama and her little ones recapture their home, too."

"Colonel Sevier did the right thing." O'Keeffe sipped the coffee, and made a face. "He had to, for good order and discipline. Besides, lieutenant or private, it's not like any of us will ever see a shilling for our work here."

"So . . . you was saying," Folson said. "About Ferguson?"

O'Keeffe nodded. "I was talking to Mister Hampton. He says, from what he learned, the major did not think we had a force of this size. Not even half our number. Now, he would not run from that, not if I know him, or, rather, his type."

"But he's gone," Teever Barnes said. "Riding south for Fort Ninety-Six."

Marty moved closer, deciding she would refill her mug with Folson's coffee, a ploy, she knew. Likely Flint O'Keeffe realized this as well, for no one ever had second helpings of Folson's stout mixture of mud and burned acorns. O'Keeffe, however, did not run off when she sat down, crossing her legs, between Folson and him.

"Nor would Ferguson go to Ninety-Six," O'Keeffe said. "This is a decoy. Ride to Ninety-Six? Risk being attacked by Clarke or Sumter? No, if I were Ferguson, I would head southeast, toward Charlotte Town, toward Tarleton and Cornwallis. He means to crush us."

"But you said he don't know how big an army we got," Barnes said.

With a grin, O'Keeffe said: "That should put the fear of God in him. Fourteen hundred men. We probably match his army."

"We got more," Barnes said. "Major Candler rode in a few hours ago with thirty Georgia boys."

"Candler." O'Keeffe spit out the name, poured the rest of his coffee onto the ground, and stood. He started to go, but Sergeant Gillespie walked into camp.

"Sentry duty, boys," he said. "For the horse herd."

She knew O'Keeffe would volunteer, and tried to beat him, but they both shouted at the same time.

"Thunderation, Flint," Folson said. "I'm beginning to wonder if you don't like my company."

Or mine, Marty thought.

"Lieu . . . O'Keeffe . . . and you, too, McKidrict. We're doubling the guards. Off with the both of you now. Folson and Bickley, you spell them at midnight."

* * * * *

It didn't work out the way she had planned, but she should have known better. Marty spent the next four hours on one side of the horse herd, shivering in the cold, alternating the Deckard from one shoulder to the other, while Flint O'Keeffe stood somewhere east of her. So much for getting a chance to apologize to him, talk to him. Maybe he hated her. She couldn't blame him.

A twig snapped, and the Deckard rolled in her arms, came to her shoulder. She peered into the shadows, waiting.

"I am no Tory," Ryan Folson grumbled, "but, if you shoot me, at least I won't have to wait in the damp till Vance relieves me. Get out of here, McKidrict. Get some sleep."

She practically ran, slowing down only when Folson admonished her, told her she might spook the horses. Marty ducked into the trees, found the path, came out by the brook. She looked toward the camp, saw only a few glimmering fires, then back toward the horses. Nothing.

"Hello," Flint O'Keeffe said.

She found him there, sitting on a tree stump, pitching stones into the water. Marty felt her confidence slipping, the way it used to, before she had met this cock of the walk Irish Virginian, this cooper's apprentice turned preacher turned Patriot, this . . . this seeker—like her.

"I am sorry . . ."—she tested his name—"Flint." Liked the sound of it, the way it came out of her mouth, natural. "I'm sorry, Flint. You should not have told Colonel Sevier . . . ."

"I am glad I did, Marty." A rock skipped over the Broad. "Sometimes." He turned toward her. "If I had let you talk, however, the colonel would have discharged you, sent you home. Mayhap I should have done that."

"I wouldn't have gone," she said. "I would have followed . . . you."

Laughing, he threw the last pebble into the brook, and rose. "You are the most singular individual I have met since leaving Williamsburg."

Confident, again. Marty stepped toward him, leaned her Deckard against an elm. She waited for him to kiss her, wanted him to, but he didn't.

Instead, he sighed. "Major Candler is part of Elijah Clarke's command," he said bitterly. "He was the man who sent us to that Negro's inn. I guess I cannot ever escape that . . . ."

"War," she said, "is hypocrisy."

He looked at her, started to reach for her, but couldn't.

Marty kissed him, briefly, sweetly, and stepped back.

"We should get back to camp," he said. "Tomorrow will be a long day. We shall ride hard, chasing down Ferguson."

"Yes," Marty agreed.

O'Keeffe reached for her.

Chapter Fifteen

Beneath a blanket of wet pine straw and rotting leaves, Stuart Brodie controlled his breathing, peering into the distance as horses trotted past. Horses—and horses—and more horses. He had never seen so many. Finally men on foot, marching and singing; he didn't recognize the song. The Bulldog had been mistaken—badly mistaken—for this Ghost Legion did not comprise phantoms and shadows, but well-armed, determined rebels, flesh and blood, the bulk of them well mounted. Ten minutes after the last had vanished, Brodie pulled himself out of his hiding place. Carefully he backed into the woods, taking no chances, clutching the Ferguson rifle tightly, and did not stop until he neared the clearing. He gave the call of a night owl, waited for the blue jay's screech, and jogged forward.

Saul Pinckert held the reins to three mounts, and waited for Brodie's report.

"You should have stayed with your family," Brodie told him glumly.

"That bad?" Pinckert asked.

He nodded. "Those deserters weren't lying. Shelby and Sevier have more than a thousand men with them. Much more."

"A thousand and a half," said Ensign James Yarbrough, stepping out of the brush. Yarbrough was part of Ferguson's elite troops from the Northern colonies, a Loyalist who called Burlington, New Jersey home. The Bulldog had sent the scouts out to find the rebels, selecting Pinckert and Brodie because they knew this country, and Yarbrough because he knew armies. Yarbrough had climbed a pine, taking advantage of moonlight, to spy on the passing forces.

"They are still heading south," Yarbrough said. "Though I do not expect them to continue. Most likely they will make camp in an hour or less, and send scouts out at dawn."

"Will we fight them?" Pinckert asked.

"That is for the major to order," Yarbrough replied. "We should make haste." He had already mounted his mare.

* * * * *

Ferguson's army had left Gilbert Town three days earlier. Pinckert had arrived, to Brodie's surprise, a few hours before they rode out, saying the rebellion wouldn't be put down with him working his farm. Part of Brodie was glad to have his unlikely friend back with him. A deeper part regretted Pinckert's decision, his duty.

The Bulldog tinkered with his plan as he rode, deciding on a feint toward Ninety-Six, which he hoped would fool Isaac Shelby's Ghost Legion. Upon learning that Elijah Clarke's Georgians were on their way to join the over-mountain men, Ferguson had decided to try to intercept them. Still, he had to learn the location and, more importantly, the size of his pursuers. That's why he had sent Yarbrough, Pinckert, and Brodie on a scout.

They caught up with the Bulldog at a farm worked by a Loyalist named James Step.

"Fifteen hundred men?" Ferguson said. "Are you certain, Ensign?"

"Yes, Major. The Negro and I both reached that number. What's more, sir, they are moving fast, though still riding south. I do not think, however, that they shall be misled much longer."

Paling, Major Ferguson sat on a stool beside Step's well, stroking his chin—he had not shaved in two days—with his one good hand. The silence proved unnerving.

"If we hasten to his Lordship . . . ," Yarbrough suggested. "Charlotte Town is only sixty miles, Major."

The Bulldog did not seem to hear.

"Cleveland's Virginians have already joined Shelby and Sevier, sir," Captain DePeyster said. "John Murray has told us this. Those deserters were right, too. Campbell is with them. Others are sure to join."

Silence.

At length, the major looked up, first at DePeyster, then at Yarbrough, but did not even consider Brodie or Pinckert. Brodie took no offense. This was a discussion among officers.

"Do you think this mission foolhardy, gentlemen? Crushing Clarke?"

DePeyster did not answer. Ever loyal, he would never question the Bulldog. His comments moments earlier were as close as he would come to that. Yarbrough, however, held no such reservations about speaking his mind.

"For all we know, Major, the Georgians are already with Campbell."

Ferguson drummed a beat on his chin with his fingers, finally rose, calm now, reassured, the old Bulldog once again. "We shall move toward Cornwallis, gentlemen, but not directly. Ensign Yarbrough, have a courier send my compliments to Colonel Cruger at Ninety-Six, and ask him to send reinforcements, as many regiments as he can spare." He smiled. "Let the rebels find us. Our furloughed men will rejoin us soon, as will Colonel Cruger. And we shall still wipe out these traitors, gentlemen."

* * * * *

But Cruger wouldn't be coming.

The courier returned Sunday night, catching up with the army at Denard's Ford.

Brodie could see the tension in the men's faces, could feel it, taste it. Ferguson remained calm, however, a rock. The army would be reinforced, he said, perhaps not by Cruger, but by the returning furloughed men, not to mention Zachariah Gibbs's and Bloody Bill Cunningham's raiders. "Victory remains in our grasp," he said before dismissing the officers, then asked Brodie to join him in his chambers.

"You once told me you could write, Mister Brodie," Ferguson said. He took a drink from Virginia Sal, then asked her to take quill and paper to the freedman. She did as told, before discreetly retiring.

"Denard's Ford, Broad River," Ferguson dictated, "Tyron County, October First, Seventeen-Eighty."

Brodie wrote.

"Make it large, Mister Brodie, and legible."

Gentlemen:

Unless you wish to be eat up by an inundation of barbarians, who have begun by murdering an unarmed son before the aged father, and afterwards lopped off his arms . . .

As he wrote, Brodie tried to remember such an event happening. Certainly he had not witnessed it. In fact, that sounded more like an act performed by Bloody Bill Cunningham on Whigs. Still, those Patriots had murdered his brother. He wouldn't put any butchery beneath them.

. . . and who by their shocking cruelties and irregularities, give the best proof of their cowardice and want of discipline; I say, if you

wish to be pinioned, robbed, and murdered, and see your wives and daughters, in four days, abused by the dregs of mankind—in short, if you wish or deserve to live, and bear the name of men, grasp your arms in a moment and run to camp.

The Backwater men have crossed the mountains; McDowell, Hampton, Shelby, and Cleveland are at their head, so that you know what you have to depend upon. If you choose to be degraded forever and ever by a set of mongrels, say so at once, and let your women turn their backs upon you, and look out for real men to protect them.

Finished, Brodie handed the letter back to the Bulldog for his signature. The major looked exhausted as he dipped the quill into an inkwell and signed his name, rank, and regiment. Brodie set the letter out to dry.

"Make four copies," Ferguson ordered. "Send couriers out at dawn in each direction. Keep the original for my papers. We shall see if anyone responds."

The letter sounded desperate to Brodie. Maybe Ferguson had become desperate, realizing that this force of well-trained men loyal to the King had not one whit of a chance against the ruffians from over the mountains. Brodie answered with a nod. He had one courier already in mind. He would send Saul Pinckert north, toward South Mountain Gap. He'd tell that stubborn lout not to come back.

* * * * *

From Denard's Ford, the army moved laggardly, covering barely four miles before they made camp, a cold camp that night, no fires, all the men in line, lying on the wet earth, shivering from the chill and fright of impending battle, waiting with their firelocks and bayonets, waiting.

Waiting . . . for nothing.

The rebels never showed.

It took the Loyalists two days to travel from the Broad River to the Cowpens, just below the Carolina border, a journey that normally would take even a force the size of Ferguson's no more than one day. Then, they tarried two days at Tate's plantation.

By that time, Brodie found his own nerves raw. Why wait? It seemed as if the Bulldog had lost his mind, petrified by fear, paralyzed, indecisive. Brodie couldn't blame that on Virginia Sal or Virginia Paul. Cruger wasn't coming, and few furloughed men had arrived in camp, although they caused cheers when they did ride or walk in. Brodie cursed when he recognized one of the men.

"I told you to stay with your family, Saul!" he screamed at Pinckert—the first time he had ever called the big man by his given name.

"Don't ye preach at me, darky!" the big man bellowed. "Them swine was at me farm, made camp there after we had left." He cursed, trembling with rage. "Turned me cabin into a hospital, sent me wife and young ones to the bloody barn. The barn! It raining, stormy, and cold. Left Matilda, I did, left her holding Nellie, me youngest, sick with fever. Fever from the rain, from sleeping in a barn. Dying, she is. No, sir, I sha'n't shirk me duty, not and let them *Patriots* stain this land with their terror. No, sir. Saul Pinckert aims to fight."

Brodie bowed his head, remembering the shy little girl, Pinckert's lovely wife, the peacefulness of that brief interlude he had spent at Saul Pinckert's home. After a moment, he gathered the reins to the big man's horse and led it away, leaving Saul Pinckert standing in the middle of camp, blubbering like a toddler.

That night, Brodie and Yarbrough rode out on another scout, and, after finding sign of the rebel camp, galloped back to Ferguson.

Midnight had passed. It was Friday, October 6th.

"Suggestions, gentlemen?" Ferguson asked.

"Major," Yarbrough began, "we know we can expect no help from Colonel Cruger, and it seems unlikely that Captains Gibbs or Cunningham will reach us in time. We do not know even where they are, sir. They could be anywhere betwixt Charlotte Town and Savannah. Or dead. I deem it wise, sir, to make haste to Cornwallis. Find and fight these brigands another day."

"Run!" The word shot out of the Bulldog's throat like a cough.

Yarbrough bristled as if the major had called him a coward. Brodie half expected the eager ensign to strike the major with his gauntlet.

"You were searching for your own ground, Major," Captain DePeyster said soothingly. "To fight them."

"Aye," Ferguson said. "But now I have a more pressing concern."

Yarbrough spoke again. "Sir, Charlotte Town is within our grasp . . . ."

The Bulldog's fist pounded on the writing desk set up in his quarters. "And what of our furloughed men, Mister Yarbrough? You would have me abandon them, leave them to the mercy of those backwater butchers? No, sir. By God, I will not leave any of our boys behind, Ensign. We must give them a chance to find us, and fight these rebels if need be."

Another silence, broken by a visibly shaking Yarbrough. "And what if those men you furloughed are not returning, Major?"

"That North Carolinian, Pinckert, he came back, Mister Yarbrough. Twice. What chance will Loyalists have if they do not fight? They shall return, mister. I believe in them, and I sha'n't abandon them. We must give them a chance to find us."

"King's Mountain." Brodie blinked, realizing he had spoken those words. In the flaring light, he saw all eyes staring at him, questioning him. "It's not much of a mountain," he explained, "but the top is wide open. Easy for our boys to find us, and easy for us to see our boys."

"Or enemy movement," Ferguson added.

"It would also be easy for Shelby and Campbell to spy us," Ensign Yarbrough argued.

"Mayhap, but the terrain is fierce," Brodie said. "Sentries should alert us and we could be ready for them, if it came to that. Plus, we would be closer to Colonel Tarleton and Lord Cornwallis. Don't get me wrong. 'Tis no place I would desire a fight, not atop that knob." He remembered standing on that ridge with Saul Pinckert, before they had discovered Virginia Sal. He remembered shuddering uncontrollably, Pinckert's comment echoing louder and louder: *Ye must have just stepped on ye grave, Preacher Darky.*

A Negro superstition. That's what the major would call it. Yet Brodie couldn't shuck the feeling, the foreboding.

"We leave in three hours," Ferguson announced. "Mister Brodie, you will guide us to this King's Mountain. Dismissed, gentlemen. Mister Brodie, I have a letter to dictate to you, a letter to Lord Cornwallis.

My Lord:

I am on my march toward you, by a road leading from Cherokee Ford, north of King's Mountain. Three or four hundred good soldiers, part dragoons, would finish the business. Something must be done soon. This is their last push in this quarter.

The part about the dragoons, Brodie guessed, came close to begging. Begging for Banastre Tarleton to bring his Green Dragoons. That must have settled in the proud Patrick Ferguson's stomach like soured milk, for the Bulldog despised Tarleton and his unholy methods. Brodie wanted to give the letter to Pinckert, but knew—speaking of prideful men—that the big farmer would refuse. Instead, he handed the letter to a capable rider named John Ponder, a young Loyalist not more than fourteen, and wished him godspeed.

The Loyalist militia rode out before dawn. Most of the men seemed cheerful, thinking they were bound for Charlotte Town and the forces of Cornwallis and Tarleton. The officers saw no need to correct them.

Down Cherokee Ford along the narrow trail between Buffalo Creek and King's Creek. After crossing King's Creek near the old mill, they headed through a narrow gap. King's Mountain loomed ahead, rising out of the landscape like a tombstone. Brodie didn't like the allusion.

Thirty-five miles from Cornwallis. We should keep moving. He shook off the thought. Ferguson was right. He wanted to save his men, but, as they climbed over the rocks, fallen trees, slipping, sliding, and stumbling through the dense forest to the top of the mountain, Brodie had regrets. He should never have brought up King's Mountain.

"This is a deathtrap," he overheard Ensign Yarbrough whisper to DePeyster once they reached the crest.

Angrily the captain whirled. Men had started calling DePeyster "the Bulldog's Pup"—ever loyal, he was, loving Ferguson like a son loves his father, loyal, even more loyal than Stuart Brodie.

"You will hold your tongue, Mister Yarbrough," DePeyster snapped. "We shall do our duty. Position sentries, double sentries, down below. Have the wagons placed on the northeast corner, facing north, positioned as a redoubt. Let the men fill their canteens. They shall have need of water directly."

Both men snapped to attention at Major Ferguson's approach. The Bulldog's head kept bobbing in satisfaction.

"Welcome, Major," DePeyster said stiffly. "You are king of the mountain, sir." The joke tumbled like a stone down the ridge. DePeyster's grin came forced, but Ferguson did not notice.

"A wise choice, Brodie." Ferguson continued to nod approval, only Brodie didn't think that way. Nor, from their faces, did DePeyster or Yarbrough. "I do not think, nay, I know for sure, that we cannot be forced from this position by an enemy the size of those barbarians after us." He nodded again, his hand clutching his sword.

The Bulldog had regained his swagger, his confidence. False confidence, Brodie thought.

"Aye," Ferguson said, his voice oddly distant. "Almighty God could not drive me off this mountain."

Chapter Sixteen

The legion had grown even more by the time the Patriots reached Alexander's Ford on the Green River. At Probit's Place on the Broad, Major William Chronicle and twenty Lincoln County men had ridden in. The following evening, another rider bolted into camp, claiming he had urgent news. His name was Edward Lacey.

"Me thinks you're a Tory spy," Ryan Folson told the man. "Keep your rifle aimed on this boy, McKidrict. If he blinks, kill him."

Marty did as she was told, although her finger remained relaxed inside the trigger guard. The man called Lacey eyed her contemptuously, but she refused to waver, even if she had doubts. The bay horse was lathered; the rider looked half dead himself. She had heard talk, too, of an Edward Lacey, a good South Carolina Patriot who had been riding for the past few days, searching for Ferguson. Folson went off to find Sergeant Gillespie; Edisto Bickley and Eugene Vance joined Marty at the edge of camp. She wished Flint O'Keeffe would come.

"My horse is nigh done for," Lacey said. "Would you gentlemen mind if I dismounted?"

"Well," Vance said, "I have cut off the heads of a dozen Tories"—Marty grimaced, recalling the beheading of her husband—"but I sha'n't see a horse suffer. Get off, you Tory, but mind ye. McKidrict, there, he can shoot better than Chucky Jack Sevier."

She kept the barrel trained on the tall Carolinian as he slipped off the mount, holding the reins. The bay snorted, pawed the earth, and pointed its nose toward the riverbank, but Lacey knew better than to let a hot horse drink. "In a little while," he said softly.

"You boys are heading the wrong way," Lacey spoke calmly. "The Old Iron Works? You shall never find Ferguson down that way. He is bound for Charlotte Town, for Cornwallis."

"Speak again, Tory," Vance said, "and I shall test my blade against your throat."

Marty exhaled when Sergeant Gillespie trotted over.

"Where is Colonel Campbell, Colonel Shelby?" Lacey demanded.

"Meeting. Been meeting all night. Who do you say you are?"

"Edward Lacey, damn your eyes. Edward Lacey of Chester District, South Carolina."

"He's a Tory spy," Vance grumbled.

"I am a true Whig, sir," the man snapped. "But a spy of ours has located Ferguson's force, and, you are going the wrong way. Now take me to Colonel Campbell. Immediately."

Gillespie hesitated.

"Take him." Flint O'Keeffe stepped out of the brush. "This is Edward Lacey."

"You know him, Lieu . . . you know him?"

"Indeed. Lower your rifle, Marty. Captain Lacey read aloud our Declaration of Independence when it reached us four years ago. He is no more a Tory than you are Vance, or you, Sergeant. Take him." O'Keeffe stepped forward, grasping the lean rider's hand. "We are comrades," O'Keeffe said. "Captain Lacey ran away from Pennsylvania. I fled Virginia."

"You look fit, Lieutenant," Lacey said, "but, allow me to inform you, my rank is now colonel."

O'Keeffe shrugged. "My apologies and congratulations. But allow me to inform you, sir, my rank is now private."

Oddly they both laughed.

"I deem it best if you come with us," Gillespie told O'Keeffe, then led them toward the main camp, ordering Eugene Vance to tend to the captain's horse.

* * * * *

He left a private, but returned a lieutenant. The men in the company cheered the news, and even Sergeant Gillespie looked relieved.

"We are bound for the Cowpens," Lieutenant O'Keeffe said. "To join forces with Colonel Lacey's troops and other Patriots. Then we will find and smash Ferguson, but we must travel quickly. So only the best horses, the best riders. This is the order of Colonel Campbell."

Marty felt her stomach roiling. *Flint will choose me to stay behind.*

"How many men?" Sergeant Gillespie asked.

"Seven hundred. The rest will wait for us, and cover our backs. 'Tis noble. There is no shame in not being chosen. Indeed, we will have need of your services after our engagement with the enemy. You must watch for Gibbs or Cunningham, Bloody Tarleton or Cornwallis." He looked directly at Marty when he said this, trying to relieve the disappointment that she knew would come. He would not put her in harm's way.

"Vance, your horse is done in. Bullen, Dryden, England, Jamison. You, too, McKidrict. I must ask you to wait behind."

Her lips trembled, and she wanted to plead, to beg. Abimelech could outrun many younger mounts, and Marty had proved her loyalty, her worth. She had already shed her blood. Yet she wouldn't challenge Flint O'Keeffe, would not question his authority in front of the men.

"Lieutenant O'Keeffe, would you allow me to make a suggestion?"

Everyone snapped to attention at the sound of John Sevier's voice. The colonel walked forward, nodding his approval.

"By all means, sir," O'Keeffe said.

"I would loathe the loss of a good-shooting mountaineer like McKidrict. Any son-of-a-bitch who can shoot better than this old son-of-a-bitch deserves a chance at killing Ferguson himself."

Now, it was Flint O'Keeffe's lips that trembled. Tears welled in his eyes, and not from shame.

"Very good, sir," he said woodenly. "McKidrict, see to your horse. And the rest of you. We ride within the hour."

* * * * *

Approximatly 1,000 men, plus Marty McKidrict, had left Sycamore Shoals in September. Now that army had grown to more than 1,800, although several hundred, including the foot soldiers, had been left behind on the Green. They rode hard to the Cowpens, joined there by Lacey's men and others, including several hundred Carolinians led by Colonel James Williams. The Ghost Legion grew again.

Yet the men didn't seem overly confident.

Ferguson was heading toward Charlotte Town, and even Colonel Sevier realized this army could not defeat the enemy if it joined forces with Cornwallis. Plus, nobody could pinpoint the location and strength of the Tory raiders led by Cunningham and Gibbs. For that matter, nobody had an inkling where Ferguson was. For all anyone knew, he had already reached Cornwallis's troops. To complicate matters, it had started to rain by the time they reached the Cowpens in South Carolina.

The Cowpens got its name from the cattle corrals built by a Tory named Hiram Saunders. Colonel Cleveland sent several of his men to the stockman's home, pulled him out of bed, and demanded that he tell them Ferguson's location. The Tory refused, claiming ignorance, so the Patriots helped themselves to his beef, slaughtering more cattle than they could eat or carry, using his fence rails for fires. The McDowell brothers had given the legion cattle and firewood a few days ago, but they had done so willingly.

Colonel Campbell had selected 200 Carolinians to ride on with the army; the rest would remain behind at the Cowpens.

In a drizzling rain, Marty saddled Abimelech, her stomach queasy from Tory beef, or maybe nerves. Her side didn't hurt—well, not too much—until the drizzle turned into a downpour and the temperature dropped. Then she felt a dull ache, which she did her best to ignore. She gave the old stallion a lick of salt before slipping the bit into his mouth.

Boots sloshed in the rain water, and her stomach fluttered again. She knew it was Flint O'Keeffe, even before he put his arm gently on her shoulder and turned her around. Looking up at him, she tried to smile, but couldn't.

After a quick glance over his shoulder, he studied her. "I have tried to keep you out of this," he said, "but it must be God's will. When we fight, you stay close to me, and keep your head down. I will not see you die, Marty. I could not bear to lose another . . . ." He swallowed hard, turned around again. When he spun back, Marty wrapped her arms around his neck, and pulled him toward her.

The kiss was brief—had to be, with all that was going on. His lips tasted like rain water. He held her tightly for a second, then whirled back around, saying something she couldn't quite catch. She wanted to run after him, to tell him she loved him. *Loved him*. How had that happened? After Seb, she had never thought she would love anyone, especially this arrogant Irish Virginian. Abimelech snorted and pawed the earth. She blinked away tears, caught her breath, and checked the saddle cinch.

"Mount up!" someone shouted, and Marty put her foot in the stirrup and swung up. She looked for O'Keeffe, but couldn't find him in the rain.

"Keep your powder dry!" This came from Sergeant Gillespie, a few rods ahead.

All was darkness as they rode.

Rumors reached her after hours in the saddle. Her fingers were numb, her clothes drenched, and she shivered as they rode through the muck. They were lost, someone reported. Foolhardy it was, to be riding in this weather. Bloody Bill Cunningham was camped not six miles from the Cowpens; maybe they would abandon Ferguson's trail and go after that Tory butcher. He had 600 Tories with him. On they rode, though, eastward, the only change in course when they opted to cross the Broad at Cherokee Ford, rather than Tate's.

As they neared the Broad River, she heard someone singing "Barney Lynn"—she recognized the tune.

"That's Enoch Gilmer," Edisto Bickley said. "That's the signal. Means it's safe to cross."

The river ran high, the current swift, and Abimelech struggled before reaching the far bank. Marty caught her breath, leaned forward, and patted the stallion's neck.

"How's your stallion?"

She blinked in the rain, staring ahead, recognizing the voice if not the darkened face. Sergeant Gillespie.

"He's fine."

"Aye, are you up for a scout, McKidrict? You and Bickley?"

Riding behind her, Bickley, grumbled. "We going to stop for a spell, Sergeant? It will be dawn directly."

"Some bantam rooster asked Colonel Shelby that an hour ago, and the colonel came close to turning him into a capon," Gillespie said. "Said the colonel . . . 'I will not stop until night, if I follow Ferguson into Cornwallis's lines!'"

"If the rain doesn't stop us, Sergeant, dead horses will," Bickley said. "We cannot keep this up much longer."

Gillespie ignored the comment, and repeated his question. Bickley answered for both. "Of course, we're game for a scout. Come on, McKidrict, let's find those Tories."

They didn't, though. All they saw was more rain. Any sign would have been washed out by now, Bickley said, and, two hours past dawn, they had given up, about to ride back when a high-pitched voice blurted out: "Hallo!"

A balding string-bean of a man lifted his black hat in greeting, riding a mule that was blind in one eye. Instinctively Marty leveled the Deckard on him, although, after all this rain, she wasn't sure the rifle would fire.

"I am Solomon Beason," he said, ignoring the rifle.

Bickley made introductions; Marty's rifle never wavered. "Are you Whig or Loyalist?" Bickley asked.

The stranger's smile revealed rotten teeth. "Half Whig, half Loyalist," he said, "as occasion requires. In this part of the world, it pays to be, well, as fickle as the wind."

She smiled in spite of herself. Solomon Beason made sense.

"And which way is the wind blowing?" Bickley said.

He sniffed the air. "It blows for liberty," he said. "The game you seek, gentlemen, lies eight miles ahead, atop King's Mountain."

* * * * *

Flint O'Keeffe considered this information with skepticism. Marty and Bickley had ridden hard in the slacking rain, finding the Patriot army taking a forced rest—apparently someone had persuaded Colonel Shelby that they *had* to stop or kill half their horses—near Cashion's Crossroads.

"Ferguson is not stupid," O'Keeffe said. "I hunted on King's Mountain. Caitrín . . . ." He paused, his eyes briefly finding Marty, then looked away. "It's no place to defend."

Yet other scouting parties returned with similar reports. A Tory lady, threatened with one of Chronicle's men's bayonets, said she had delivered a mess of chickens to Ferguson's army on King's Mountain shortly before the skies opened. A Surry County stonemason had captured a Tory dispatch rider, a young lad not old enough to shave, carrying a message from Ferguson to Cornwallis.

The British officer and his Tories, indeed, were camped at King's Mountain, according to the letter. Seventeen wagons, 1,000 troops, most of those Carolina Loyalists and perhaps 100 Northern volunteers.

"That's a Tory each, more or less, for us," Ryan Folson said.

Suddenly the rain stopped, and the sun peeked from the behind the gray clouds.

"A sign!" Marty heard Isaac Shelby yelling. "A sign from the Almighty! Victory is ours!"

Men applauded. Others prayed. Marty felt crushed by the men in her company trying to get closer to hear what O'Keeffe and the others had to say. Eager for a fight. Ready to kill. "Let's go," Teever Barnes demanded. "And if any of you boys see one of my kinfolk, you leave me kill them, you hear!"

The crowd parted briefly, crushing Marty against rancid Edisto Bickley, and a murmur rose from those around her. Chucky Jack Sevier was here.

"Pray tell, how well do you know King's Mountain?" Sevier asked O'Keeffe.

"I used to come down from North Carolina to hunt here, Colonel," he said. "There's a road between two ridges. We're only nine hundred men . . . we can follow that road, sir, then use the forest for cover, reach the ridge, start climbing. If they don't spot us before we enter the timbers, we could surprise them."

Marty steeled herself, trying to stop shaking, from nerves, anticipation, blood lust. She wasn't sure. For days, they had talked of battle, but it had only seemed like idle chatter, even after her shooting scrape with Seb McKidrict, and that had been little better than one of his savage beatings back along the Tiger. But this—suddenly it seemed real, too real. Soon, there would be a battle between Patriots and Ferguson's Tories.

"Very good," Sevier said. "I am glad I did not cashier you, Mister O'Keeffe, when we had our disagreement, and send you home to Washington County."

I wish you had, Marty's lips mouthed.

Sevier started to leave, but, when he spotted Marty, he headed for her. The Washington County volunteers parted again, giving the colonel room, and Marty could breathe again. She tried to stand erect, to look determined, even though she was frightened to death as Sevier put his right hand on her shoulder. "I have an especial assignment for you, McKidrict."

"Yes, sir." Her voice creaked.

"During our interrogation of this Ponder boy, the Tory messenger, he informed us that Colonel Ferguson is wearing a checked shirt and duster, often blows a pair of whistles. His right arm is crippled, from a wound sustained at Brandywine."

"Yes, sir."

"Kill this man, McKidrict. The Tories are like a serpent, and Ferguson is the head. Chop off the head, and the snake dies. Kill the snake, McKidrict. Kill Ferguson."

Men around her cheered, and Sevier's eyes beamed. He patted her back and left. Marty just stood there, frozen, her stomach queasy again, confused and sick. She located Flint O'Keeffe, his face granite, eyes drilling her with Irish intensity. Sevier's order disgusted her.

War is hypocrisy, she told herself.

"Don't set yourself up as holier than thou, McKidrict," Ryan Folson told her. "Chucky Jack has been giving that order to practically anyone who can hit a barn door at one hundred yards."

Chapter Seventeen

The rain had stopped.

Gingerly Marty swung out of the saddle and tethered Abimelech to a young pine. She loosened the cinch and tied her coat and blanket behind the saddle. Beside her, others did the same. Few spoke; those who did mostly prayed.

"Fresh prime," Sergeant Gillespie whispered as he hurried by, crouching, gripping a flintlock tightly in his right hand. "Put fresh prime in your rifles, boys. Fresh prime. And remember Colonel Shelby's words. 'Never shoot until you see an enemy, and never see an enemy without bringing him down.'"

She took the Deckard, following the order, then tried to work up a spit. Her throat was dry. Her heart pounded.

Minutes later, Gillespie was heading back with new instructions. "We fight until we die, boys. Make your peace with your Maker, and remember . . . kill the cripple wearing the pig shirt."

What I am doing here? She had to beat down the rising panic, realized she had spilled most of the priming powder onto the wet ground, instead of the pan. Her hands shook uncontrollably, and she bit her lower lip, tried to concentrate.

Suddenly calm hands reached over and removed the powder horn and rifle. Looking up, Marty watched with relief as Flint O'Keeffe shook powder into the pan, closed it, and handed both weapon and horn back to her. Their eyes met, held briefly, but neither spoke. A few rods away, fifteen-year-old Reginald

Golf sputtered out protests as Sergeant Gillespie ordered him to remain behind with the horses. She could read O'Keeffe's thoughts, understanding that he wished he could countermand that order, have Marty stay instead. Indeed, he was about to do just that, but Colonel Sevier rode by at that moment, muttering encouragement to the men. "Do your duty, boys. Do your duty, McKidrict."

O'Keeffe's eyes filled with tears, and Marty felt her own heart bursting. Young Golf started protesting again, petulant, pouting. O'Keeffe patted Marty's arm, smiled without humor, and moved away, telling Golf to be quiet, lest he give away their position, that he had his orders and he would follow them, or go home, immediately. Golf mumbled an apology, although he still said it wasn't fair.

Tranquil, she thought, studying King's Mountain for the first time. The afternoon sun set the thick forest ablaze with light, glimmering from the rains, the remaining leaves on the trees still ablaze with color, the ground carpeted with those that had turned brown and fallen. A cool breeze—bright sun—skies slowly becoming more blue and less gray. Such a beautiful autumn afternoon. She wiped sweat from her brow.

"God loves us," Teever Barnes said. "All that rain, ground will be so soft, we shall climb that little hill and make nary a sound."

War is hypocrisy.

Only once did she look above the trees, at the mountain top, catching an occasional glimpse of movement by the Tories above. Wood smoke serpentined from campfires into the sky, and she caught distant scents of tea, of food being cooked.

Making his final rounds, Colonel Campbell walked by, erect, tall, confident, informing his troops that anyone could leave now, without penalty or shame (although Marty knew better than to believe the *shame* part). Merely a formality, she thought. No one would turn back now, no matter how frightened. She was proof of that.

A movement to her right caught her eye, and she watched Edisto Bickley put something in his mouth. Not tobacco, either. Beside Bickley, Ryan Folson did the same. Spotting her, the big man motioned to her shot pouch. Next, he smiled, revealing a rifle ball clamped between his teeth.

With a mouthful of ammunition, Bickley whispered to her. "Take four or five balls," he said. "Shall prevent thirst, be easy to get to when the fighting commences."

"Careful, McKidrict," Folson added. "Do not swallow them. Tories might hear them rolling around in your belly."

Marty dumped a handful in an unsteady hand, shoved them in her mouth, disliking the taste of lead, but realizing almost immediately that they produced saliva, easing her parched mouth.

"The counter sign," Colonel Sevier called out as he made his way back, "is Buford!"

"Aye," Teever Barnes said after the colonel had disappeared down the line. "'Tis fitting. We shall avenge what happened at the Waxhaws, friends."

Waxhaws. Marty didn't understand everything about this war, but she knew Ferguson and those men camped atop this mountain had nothing to do with the massacre of Buford's troops. Yet all around her, men nodded, approving of the counter sign as well as Barnes's comment. Nicholas Waldrin, who owned a tavern on the Nolichucky, began honing his hatchet blade, whispering— "Tarleton's quarter."—over and over.

Sergeant Gillespie moved back quickly, telling everyone to stick a piece of paper or cloth into his hat, something that could identify everyone as a Patriot, so they wouldn't be shot by mistake by some comrade.

"Jupiter!" Edisto Bickley tugged on his stinking wolf cap. "If nobody can recognize this as belonging to Edisto Bickley . . . ."

"Shut up!" Folson snapped.

A moment later, Richard Lewis, a miller and sometimes Methodist preacher, told Waldrin to put away his hatchet and keep quiet.

Nerves were taut now. Marty found a patch of calico, stuck it in the brim of her hat.

They were moving into the woods at the base of the mountain. Marty hadn't heard the order to advance. Not marching, really, but going slowly, carefully, creeping into the woods at the bottom of the ridge, then climbing. Bickley and Folson bolted ahead of the main party, on a scout, she presumed. Rifle balls moved around in her mouth, and she almost swallowed them when she tripped over a fallen branch.

"Careful," O'Keeffe whispered.

O'Keeffe had explained the battle plan, not that Marty could make much sense of it. The Patriots would circle the mountain, hit on all sides, surround the Tories and crush them. When the center columns, led by Shelby and Campbell, had formed their battle lines, they would scream like Indians and charge. That would be the signal for the others to begin the attack.

On the north side of King's Mountain, Colonel Sevier's men would climb the highest point of the ridge, Shelby's men to their left, and beyond them groups led by James Williams's Carolinians, Colonel Lacey's men, Major Candler's Georgians, Cleveland's Virginians, and finally, coming up from Clark's Ford, the fifty troops with the German, Hambright, and William Chronicle. Attacking the south side, next to Sevier's command, would be Campbell and his Virginians, 200 strong, with the commands of McDowell and Winston farther to the right.

Darting from tree to tree, oddly quiet. Teever Barnes had been right. Rain had softened the terrain so they barely made a sound. Leaves rustled overhead in the cooling breeze. Cartridge boxes, canisters, canteens, shot pouches, and powder horns rattled softly. Those were the only sounds she could make out.

She moved to the next tree, hugged it briefly, then glanced into the ditch a few rods to her right, spotting the Tory. As she aimed the rifle, a cry rose in her throat, but she choked it off, somehow, some way, not really knowing why. Maybe she feared a scream would let the Tories know they were coming, although once she pulled the trigger, they would certainly understand something was afoot. She jammed the stock against her shoulder, pulled back the Deckard's hammer.

Flint O'Keeffe gripped the rifle, and he said something urgently, whispering. Marty blinked, stared, focusing on the body in the ditch.

"He's done for," O'Keeffe repeated. "A sentry."

Now, she could smell the blood, which covered the dead man's chest. *Man?* A boy, maybe, no older that Reginald Golf. Her stomach went south, but she choked down the bile, made herself look away. Edisto Bickley or Ryan Folson had found him, slit his throat from ear to ear.

The first casualty of King's Mountain.

"Another glorious omen," Teever Barnes said.

She thumbed the hammer, set it down easy, and went to the next tree, O'Keeffe just steps behind her.

Sweating more now. The terrain turned slick, treacherous. Thick trees trapped in heat, and she no longer felt any breeze. She climbed over a rock, slid down, felt a jagged corner rip through her left sleeve. Blood trickled onto her hand. Her side ached, and she fought for breath.

Their pace slackened, and now she could hear movement, even see a few of Shelby's men, higher up, never faltering, determined. Sounds came from the ridge top, too. Laughter—and singing. She remembered the tune; Seb had sung it back on the Yadkin, back before she knew what a demon he truly was.

Again, she stumbled, tried to regain her footing, couldn't, and splashed into a pool of water, soaking her knees, almost swallowing the rifle balls stuck in her cheek. What she wanted to do, suddenly, the urge almost uncontrollable, despite the rifle balls in her mouth, was to scoop up the water, drink, drink, drink, and wash her face. Yet she couldn't. Strong hands lifted her to her feet, pushed her forward.

Higher she climbed, closer to the laughter and music.

She choked the Deckard with both hands, steeling herself for the battle, yet she was unprepared when the first shot sounded. A scream followed, a shout, then musketry, and whoops, yells, screams of Shelby's men.

O'Keeffe crouched beside her, his face contorted from pressure. He muttered an oath. "Too soon," he said. "Campbell's not in position."

To her right, though, came Campbell's booming voice: "Here they are my brave boys! Shout like hell and fight like devils!"

More whoops, sounding like the high-pitched scream of Indians. Cracking muskets. Shouts—groans—war.

They ran, swept up, moving toward the crest, the staccato of battle all around them. "Stay close . . . ," O'Keeffe seemed to plead. Then she lost sight of him. She charged on, trying to find him, veering to her left because she had no choice. Others ran to the right, toward Campbell. She didn't know which direction Flint O'Keeffe had gone.

A musket ball clipped a branch over her head. Another whined off a boulder.

Smoke burned her eyes.

"Here they come! Send them to hell!" It was Colonel Shelby's voice.

She had been swept up into his command. Confused, she turned. A shot clipped her hat. Kneeling, she brought up the Deckard. *Stay here! But where's Flint? I'm supposed to be with Colonel Sevier . . . .*

Teever Barnes squatted beside her, and behind him she recognized Edisto Bickley, firing, reloading. Still, she couldn't find Flint O'Keeffe anywhere.

"Reload, McKidrict! Tories will be on us in an instant!"

She blinked, recognized Ryan Folson's snowy hair. He spit a ball into his hand, drew his ramrod, rammed the charge down the rifle barrel. Quickly Marty looked at the Deckard, realized she had fired—couldn't remember when, or at what. She pulled a ball from her mouth, set the Deckard at half cock. Another shot spanged off a rock to her right. She shook powder into the pan. Another ball whistled, too close, this one fired by someone behind her.

Bickley turned and swore. "Don't shoot us, you ignorant . . . !" Screams, curses, musketry drowned out the rest of his tirade.

She shut the pan, charged and loaded the rifle, working the ramrod furiously. Her ears rang from the gunfire around her. Other noises, too. A pattern of drumbeats from atop the mountain—short blasts from a whistle—a strangle whirling in the air, which, she later realized, came from a nervous Tory who had accidentally fired his musket with the ramrod still in the barrel—a mistake she almost made herself. Her own ramrod remained in the Deckard's barrel. Quickly she snatched it, secured it, brought the rifle up.

"Good God!" Bickley shouted.

Through suffocating white smoke, she saw the Tories, marching down the mountainside, bayonets glistening, moving so slowly, so orderly, it befuddled Marty. A red-coated officer on horseback, both man and beast equally calm, led the charge.

"It's Ferguson!" came a shout.

Marty looked again. No, this man had no crippled arm. His right hand held the horse's reins, his left gripped a massive sword.

A Patriot stepped toward the charge, turned to run. The Tory's sword split his head.

Marty shot into the mass, reloaded, pulled the trigger again. The Tories had stopped firing after several volleys, now just marched with their intimidating bayonets. The Deckard kicked, ripping off bark from the tree. She reloaded, spitting out another ball, heard screams of agony, begs for mercy. Not aiming really. She could hardly see, from the thick smoke and bits of bark that burned her eyes. Reload—fire.

"They are cowards!" a voice bellowed. "One more round, boys! One more round. The Tory cowards will run!"

Only, the Tories didn't retreat. On they came, some of them yipping now, their furious howls matching the screeches and whoops of the mountain men. Cowards? Not hardly. A rifle ball, likely fired by a nervous Whig, knocked off her hat, and, stupidly, she bent over to pick it up, surprised to find four or five holes in the brim and crown.

She fired, backing up now, stumbling with the rest of the Patriots, reloading as she moved, spitting the last rifle ball into her hand.

The sea of Tories swarmed.

"Let's get out of here!"

Her next shot struck someone. He was so close, she saw the shock in his eyes, the green, pine bough pinned in his cocked hat, the splotch of blood spreading across his shirt, crimson liquid pouring from his mouth before he stumbled and fell. It didn't seem real, though. Things moved slowly, dreamily.

At first. An instant later, the world spun out of control, moving so fast, she could barely breathe.

She raised the rifle, took it with both hands, lunged forward and upward, deflecting another man's bayonet thrust. His brown eyes blazed at her, so close she could see beads of sweat on his nose, smell cinnamon on his breath. Another musket barrel suddenly appeared at her head. She tilted her head as the firelock roared, deafening, singeing her hair, burning her ear lobe. Her head pounded, and she fell.

On the ground, crushed by a man's weight, the bayonet stuck in a tree root to her side. Desperately trying to free the weapon, the Tory cursed, then shuddered as a hatchet blade slammed into his forehead. A massive hand jerked the weapon free, and the Tory fell backward, atop another dying man. She smelled their blood, their urine.

"This is a hog killing!" a Scottish voice shouted. She didn't know if it came from a Tory or a Patriot.

A hand jerked Marty to her feet.

Ryan Folson. "Move!" the big man shouted, shoved her, dived into a sinkhole.

Marty tumbled, somehow holding onto the rifle, followed Folson, crashing beside him, rolling over. A Tory jumped in after them, brought the bayonet down. Folson screamed as the blade pierced his calf. Enraged, Marty leaped up, clawing the soldier's face, biting his ear, hitting him, screaming, spitting on his face. They moved around, like a pair of comical dancers, until he shoved her off.

Breath exploded from her lungs. She lay stunned, gasping for air, her back against a slab of granite. The Tory wiped blood off his face, staggered, brought the musket back up, then fell like a pine, the back of his head blown off.

Folson was sitting, wrapping a strip of cloth around his leg, biting his lip so hard that it bled. Lungs working again, barely, Marty dragged herself toward him, to help. He glared at her, cursed.

"Reload, damn you. Reload!"

She spit, forgetting she had used the last ball in her mouth, saw a bit of tooth in her hand. Tossed it aside. Reached into her pouch.

Too late. Another Tory jumped in after her, but she saw him coming. Marty dived, found a dead soldier's musket, and rammed the bayonet into him. He staggered backward, jerking the Brown Bess from Marty's hands, falling down, trying to pull the bayonet from his chest.

She ignored him, opened the pan, grabbed her powder horn . . . .

Whistles blasted. She could hear again, above the din of battle. Men rushed over her, Tories, but none gave her or Folson any notice. One slammed into the tree, clutching it, blood pouring from a hole in his back. Another hole. Then another.

"God . . . ," the man gasped, and slid beside Folson, who kicked the dead man with his good leg.

"After them, boys! After them! See them run like cowards!"

She finished reloading the Deckard, shoved a handful of balls into her mouth, and bent over to look at Folson.

"Off with you, lad," he said through clenched teeth. "I will be fine! Got plenty of company." He attempted a smile, motioning at the dead Tories surrounding him. Marty didn't look at the bodies littering the killing field, tried not to think of the ones she had sent to Glory herself.

War whoops grew louder, and men—some whose faces she recognized—rushed forward, charging after the retreating Tories. Marty climbed out of the depression, glanced back at Folson, then rushed ahead, firing, reloading, firing.

Off to her right, she saw Teever Barnes. He sat on the ground, rocking back and forth, back and forth, tears streaming down his face, caressing a dead man's head in his lap. The dead man wore a red coat, and he looked a lot like Teever Barnes.

She wanted to stop, knew she couldn't. She wanted to find Flint O'Keeffe. Instead, she followed Isaac Shelby, running, slipping, ducking, screaming, heading toward the top of the ridge.

It was 3:15 p.m.

Chapter Eighteen

The rain had stopped.

One more time—he had long since lost track of the exact number—Stuart Brodie circled the ridge. The mountain top, he had decided, was shaped like a spoon, or drumstick, maybe a footprint, perhaps something totally different. He had quit thinking about it. As he came back toward the widest part, he stopped and listened. Brodie studied the trees and boulders, wet his lips, wondering. Probably just one of the pickets below, he told himself, answering nature's call. Suddenly he noticed movement, and his eyes widened.

He aimed the Ferguson rifle, holding his breath, then slowly let it out. A man in a red coat riding a roan horse maneuvered through the thick woods, picking a roundabout path through the rocks and trees, the horse's hoofs clattering on the rocks. With a final lunge, both horse and rider were on the top, beside Brodie.

The officer, a captain named Alexander Chesney who served as Ferguson's adjutant, gave Brodie a hard stare.

"Sorry," Brodie said immediately embarrassed, and lowered the rifle.

"Where is the major?" Chesney asked.

"At his tent, sir."

With a curt nod, Chesney kicked the roan into a walk and headed away. Brodie wanted to ask if the captain had seen anything, but realized he knew the answer, for Chesney rode with no urgency. There's nothing to see, he tried to tell himself. The Ghost Legion, more than likely, was more than fifty miles from here, riding hard for the Old Iron Works and on to Ninety-Six. *Relax, stop pacing this hilltop.* He took another breath, exhaled, and walked through camp. He smelled tea as he passed Uzal Johnson's tent, saw the surgeon checking his timepiece. Other soldiers broiled squirrels, some slept, a few wrote letters, and a black-bearded man from Ninety-Six invited Brodie to take part in a game of lanterloo.

With a sociable grin, Brodie declined. Over the years, he had lost a lot of money gambling on cards, especially lanterloo. Nor was he in the mood to play cards at the moment.

He approached Major Ferguson's tent a few minutes after Captain Chesney had dismounted. With a smile, Ferguson nodded at Chesney's report and handed his cup to Virginia Sal. She refilled it from a teapot. Standing beside the campfire, Captain DePeyster spotted Brodie and motioned him forward.

"Captain Chesney has just returned from a reconnaissance," DePeyster said. "After interviewing our pickets, he reports that all is quiet. Have you seen anything on your surveillance?"

"No, sir. All this rain, though, even a force the size of the rebels would not raise dust."

"I am just glad the bloody rain has stopped." Ferguson set his teacup on a rock and massaged his bad arm. "Makes a body stiff."

DePeyster held a Ferguson rifle in his hands, and had two pistols stuck in his belt. Until now, Brodie had not noticed the weapons.

"Where is Mister Yarbrough?" Ferguson asked.

"On a reconnaissance, too, Major," DePeyster replied.

The Bulldog chuckled. "You are cautious, Captain."

"Aye, sir. That I am."

The major's eyes found Brodie. "As are you, Brodie."

Brodie agreed.

"How is the weapon?" Ferguson nodded at the rifle.

"A fine rifle, sir. I have grown accustomed to it."

"Indeed, and, if our army were not so myopic, every regiment would have a Ferguson rifle instead of those archaic Brown Bess muskets. Alas, His Majesty's military does not move with due haste. Carry on, Brodie. And you, Captains."

Brodie started to turn, but realized he might not have another opportunity. One question had been nagging him for months, and Ferguson had brought up the rifle.

"Major?"

"Yes, Brodie."

He hefted the rifle. "Why did you give me this, sir? I mean, Major, why choose me to have your rifle? Why not Captain Chesney or any Loyalist?"

The Bulldog chuckled slightly, finished his tea, and stood. "You have a select memory, Brodie. When I came to your inn, you held a burned, busted, utterly worthless weapon in your hands. Remember?" After Brodie's nod, Ferguson continued. "I could not very well have a volunteer of mine go up against these backwater mongrels with no weapon."

So utterly simple. Brodie shook off his bewilderment. He started to speak, then laughed. "There was a Hussar carbine with my mule," he said, remembering. He had left his weapons with the jenny, had only his dead brother's ruined flintlock handy, had been running a bluff in case the riders coming to the cabin were Whigs, not men true to King George. He had kept the carbine for a long time, too, though never using it, before trading it to Saul Pinckert back at Gilbert Town.

"Well," Ferguson said at last, "nor could I have one of my men with a *French* weapon." He patted Brodie's shoulder. "I am

175

glad you are with us, Brodie. You are a good man, too good, in fact, for the colonies. Remember the words of Lord Mansfield . . . 'The air of England is too pure for a slave to breathe in.' Mayhap you will remember that after this insurrection, visit England . . . or, better yet, Scotland. Be free."

I am free, Brodie wanted to tell him. *I was born free.*

"Now, carry on," Ferguson said. "And, Mister DePeyster, please, when Ensign Yarbrough returns, send no more officers out on a fool's errand."

A gunshot came from the southwest, somewhere down the mountain. Brodie turned, his mouth parched.

"From the pickets . . . ," Chesney began.

One shot, then another, and an answering cannonade of musketry. Screams. Shouts. A cacophony of savage whoops. Like Cherokees or Shawnees. An Indian raid? No, certainly not against the British, not this far east. Brodie took one step, stopped, remembering the terrifying yells of the rebels back at Musgrove's Mill.

"These things are ominous," DePeyster began. His face hardened, and he shouted: "These are the damned yelling boys!"

Men stood and stared, uncertain, some turning toward the Bulldog.

"Belay those orders!" Ferguson shouted. He brought a whistle to his lips, and the shrill blast hurt Brodie's ears. "Captain DePeyster, follow me! Captain Chesney!" Another whistle blast. Brodie couldn't hear for a second, then saw the Bulldog standing inches from his face.

"Escort the ladies, Brodie, to Doctor Johnson. Then find your place. The battle has begun!"

Gamely, moving unlike a cripple, Ferguson leaped onto Captain Chesney's mount, blowing his whistle, wielding his saber, galloping toward the din of gunfire, DePeyster and Chesney running after him.

Brodie started to follow, but remembered his orders. The redheaded woman knelt on the ground beside the major's tent, both hands covering her ears. He grabbed Virginia Sal's hand, lifted her to her feet, looked for the other woman. She stood, shocked, a few feet away.

"Come on!" he shouted, pulling, practically dragging Virginia Sal behind him. He stopped briefly, looked behind him. He had to let go of Sal's hand to shove Virginia Paul forward. Either that, or lose the rifle, and he would have need of it before long.

"I am all right!"

He blinked, turned. Virginia Sal repeated the sentence, and took off, lifting the hems of her skirt, leading the way toward Dr. Johnson's tent. Brodie followed, tugging the other Virginia behind him.

War cries of the rebels unnerved him, and Brodie considered himself an experienced backcountry fighter. Loyalists ran past him, their faces pale, strapping on cartridge boxes, buttoning their breeches, many hatless, some even barefoot. Drummers beat out orders. Muskets volleyed. Ferguson's whistles screeched.

Brodie dodged a runaway mule, tripped over a tent stake, somehow managed to keep his feet, but had to stop, help Virginia Paul to her feet. They ran, chasing Virginia Sal. More soldiers rushed by him, hurriedly fixing bayonets to their firelocks. Officers bellowed orders. A ball whizzed past Brodie's ear.

How had those rebels managed to get this close to camp? What had happened to the pickets? Other questions raced through his mind. Then he stopped thinking. Stuart Brodie was a fighter, not some coward. Today, he would live or he would die.

That was up to fate. A sudden calmness overcame him, and he slowed down, brought Virginia Paul closer.

"Everything will be all right," he reassured her. "There." He pointed to the tent where Dr. Johnson stood ordering his assistants around. Virginia Sal was already there, motioning for Brodie and Mrs. Paul to hurry. He covered the distance quickly, but not in a panic.

"Doctor," he said when he reached the surgeon's tent. "Major Ferguson wishes these ladies . . . ."

"Yes, yes. Be gone, lad. You have work to do, as shall I, very soon."

He turned. Virginia Sal smiled at him. He remembered finding her with Pinckert on the mountain, never once dreaming they would be back here, for a battle.

More whistle blasts, drum beats. Pounding hoofs. Shrieks. Groans.

Brodie checked the rifle in his hands, and started off toward the sound of battle, stopped, blinked. Virginia Sal sat gently on the ground, her back and head resting against a water keg, so natural, eyes open, red hair blowing in the wind. He started to ask her if she were all right, then saw the small hole in her temple. That bright orange hair would have made such a grand target for some assassin. Her head tilted forward.

He turned, started to tell Dr. Johnson to help her, but realized that this lovely widow was beyond help.

Brodie saw Pinckert, and ran after him, hurrying to fight off the rebel charge.

They reached the trees, moving forward, then stopped. Loyalists were heading back, retreating, chased by a man on horseback. Pinckert raised his carbine, lowered it. "That's Yarbrough!"

Sure enough, and the young ensign was not chasing his men, but rallying them. Or trying to. To stop the retreat. DePeyster suddenly showed up beside them.

"Fall in, lads. Fall in! We shall turn back those mongrels!"

The captain fired, reloaded, fired again.

Brodie aimed, pulled the trigger. Beside him, Saul Pinckert cursed, fumbling with his bayonet, finally tossing it to the ground. "Lot of bloody good this thing will do us now!"

Yarbrough rode past, leaped off his horse, stumbling. Blood flowed in rivulets down both cheeks, over his right eye.

"Report to Doctor Johnson, Ensign!" DePeyster shouted, and reloaded.

"No, sir," Yarbrough replied. "Respectfully, sir!"

Whistle blasts. The Loyalists rushed past, stopped, milling. Brodie fired, and fired. The barrel was hot, and smoke stung his eyes. He could see the rebels, whooping, climbing forward.

"Put a twig, a pine bough, something in your hats, laddies!" It was Ferguson.

Brodie snapped a stem off a tree, reached, stopped. He had lost his hat. He tossed the stem to the ground.

The Loyalists gathered, following orders, listening. One deafening volley followed a second, then a third. And finally: "Charge!"

Ferguson's whistle blared.

He was marching forward now, caught up with DePeyster's men, even though he had no bayonet. They went down the slopes, screaming, answering the rebels' war cry with one of their own despite condemnations from officers that they were His Majesty's soldiers, not barbarians. A bayonet charge was meant to intimidate as much as inflict casualties. Pinckert, his blood up, raced ahead of him, swearing, shucking his carbine for his hatchet. Brodie followed into the thick of battle. The two forces seemed to collide, ramming each other like hundreds of ships.

Savagery all around him. He fired, so close the muzzle blast set a dying Whig's hunting frock ablaze. Swung the rifle, cracking another man's skull. Bayonets ripped into bodies. Blood spurted skyward from dying men, like some unholy artesian well. The rebels were fleeing now, back down the hill.

"Look at them run!" a Loyalist bellowed. "Let us send them back over those damned mountains!"

Brodie tugged on the knife handle, reached down, slit the throat of the man whose head he had just smashed.

He stared, standing, unbelieving.

A black man, a Negro Whig, looking at him, but not seeing. Death's film coated his eyes.

"Come on!" Pinckert screamed, somewhere ahead of him. "We have these cowards on the run!"

The Tory charge halted in the rocks below, though. A volley cut through them like a scythe. Brodie's thigh burned, and he felt the warm, sticky blood soaking his breeches. He fell against a tree. Bark showered his face and hair. Another rifle ball tore off his left earlobe. Brodie took aim at a rebel high in the rocks, squeezed the trigger, saw—or thought he saw—the man tumble below, his rifle bouncing off the rocks. He licked his lips, tasting salty sweat, blood.

Muskets and rifles boomed all around him, some close, some far. Ferguson's whistle blasts seemed distant, and he realized the battle wasn't just here, on the southwestern ridge, but all around King's Mountain. Another mass scream answered a deadly volley, and the Loyalists fell back again, heading uphill, racing past Brodie as he reloaded. He triggered one more round before climbing up the ridge, taking cover behind another tree. Balls thudded around him. Sap coated his hair.

He fired, not knowing if he hit anyone, moved again, stumbling a bit more, his left leg aching from the round that had pierced his thigh. Taking shelter behind another tree, he leaned the rifle beside him, clamped his hands on the wound, grimacing. At least it hadn't struck a bone, or cut an artery. He bit back pain, hurriedly untied the bandanna around his neck, and wrapped it over the bloody holes. Tied it as tight as he could. A shot splintered the stock of his rifle.

Run . . . get back to the ridge! Or be killed.

He tried to step over a rebel's body, but the hand reached out, jerked him to the ground. Brodie crashed with a thud, rolled over. The rebel leaped up, clawing, digging his fingers into the thigh wound, pulling, ripping.

The man looked like the devil himself. At least, his bearded face did, masked in violence, eyes rimmed red, bulging, malevolent. A ugly wolf-skin hat covered much of his dark, dirty hair. He stank of sweat and blood, of wood smoke and greasy buckskins. The hands left Brodie's leg, reached, and grasped his throat, crushing down.

Brodie fought for breath. Knowing he couldn't break the man's hold on his throat, he reached forward slowly, but urgently, trying to find the man's testicles, to squeeze them, twist them. Anything. His hand gripped something else, though, solid, and he realized it was the rebel's knife handle. He jerked the weapon free.

His attacker realized this, cursed, released his grip, straightened. He tried to stop Brodie's thrust, but couldn't. Brodie buried the knife into the man's gut, to the hilt, tried to push it all the way through him, then twisted, and twisted, twisted until the man swayed and toppled, groaning, kicking, tugging at the knife handle with both hands. Blood spilled from both corners of his mouth. He spit, made some gurgling noise, choking on his own blood.

Brodie left the man dying, saw the rebels charging forward, closer, whooping. He picked up the rifle, moved forward, clearing the trees. The battle sounded all around him as he turned, looked for Pinckert, couldn't find him.

"Fall in, lads! Fall in! Regroup. Reload!"

Drumbeats. Blaring whistles. Rifle fire.

"Are you all right?"

Brodie wiped sweat and blood from his eyes, saw Ensign Yarbrough in front of him, his face a bloody mess. *And he's asking me if I am all right!*

"It's kill or be killed, lads!" Major Ferguson loped past, wielding his saber. "Expect no quarter from those monsters, and give them none!" One volley. Another. The Bulldog reined up as the din of gunfire subsided, now only coming in pockets, pockets that surrounded the Loyalist camp. Ferguson lay the sword across his pommel, reached for the longer whistle, brought it to his lips, and blew.

"Charge!"

A murderous cry rose from the throats of the Loyalists—this time, the officers did not object—and down they went again, shouting, firing, stumbling, dying. At first, Brodie moved with them, in that slow march, but that wasn't his nature, and he left, moving from tree to tree, fighting as the rebels did, like Indians, not charging to their deaths with bayonets. He thought he saw Pinckert, but couldn't be sure.

It was 3:15 p.m.

Chapter Nineteen

Almost instantly the Patriots' charge stopped. From the ridge, Tories screamed and attacked, fixed bayonets turning Brown Bess muskets into long, deadly pikes, their volleys noisy, and deadly. The mountaineers did not meet this charge head-on. Instead—wisely, Marty figured—they fell back toward the mountain's base. She dodged between trees, trying to keep her balance running downhill over the terrain, stopping only to aim and fire, covering the retreating comrades. She slid behind an elm, exhausted, barely able to use the ramrod. Her mouth tasted like gunpowder.

A dead man lay less than a rod from her, and she recognized the wolf-skin hat. Edisto Bickley, blood-soaked hands gripping the hilt of a knife in his stomach, mouth open, eyes closed, lips and throat caked with drying blood, and a scarlet pool puddled all around him. He had been gutted like a fish.

She couldn't think about that now, though. A musket ball clipped a piece of bark above her, and she turned, cocked the Deckard, and pulled the trigger. Her shoulder throbbed, already bruised from the rifle's kick. Marty drew the ramrod, spit another ball into her hand, climbed to her feet, and darted to another tree. A man joined her. She started to club him with the stock of her rifle, but noticed a piece of paper pinned to his hat.

"Afternoon," he said, "I am Josiah Culbertson of Sullivan County." Spoken as if he had met her on the streets of George Town.

"Marty," she said, pouring a charge down the barrel. "McKidrict."

They turned at the same time. Marty took the left side of the tree, Culbertson the right. Their rifles bellowed simultaneously.

"Aim for them on horseback, McKidrict," Culbertson said. "Those are the officers. Shoot 'em in the head."

After reloading, they took the same positions. This time, however, Marty's rifle misfired, but she saw a young man on a bay horse wheel from the saddle. Several Tories rushed to him. A few broke and ran back toward the ridge.

She started to move to another position, but Culbertson stopped her. "We got us a good place here, McKidrict." He had already reloaded, and, taking aim, he continued to speak calmly. "They are shooting high, and we can pick them off like . . . ."

His long rifle boomed, answered by dozens of shots from other Patriots. Sheltered by trees, over-mountain men picked off the Tories easily, repulsing the charge. Tory muskets could fire quicker than long rifles, but lacked their accuracy, and bayonets were proving ineffective. "That's bloody unfair!" she heard a Tory officer cry out. "You are fighting like savages!"

"Amen," Culbertson said, chuckling. "And you are fighting like idiots."

She lay under the thick smoke, eyes tearing as she watched the slaughter. A loud hurrah swept through the ranks, and Colonel Shelby rode past, wielding a saber, shouting: "Now boys, quickly reload your rifles, and let's advance upon them! Give them another hell of fire!" Blood streamed down the colonel's head, his balding pate blackened by gunpowder, but he didn't seem to notice the wound. Spurring the horse, he charged uphill, and men followed him.

Marty scrambled to her feet.

"Be seeing you, Marty," Josiah Culbertson said. "I am going to find me a spot higher up, kill some more officers."

"Good luck." She wondered about such a statement as she followed Shelby.

She leaped over dead bodies, most of them Tories. White smoke hovered in the trees like fog, and the whole mountain smelled of sulphur, brimstone, human waste, blood. It stank of hell.

Again, the charge stalled. A man in front of her gasped, dropping his rifle, and stumbled out of control, smashing against a boulder and sliding down. She didn't stop, ran by him, didn't look back. Another ball creased her arm.

Keep your head down, O'Keeffe had told her, an impossible suggestion. Well, maybe not. Josiah Culbertson was keeping his head down, playing the sniper, a role that, while not glorious and certainly not deemed honorable, proved brutally effective. Marty couldn't keep her head down, wouldn't fight like Culbertson, if for no other reason than she wanted to find Flint O'Keeffe, make sure he wasn't hurt—or dead.

She slid to a stop, fired, reloaded, realized Shelby's men were falling back, again, stopped at the summit by Ferguson's men. They had made it farther up the mountain this time, but still could not hold that position. A sword chopped the tree just inches above her head, and Marty fell backward, bringing the rifle up. A man on horseback, in a red coat and plaid kilt, worked wildly to free the weapon, but stopped, buckling in the saddle, a tiny hole in the center of his forehead. She thought about Josiah Culbertson as the Tory officer fell dead, wondered if this had been his handiwork, if that Sullivan County killer had just saved her life.

On her feet again, stumbling, finding shelter in the rocks. She reached into her shot pouch, kept one ball in her fingers, tossed five or six more in her mouth, looked again.

"I'm almost out of lead," she told the man beside her.

"Pick up a dead man's weapon," came the reply, "and his cartridge box. Or use your hatchet." She recognized the voice, looked over. Ryan Folson nodded curtly, squeezed the trigger, and ducked. A ball ricocheted off the rock above his head.

Blood soaked the bottom half of his trouser leg, where he had been stabbed with a bayonet. Powder and dirt, smeared from sweat, covered his face.

"Have you seen Bickley?" he asked as he charged his rifle.

Briefly she closed her eyes, picturing Bickley lying up the mountain, then tried to remember him alive, but couldn't.

"He's dead." The words were flat.

"Aye." That was all Folson said. He pulled back the hammer, lifted his head, and fired without hardly aiming.

"Have you seen Flint . . . the lieutenant?"

Folson didn't answer. Most likely he had not heard. He primed the pan, rammed another charge down the barrel. Suddenly his entire body trembled with rage, and, after he triggered another round, he let out some primal scream.

"The vermin are running again!" Shelby was shouting, still mounted on that horse, which bled from a half dozen wounds. "Onward, boys! Onward to glory!"

Another whoop, another charge. Marty ran, unable to keep up with the limping Ryan Folson, who fired once, then tossed the rifle away and drew his bloody hatchet, moving like a man possessed, the way Seb would attack her when in his cups. Once, she fell to her knees, saw the gory ground, and climbed up, ran, coughing from the smoke, trying to find fresh air. Running . . . yelling . . . .

Ahead of her, Ryan Folson had bent over a log, working feverishly, gripping something. She couldn't see exactly what, at first, then spotted the boots. A Tory had hidden in a hollow sycamore, and Folson had pulled him out, him kicking, squealing, begging.

"Mercy," the man pleaded. "I surrender. I surrender! Mercy!"

Folson buried the hatchet in the man's chest, jerked it free, raised it.

"*Grosser Gott!*" a harsh accented voice called behind her.

Still alive, though spitting out blood, the Tory lifted his hands again, begging. Folson's blade cut off several fingers. The hatchet came up, over Folson's head, then down. Again, and again, and again.

"I'll show you mercy . . . for Edisto Bickley . . . for Buford and his boys."

"*Grosser Gott . . . .*"

Folson stopped at last, bellowing like a bear, moving forward, chopping, swinging, cursing, killing anyone who crawled across the killing fields, anyone with a twig or pine bough pinned to his hat.

She heard cries then, pitiful moans, coughing, choking, men begging for water, a handful of prayers.

"*Grosser Gott.*"

Marty didn't stop. She spit another rifle ball into her hand, drew the ramrod, and ran. Her ears still rang, her head ached. Another man fell before her, and she leaped over his body as it twisted on branches clipped off trees during the battle. Ryan Folson slashed, hacked, and roared. Isaac Shelby spouted out orders, not that anyone could hear him. Tories tried to surrender, only to be shot, stabbed, bludgeoned. She fired, spit, realized she had used all the rounds in her mouth—or had swallowed them. She reached into the pouch. Empty. A man charged her, his eyes wide, blood spewing from his nostrils. She swung the Deckard, the stock crushing his head. Down he went, and Marty tossed the rifle away, grabbed at the man's cartridge box belted around his waist. He groaned.

When she spied his canteen, she ripped it from his body, uncorked it, drank greedily, water spilling out of her mouth, down her chin, cascading onto the front of her frock. Able to breathe again, she looked down at the unconscious soldier. A silver medallion dangled from his neck, and she caught her reflection in the coin. Gunpowder and blood blackened her face, her hair was a mess, her ear almost raw from the musket blast that had come close to killing her. Water from the canteen had washed away some of the grime, but the streaks only made her look more like some monster.

I am a monster, she realized, and she took the man's ammunition, found his musket, picked it up, tried to stand, but her legs did not want to work.

"Major Chronicle's dead!" someone shouted.

"Avenge him! Send these demons to their maker!"

"*Huzza! Huzza!*" An officer on horseback looked down at her. She didn't recognize him, but he wore a piece of white cloth in his hat. "Fight on a few more minutes. Just a few more minutes, and the battle will be over!"

She propelled herself to her feet using the Brown Bess, tripped again, staggered against a tent. A tent! Scores of them. They were out of the forest, on top of the ridge, driving the Tories back in their own camp. The Patriot army seemed larger now, and she realized some of the forces had finally converged. Colonel Sevier rode past, pounding a lathered stallion with the flat of his sword.

She heard more rumors, or maybe fact, that jumped among the men as they stopped to reload, to drink, to mutilate wounded Tories.

"Colonel Williams had been mortally wounded."

"Banastre Tarleton's Green Dragoons were coming up the mountain to crush the rebels."

"Let him come!" Colonel Sevier dared. "We shall whip him, too, but first . . . remember Ferguson's boast! There's your enemy! Kill him!" He bolted ahead, leading weary but determined men running behind him, yelling out huzzas and war cries.

Another voice: "Boys, remember your liberty!"

She recognized the accent and, turning, found Colonel Campbell standing atop a mass of rocks. "Come on! Come on, my brave fellows . . . ."

And then—"Marty!"

She whirled, dropping the musket, leaping into Flint O'Keeffe's arms. They fell against a tent. Tears flowed freely, washing her face. She couldn't stop them. O'Keeffe pried her arms away. His thumbs brushed her tears, and his mouth fell open.

"You . . . you . . . you look . . . are you . . . ?"

"I am all right," she said. She wanted to kiss him, but knew she couldn't. Not here. Not now.

"You . . . y-you . . . you don't look . . . are you sure?"

Musket balls had riddled her hat, her clothes. Her ear burned from the muzzle blast, and her hair had been scorched. She could smell it. Another shot had grazed her arm, but she was fine, especially now. She grimaced, although staring at O'Keeffe, this close to him. Blood trickled down his scalp, turning his curly hair into an ugly mass, thick and sticky like tar. His face, like hers, had been blackened, and his lips were caked, crusted with gunpowder. Another wound spilled blood from the side of his neck, soaking his shoulder.

She reached up urgently. "You're . . . ."

"It's nothing," he said, smiled, then his eyes narrowed. "I told you to keep your head down."

Men rushed around them, shooting at the fleeing enemy, and O'Keeffe halted his scolding. Gripping his rifle, he stood, but, when she started to rise, he pushed her down.

"You stay here!" he ordered, turned, and ran after his men. "I mean it!"

Marty didn't hesitate. She scrambled to her feet, took off after him. She wouldn't lose him. Not again.

He turned, eyes blazing, as if he had expected her. "I said . . . ."

"No!" she shouted back. "I won't!"

With a curse, he reloaded. She knelt beside him, pulled the trigger, began reloading, but found it awkward, clumsy. The Brown Bess was lighter, shorter than the Deckard, and she wasn't used to having a bayonet mounted beneath the barrel. Obviously trained Tories had no problem loading muskets with bayonets in place for they had been doing it since the battle began, but Marty wasn't trained. She sliced her hand, yelped, jerked the hand to her mouth, sucked the blood.

"Here," O'Keeffe said, and he twisted the long blade, removed it from the socket, tossed it aside. He pulled a rag from his pocket, handed it to her, helped her wrap it around her hand.

"Now will you go back . . . ," he started.

"I'm not leaving," she said, and thought to add: "you!"

"Stubborn . . . ."

He didn't finish, just grabbed the rifle, and ran, Marty just steps behind him.

"Give them Buford's play, boys!" Ryan Folson's voice boomed over the musketry. Blood smeared his Cross of Lorraine. "Tarleton's quarter!"

It was no longer a battle, but a slaughter. Tories held out white handkerchiefs, only to be shot down. Others fell to their knees, begging for mercy, their cries denied. Ahead of her, O'Keeffe used his rifle to ram one of his own men, sent him sprawling. It took a few seconds for what had happened to register, but O'Keeffe stood in front of a tent, shrieking, telling his men that this Tory would not be harmed. She saw the man he was protecting, a lanky, young man, coatless, his white shirt sleeves stained crimson, dripping blood. Marty ran to help O'Keeffe.

"He's a surgeon, damn you!" O'Keeffe blared.

"He's a Tory!"

"He will not be harmed!"

The man on the ground cursed, spit, picked up his knife, and ran away.

Visibly shaking, O'Keeffe spun back to the Tory. "Doctor, do you need assistance?"

The doctor coughed out something that resembled a laugh, ignored the question, and turned back to a table, and, picking up a pair of metal forceps, went to work. The wreck of a body lying on the table screamed.

They ran forward. Ahead of her, a Tory boy sprang from behind a wagon, and threw his arms around Sergeant Gillespie. She hadn't seen the sergeant since the battle began.

"Please," the boy said. "I am not fighting."

Gillespie clubbed him to the ground. "Then let me go," he said, "so that I might fight!"

She hadn't fired the musket in minutes, hadn't even bothered to reload, and couldn't. She had lost the ramrod, or fired it by mistake. Now, she stood next to O'Keeffe, watching the carnage. They had driven Ferguson's men through their own camp, into the open. Ahead, the Tories milled like frightened cattle. What was that she had heard someone declare earlier? *This is a hog killing!* Only worse. Officers on horseback tumbled from their saddles. One man raised a white flag, but another redcoat galloped to him, swung his saber, clipping the flag. He bellowed something, but the words were lost. She recognized the redcoat, though, saw that useless arm dangling at his side, the reflections of sunlight from whistles tied around his neck. Ferguson. Tories fired their muskets, those that hadn't dropped them, tried to reload, only to be shot down. Rifles sang from all directions.

Hopeless.

Hundreds of over-mountain men hid just behind the trees, firing from cover, taking an exacting toll. Ferguson and a handful of men raced forward, the gallant cripple swinging his sword on a last-gasp dash for the woods.

"There's Ferguson!" Sergeant Gillespie shouted. "Shoot him!"

She couldn't see now, from tears.

A volley of rifle fire, shouts, hurrahs. She buried her head against Flint O'Keeffe's chest, felt him stroke her unruly hair. Then he lifted her chin with his fingers.

"Keep your head up," he said. Tears rolled down his face.

A black man rode forward, waving a white shirt tied to his rifle barrel. Another volley dropped both rider and animal.

O'Keeffe ran forward, screaming: "Stop it! Stop it, men! This is murder! These men are trying to surrender!"

"So was Buford!" Ryan Folson shrieked back.

"Quarter! Quarter!" More white flags appeared.

Marty had dropped the musket. She just stared at the carnage, in horror, shock, disgust.

Shelby galloped by, jerking the reins, bringing his horse to a stop, bellowing at the Tories: "Damn you, if you want quarter, throw down your arms!"

A few did. Some of those died with another round of fire.

O'Keeffe yelled again: "Stop it! Stop it! Stop this wanton murder!"

Joseph Sevier, a young lad whose face was drenched with tears, whirled on the lieutenant, shouting as he worked powder horn and ramrod. "The damned rascals have killed my father! And I will keep loading and shooting until I kill every son-of-a-bitch!"

Marty bolted to young Sevier, grabbing his rifle, pulling it. He tugged, tried to break her hold, but she wouldn't let go. "There!" she yelled. "There! There is your father! He isn't dead!"

The boy's mouth dropped as Colonel John Sevier rode up, barking out orders that were drowned out by shouts and gunfire. Joseph Sevier staggered back, leaving his rifle in Marty's hands, and fell to his knees, burying his face in his hands, sobbing, shaking, begging for God's forgiveness.

Slowly the sound of gunfire lessened, finally stopped altogether, and Marty tried to swallow, couldn't, took a step toward Flint O'Keeffe, watched the Tories, those still alive, saw their white flags waving in the wind. All around her, she heard the moans again, the begging for water, pleading for mercy, for mothers, for death.

Behind her came that harsh voice, like her conscience. She didn't understand the words, the language, but she knew the meaning.

"Grosser Gott . . . ."

Chapter Twenty

He watched Ensign James Yarbrough die.

"That's bloody unfair!" the young officer had just called out to the enemy. "You are fighting like savages!"

The *banditti* answered with their long rifles, and a ball struck Yarbrough just below his right eye. Another hit him in the throat, and a third round found his chest. Pinckert and another Loyalist helped the ensign from the saddle, and, once freed of its burden, the dun bolted up the mountain. They laid Yarbrough on the ground, folded his arms across his chest.

"Ensign!" shrieked a Loyalist, a mere teenager. "Ensign Yarbrough!"

"He's dead," Brodie spoke hollowly. Poor Yarbrough—a boy, really, not much older than that blubbering teenager—was dead before they helped him out of the saddle. The hysterical Loyalist turned and fled, and a handful followed him. Brodie ignored them, reloaded his rifle, and squeezed the trigger. Only the pan flashed, however, and he cursed.

The counterattack had stopped the rebel charge, but now the Loyalists faltered, stumbled, died. Saul Pinckert had been right back at Gilbert Town. Bayonets were useless against the enemy. *A bloody waste of time. It's the drill that will kill us all . . . .* You couldn't use those long knifes in these woods, not effectively. The Whigs hid behind trees, picking off Loyalists as easily as they would squirrels.

Pinckert surprised Brodie, the way the big ruffian took charge after Yarbrough's death, rallying the men, maintaining order through all the bedlam.

"Get rid of ye pig-stickers!" he yelled. "Take cover behind the trees, the rocks. Fight them like they fight us!"

"But . . . ."

"Just ye do it, boy. Do it or die like Ensign Yarbrough yonder!"

Brodie worked the Ferguson rifle, its barrel burning hot, while Pinckert charged his musket, pulling a cartridge from the box on his hip, biting off the top, and covering it with his thumb. He never got to finish, though. The rebels charged again, screaming, yipping, shooting.

"Fall back!" Pinckert yelled. "Fall back! Let us whip them at the top of the mountain!"

They retreated orderly, or as disciplined as they could, stumbling over the dead and dying. Balls splintered trees, peppering the fleeing militiamen with bark and bits of hot lead. One man leaned against an elm for support, only to fall with the tree, cut apart by rifle balls. A shot splintered the Ferguson rifle's stock, knocking the weapon from Brodie's hands, and he couldn't stop to pick it up, had to keep moving, unarmed, following Pinckert. Back to the ridge, past a line of kneeling Loyalists. Once the last of the retreating soldiers cleared the line of fire, Captain DePeyster lowered his sword. A sergeant gave the order; the muskets rang out.

"*Charge!*"

Brodie looked around, found Saul Pinckert leading the way. He wanted to report Ensign Yarbrough's death to Captain DePeyster. Instead, he pried a musket from a dead man's hands, and stumbled down the mountain one more time.

Caught in an enfilade, the Loyalists fell, screaming, shot to pieces. Brodie slid beside Pinckert as a ball burned his armpit.

He shouldered the musket, but the Brown Bess misfired, and he cursed his stupidity. On the mountain top, he had grabbed the dead man's weapon, but not a cartridge box. He crawled to the nearest body, fumbling with the tin box strapped to the front of the waist belt.

The man's head turned, eyes locking on Brodie.

"Water . . . ," the lips pleaded. Blood frothed from the soldier's mouth.

"I cannot help you," Brodie said, hating himself, removing the waterproof canister before backing away.

They had not reached Ensign Yarbrough's body on this charge, meaning the rebels were gaining ground—*kept gaining ground.* Another attack and they would be in camp, with a clear, open killing field. They had to stop them, here. Now.

"Hold ye ground, boys!" Pinckert shouted. "And show them no mercy. For they shall give you none."

Brodie let out a mirthless laugh when he opened the lid. When full, the japanned canister would hold thirty-six cartridges for Brown Bess muskets. The one he had scavenged held two.

"Come on ye vermin!" Pinckert roared at the hiding rebels. "Fight us, ye cowards!" Then to his men: "We shall kill them all this time, boys. Aim low!"

After another volley, they sank back behind the shelter of the trees, and began to reload. Pinckert looked at Brodie.

"It's hopeless," he said softly.

"I know," Brodie agreed.

"Give them hell, boys!" Pinckert's voice boomed again. "Ye cannot live forever! Glory will be ours!"

Pinckert shut the pan, charged the barrel, and was drawing the ramrod when Brodie saw the puff of dust fly off his friend's chest. Pinckert's groan was lost in an explosion of rifle fire, followed by the unholy whoops of the rebels.

"Now, boys, quickly reload your rifles, and let's advance upon them!" a rebel officer called from somewhere in the thicket. "Give them another hell of fire!"

Pinckert rolled on his back, trying to catch his breath. Then he cursed, spitting out a bit of blood. Brodie tossed the empty musket aside, pressed both hands on Pinckert's wound, stanching the flow.

"Saul's dead!" someone cried. "Saul's dead, too!"

Pinckert managed to say—"I am not dead."—but only Brodie could hear him.

The Loyalists were running back up the mountain, chased by those yelling bandits. Brodie tried to pull Pinckert to his feet, but another ball slammed into the small of his friend's back, driving both into the wet leaves.

"Save yeself . . . ," Pinckert began, but cried out in agony when Brodie lifted him, grunting, throwing the man over his shoulder. They stumbled. A rifle ball pierced Brodie's hand. He winced, more from Pinckert's weight than the wound. Then tripped, jamming his fingers against a rock, rolled over, tried to pull Pinckert up, but couldn't. Gasping for breath, choking on the acrid smoke, he collapsed beside the big farmer.

Another ball whined off a rock.

Brodie lunged for his friend, snatching the bloody buckskin shirt. Pinckert gripped Brodie's hands, surprisingly strong, pulled them away.

"Ye will not die with me . . . ." He spit out flakes of blood. "Go on . . . Stuart." Pinckert sank back into the brush, resting his head against a rock. His eyes focused on something beyond Brodie, maybe the sky, if he could see that far through the smoke and trees. "Oh, Lord," he said softly. "If I could only hold me sweet Nellie, me angel Matilda, me boys . . . once more . . . ." He looked at Brodie again. "Be gone, friend." He coughed, shuddered.

A ball tore through Pinckert's shoulder. He didn't seem to feel it.

"I shall see you in the morning, Saul," Brodie said softly.

Saul Pinckert grinned. "Aye, Preacher Darky," he whispered. "Amen."

Brodie left Pinckert there, running in a crouch as lead flew all around him. This retreat lacked any order, and Brodie knew it was finished. He cleared the woods, staggered toward camp, saw Captain DePeyster raising his sword, blaring orders that went ignored. A ball killed the captain's horse, dropped it like a stone, but DePeyster freed his boots from the stirrups, leaped aside, grabbed another horse with an empty saddle, pulled himself into the saddle, raised the sword again.

"Rally your men!" he shouted to his junior officers.

No one listened.

Finally DePeyster spurred his mount and charged through camp. Brodie followed, past the rows of tents, the wagons. He spotted Dr. Johnson helping a badly wounded man into his tent, oblivious to the tumult around him. Ahead of him, Major Ferguson went down, and Brodie's heart skipped. A second later, however, the Bulldog was up, finding another horse, pulling himself with his one good hand into the saddle. Captain Chesney handed Ferguson his sword—broken—and the Bulldog loped toward the woods and back, shrieking orders.

At the edge of the mountain, the surviving Loyalists gathered for one last stand, but the rebel noose tightened.

Bound for the cord, his mother had told him, but neither she nor Brodie had ever pictured this kind of hangman's noose.

He reached the circle of survivors, knelt, and tried to pick up another abandoned musket. Try as he might, though, his bloody, smashed fingers could not grip it.

"Major!" Captain DePeyster cried out at Ferguson. "The battle is lost, sir. We must yield or die like ducks in a coop!"

Enraged, Ferguson responded: "Never! Never shall I surrender to such damned *banditti!*" He raked the animal's sides with spurs, raced toward a white flag being waved by a Loyalist lieutenant. The broken sword slashed forward, and the flag toppled to the ground. Other Loyalists, even some of Ferguson's best troops from New York and New Jersey, broke toward the rebels, begging for mercy, tossing their muskets away.

They died, and, above the horrible din, Brodie heard the words.

"Give them Buford's play!"

"Tarleton's quarter!"

"Bloody Tarleton!"

"Remember the Waxhaws!"

Ferguson galloped back. His eyes fell on Brodie, but he didn't seem to notice the man. He didn't recognize anything, or anyone. Again, Captain DePeyster begged that they surrender. Again, the Bulldog refused to listen.

Balls whipped overhead, from all sides. The rebels had surrounded them. DePeyster was right. They would all die here if they didn't give up. But if they did? Likely they would be butchered anyway.

The man standing next to Brodie buckled, sank to his knees, and fell, face down.

Brodie just stood, numbed, resigned.

"*Ghost* Legion," he whispered. How badly had Major Ferguson been mistaken, underestimating the enemy, overestimating his chances, troops, and tactics.

"Here is our last chance, lads!" The Bulldog's horse reared. "There will be no quarter. Ride for the woods, men! Ride or die! But at least we shall die game."

Ferguson galloped ahead, swinging his saber, the silver whistles bouncing across his chest as he slashed left and right, cleared a horde of mountaineers, and bolted forward. Behind him rode a handful of officers. Brodie looked for DePeyster, but the captain wasn't with them. Behind him, he heard DePeyster's sigh. *Look away,* Brodie told himself, but he couldn't.

A volley rang out, followed by other shots echoing from the woods. Ferguson's head whipped back violently, and the saber fell under charging hoofs. Wheeling in the saddle, the Bulldog rocked as other balls struck his arm, stomach, chest. Mercifully Major Patrick Ferguson fell from the saddle. Alas, his boot caught in the stirrup, and the panicked horse dragged him over the rocks, over dead bodies. The vermin shot his body as the horse dragged him past the rebel line, then turned, galloping toward the last band of Loyalists.

Brodie ran forward, waving his hands, somehow managing to stop the horse. Three men rushed forward, freed Ferguson's boot, picked him up, laid him gently on a blanket. A second later, one of those men fell, dead from a rifle ball that pierced his heart.

"God have mercy!" Captain Chesney cried out. "He still lives!"

Brodie let the horse go, stared briefly at the Bulldog.

God is not merciful, Brodie thought. *Not today. Not after all that has happened on this awful hill. Not letting the Bulldog live.*

A rider swung onto the major's mount, bolted toward the rebels, waving a handkerchief in his hand. The brigands shot him dead.

"Quarter!" echoed all around him. "Quarter!"

"Captain! We must surrender. We must not all die here!"

"Quarter!"

"Mercy!"

"Quarter!"

Brodie knelt over Ferguson, wiped the blood off the major's face. He had been shot in the head, and Brodie could see the man's brains. Both arms had been broken, as well as the leg that had hung in the stirrup. Blood stained his duster, ripped to pieces by rocks and rebel balls. His breathing was labored, hoarse, but his eyes fluttered open, focused on Brodie.

"Lift my . . . head . . . ." He tried to rise, but sank, swallowed. "Lift my head . . . Mister . . . Brodie. Let me . . . sit . . . for a . . . while."

Gingerly Brodie pulled the major up, leaned him against a rock cairn. The major nodded, as if saying he were comfortable, and spoke again, softer this time.

"Have you . . . seen . . . Miss . . . Sal?"

Brodie remembered the lovely red-headed woman, lying dead in front of the surgeon's tent.

"Yes, sir. She is with Doctor Johnson." And thought to himself: *She is with God.*

The major said something, but Brodie couldn't hear him. Instead, the cries rang out all around him.

"Quarter!"

"For the love of God . . . ."

"Quarter!"

"Tarleton's quarter! Tarleton's quarter!"

"Mercy! Mercy!"

"Stop it! This is murder! These men are trying to surrender! That's a white flag!"

"I don't see it."

"Don't know what a white flag means!"

"Quarter!"

"Quarter!"

Ferguson could not hear the shouts, nor the gunfire. His eyes located Brodie again, but he didn't see him, not really. The Bulldog smiled. "You should have seen me, Mum, at Minden. A 'prodigy' . . . they called . . . me . . . 'of valor' . . . . Oh, what . . . wonderful . . . glory."

He would not watch this man, this soldier he loved, die. Brodie stood. Another ball whistled over his head, and he strode to Captain DePeyster, trying to forget the images of Patrick Ferguson . . . of Ensign Yarbrough . . . of countless faces of men he never knew, or knew only by sight . . . of Virginia Sal . . . of Saul Pinckert.

"We must try again to surrender!" DePeyster said.

An ensign shouted back. "Well, send the nigger! Let the barbarians kill him. For, damn you, I sha'n't go."

Brodie didn't care. Making his fingers bend, he snatched the musket from the ensign's hand, biting back pain, and grabbed the dirty homespun shirt from another officer. Captain Chesney tied the sleeves to the barrel, but would not look Brodie in the eye, knowing they were sending him, in all likelihood, to his death.

The weapon was loaded, Brodie noticed. Not that that meant anything.

Uncaring, Brodie climbed onto the horse, kicked it forward, had to kick harder. The horse hesitated, but finally eased toward the over-mountain men. He waved the flag back and forth steadily, waiting for the rebel ball to strike him.

He didn't have to wait long.

Chapter Twenty-One

It was over. The battle had lasted perhaps an hour.

Only an hour. Marty found it hard to comprehend, feeling as though she had been fighting for days, yet now the Tories began to lay down their muskets, and the Whigs, even Ryan Folson, had stopped killing them. Maybe they finally heard the pleadings, the orders from Shelby, Sevier, and Flint O'Keeffe. Maybe they, too, had at last been sickened by it all, or perhaps they were just too worn out from the blood lust to continue the slaughter.

Mounted on a lathered gray stallion, a Tory captain rode up to Colonel Campbell. Unable to hold his emotions in check, tears streamed down his face as he unbuckled his saber scabbard and handed the weapon, still sheathed, to the devout Whig. "It's damned unfair," the officer said, practically blubbering. "Damned unfair."

Campbell ignored both the comment and the saber. "Officers," he ordered the prisoners, "rank by yourselves. The rest of you, take off your hats and sit down!"

O'Keeffe stepped forward, and helped the Tory dismount, took the proffered weapon, which he passed to Marty. O'Keeffe introduced himself to the bedraggled enemy, who gave his name as Abraham DePeyster.

"Our men were trying to surrender, only to be shot down," DePeyster repeated. "Damnable actions, sir."

O'Keeffe said nothing.

Across the ridge, stories began to spread. That rumor that Banastre Tarleton's Green Dragoons were nearby had proved false. Colonel Williams, however, lay mortally wounded from a shot in the breast. Robert Sevier, the colonel's brother, was also bleeding to death somewhere. Major William Chronicle was dead. Colonel Hambright had sustained a serious leg wound. Yet victory had been complete. Blood stained King's Mountain, predominantly Tory blood. Marty looked around at the carnage. Later, she would learn the estimates: fewer than thirty Patriots killed, and only sixty or so wounded. For the Tories, almost 250 dead and more than 160 wounded. The rest, close to 600, were prisoners. Lord Cornwallis's Western flank no longer existed.

"Three huzzas for liberty!" Colonel Campbell bellowed from horseback, and, lifting his hat, he began the cheer.

"*Huzza! Huzza! Huzza!*"

Laughter seemed out of place, Marty thought, but there was Colonel John Sevier, pointing at the bloody, blackened head of Isaac Shelby. "By God, sir, they have burned off your hair!" Old Chucky Jack could hardly contain himself, giggling so hard he almost tumbled out of the saddle, pointing and laughing, first at Shelby, then at Marty herself.

"You do not look much better, McKidrict. Nor do you Mister O'Keeffe."

Shelby grunted. "I warrant we have more important matters to discuss than my appearance, Colonel," he said stiffly.

She felt Flint O'Keeffe's hand on her arm, and let him steer her away. A few celebratory rifle shots echoed in the woods, more cheers, but now Marty heard the groans again, moans as men writhed on the ground, slipping in their own blood.

"Water . . . please . . . water . . . ."

Sergeant Gillespie quickly brushed past, carrying a wounded man she didn't recognize toward the Tory surgeon's tent.

She stepped over a dead man.

"We should have one of the Tory doctors examine you, Marty," O'Keeffe said. "You look frightful, and quite pale."

Briefly she considered O'Keeffe. He didn't look that healthy himself.

I just want to leave this place, she thought, *go back over the mountains, find that place you keep dreaming about. Forget all about King's Mountain. Start over again. With you.* She wet her lips, struggling to form the words, to tell Flint O'Keeffe how she felt, but his eyes widened, and he muttered an oath, then bolted away.

"Stop it!" she heard him screaming. "Cease with these atrocities!"

Spinning around, she staggered after him, dropping the Tory's saber, her mouth falling open. Ryan Folson and a handful of other men had gathered over a body—the late Major Patrick Ferguson. Folson had unbuttoned his breeches, and stood urinating on the corpse. Others did the same, splashing urine off the dead man's bloody clothes, his face, drenching his hair.

"Well, Paddy," Folson said, after emptying his bladder and then spitting on the body until his mouth turned dry. "I guess you will not be hanging any of us. Or laying our country to waste with fire and sword. Will you? Hurry up, lads. When you are done, I think I shall commence to shat on this man's . . . ."

O'Keeffe shoved him aside. "Outrageous!" he bellowed. "Here lies a brave man, and, by Jehovah, I will not stand by and allow these transgressions."

"Lieutenant . . . ," Nicholas Waldrin began, but O'Keeffe whirled on him, pushed him backward as Waldrin buttoned his breeches.

"Abominable!" O'Keeffe shrieked. "Victory is ours, and I will not allow you to disgrace what we have accomplished here."

Another man, one she did not know, swore underneath his breath and began spraying Ferguson with yellow urine. "I do not answer to you . . . ," he began, but never finished. Flint O'Keeffe's fist sent him sprawling, splattering his moccasins with urine. The man rolled up, attempted to stand and charge, but slipped.

"Enough!" O'Keeffe yelled. "E . . . ." His knees buckled, and he suddenly gasped for air, dropping beside the dead major. A groan escaped his lips, and a second later he rolled to his side. Only then did Marty realize a gun had been fired.

She ran forward, tears welling in her eyes, looking at Folson, Waldrin, and the other savages, trying to find which one of them had just shot Flint O'Keeffe in the back. Yet they looked equally confused, and a moment later they were pointing, cursing, leaving O'Keeffe and the dead Ferguson, racing toward smoke that curled above a dead horse.

"Flint!" Marty slid beside him, lifted his head, resting it on her lap, ignoring the stench of the urine that soaked her trousers. "Oh . . . Flint."

His eyes fluttered. "What . . . ?"

Exploring his back, Marty felt the sticky, warm liquid, brought her hand up. The blood was dark.

"You'll be all right . . . ." She bawled uncontrollably, regained control, and tried to help him stand. "Can you walk?" she asked.

"I do not know . . . I think . . . so. Who?"

She wondered that herself, and looked around. Ryan Folson and the others had jerked a musket from behind a dead horse. Something was tied to the barrel, a shirt, maybe, and she remembered. A man of color had ridden forward moments before the massacre had ended, trying to surrender, and the Whigs had shot him and his mount. She figured he had been killed, but apparently he had been playing 'possum, and now the low assassin had shot Flint O'Keeffe, ambushed him when he was trying to stop his own men from disgracing Major Ferguson's corpse.

She half expected Ryan Folson to chop the assassin to bits with his hatchet. Indeed, she hoped he would, but Nicholas Waldrin had thrown a rope around the Negro's head, and Folson and the others were dragging him to the woods.

Good. Hang him. He deserves it.

The Negro would not be alone, Marty noticed. Already Tories swung from the trees, some kicking violently, some just swaying in the late afternoon breeze.

"I must get you to that doctor," Marty said.

"No!" O'Keeffe straightened, grimaced, and staggered toward the woods. "I must stop . . . ." He collapsed to his knees.

Marty, sobbing again, tried to help him up, begged him to let her take him to the surgeon, before he bled to death.

"I will not . . . they will not . . . do . . . not on . . . my conscience . . . not again."

She didn't understand him at first, but, as he struggled to his feet, wavering, trying to reach Folson's murderous party, Marty remembered O'Keeffe's story, the Negro that had been whipped and hanged around Ninety-Six back when O'Keeffe had been riding with Elijah Clarke's militia.

"Don't . . . ," he said weakly, and began coughing.

Marty made him sit on a rock. "You stay here," she ordered, and ran, screaming, trying to be heard over Ryan Folson's shouts. No use. She leaped, hoping to knock Folson off his feet, an impossible goal considering Folson's bulk and Marty's lightness. Marty bounced off him, landing so savagely the wind exploded from her lungs. At least, she had knocked the rope to the ground.

With a curse, Folson started to kick her, almost buried his foot in her wounded side, but stopped, recognizing her, seeing she no longer posed a threat. Instead, he bent over and grabbed the rope.

The Negro just stared down at her, his head and shoulder bleeding, along with his hand and leg, and his left earlobe had been shot away. He looked so resigned to his fate, not resisting as Folson tossed the rope over a sturdy limb.

"Pull him up, lads," Folson said. "Let him kick himself to death, the black cur."

"Stop it," Marty said, gasping for air, her voice barely audible. "Flint . . . don't . . . ."

The rope tightened, then slackened.

"There has been enough blood shed today," a man was saying. "This man is a prisoner and he shall be treated as such, as decency allows."

"*Decency?* This darky shot Lieutenant O'Keeffe!" Waldrin sputtered. "Killed him, he did. Murdered him!"

Having caught her breath at last, she had just pulled herself to a sitting position, but Waldrin's words made her head reel. Then the newcomer spoke again, and Marty breathed easier.

"Lieutenant O'Keeffe lives, men. There he is. He sent me to intercede. Now, you shall remove the rope from this prisoner's head or every one of you will feel the bite of hemp when you stand underneath a gallows tree."

Edward Lacey. Marty recognized him at last. Flint O'Keeffe's old friend. By the time she managed to stand, Folson had removed the noose and stormed away. The others pushed the Negro forward, hustling him toward the prisoners who sat nervously on the ground.

She thanked Colonel Lacey, but wasn't sure the South Carolinian heard her, and ran back to O'Keeffe, pulled him to his feet, lunged toward the ruined Tory camp. Mountaineers moved from tent to tent, claiming their spoils. None gave Marty or O'Keeffe any assistance. She doubted if they even noticed them, blinded as they were by the victory, by their greed. A moment later, Lacey walked beside her, helping her with her load.

* * * * *

The sight of the wounded, surrounding the surgeon's tent, shocked her. Prayers drifted over the ridge like the wind. So did pitiful wails and horrifying screams.

"Sir." Colonel Lacey addressed the only surgeon they found. The man O'Keeffe had protected during the battle held a saw. If anything, his hands, shirt sleeves, and face looked even more blood-splattered now. "I have a wounded officer, Doctor," Lacey continued, "who requires immediate attention."

"Leave him here," the doctor answered hoarsely. "I shall attend him when I can, if I can."

"Sir," Lacey said in protest, "this man is gravely wounded, wounded, I say, protecting your late commanding officer. Now . . . ."

"I am but one man," the surgeon spoke, and began sawing. The patient screamed before passing out.

Marty almost toppled over in a faint, but Flint O'Keeffe squeezed her hand gently. She squeezed back.

"Surely there are other surgeons with your army, Doctor," Lacey argued.

"There were two others," came the reply, "but you rebels killed them."

"Leave me," O'Keeffe said weakly. "Just put me in the shade. I will be all right."

"No," Colonel Lacey said forcefully. "I will make this bloke remove . . . ."

"There are men in worse condition than I," O'Keeffe said. "Go on. There is much work to be done. Go."

* * * * *

She stood guard that evening, overseeing prisoners as they buried their dead. Marty would not have left O'Keeffe, but he had insisted, so she stood, cold, numb, butting a Brown Bess musket on the ground as weary Tories tossed bodies into two rows of shallow pits.

As the sun began to dip behind the trees, Sergeant Gillespie approached her and handed her the Deckard, saying he had found it on the battlefield, figured she would want it. After he took the British musket from her cold hands, she gripped the rifle with her bandaged hand and stared into the gloaming. Not trusting her voice, she merely nodded at the sergeant. Actually part of her never really wanted to see the Deckard again. After today, she didn't know if she would be able to pull the trigger, any trigger, aim a rifle at anything, man, deer, or squirrel.

Yet another part of her wanted to kill that Negro, the Tory who had shot Flint O'Keeffe. She watched him as he laid a body in the pit, fighting the urge to kill him.

"By Jupiter," another guard said. "That is a woman."

Marty blinked, and noticed the body on the ground. A redheaded woman lay with her hands folded across her chest, hair mashed, dirty, a purple hole in her temple, surprisingly little blood. As she studied the woman, Marty felt sickened. What had she been doing here? Why had she died? Why had Flint O'Keeffe been shot when the battle was over? Why did she live?

"Do we bury her with them Tories?" the guard asked. "Does not seem Christian."

"Bury her with Major Ferguson." It was the Negro who had spoken.

Marty glared at him, then sighed. It hurt too much, drained her so, to hate this man. Even Flint O'Keeffe, wounded as he was, did not condemn the Negro.

"Why, pray tell?" the guard asked.

"They would have wished it," the Tory said.

The guard shrugged. "Well, I warrant it is better, more civilized, than leaving her in this ditch for the wolves."

An hour later, while the prisoners were still burying the dead, Marty was relieved by Nicholas Waldrin. Tucking the Deckard underneath her arm, she raced back to the surgeon's tent, trembling as prisoners and Whigs carted more dead to the burial ground. She peered at the faces, praying she would not find Flint O'Keeffe's among the dead. She didn't, mainly because in the darkness she could barely recognize anyone. It took her fifteen minutes to locate Flint O'Keeffe, lying on a blanket, his head propped up on a collection of hats and boots, a fire crackling a few rods beyond him.

"Hello." O'Keeffe's eyes danced a little when he saw Marty, although, maybe, it was from the fire.

She knelt beside him, gripping his hand, and fell asleep by his side.

* * * * *

Morning dawned heavily with smoke. Marty rose stiffly, found Flint O'Keeffe awake, sipping captured Tory tea, chatting with the Tory doctor, Uzal Johnson, and Colonel Edward

Lacey. So calm they sounded. So normal, except O'Keeffe looked so pale.

Her bones creaked as she rose, finding the source of the smoke. Tory wagons had been set afire. Officers barked orders to the prisoners, telling them they would carry rifles—with flints removed, of course—on the march, that anyone trying to escape would be shot.

They were leaving. *Going home*, Marty thought. *But what of Flint O'Keeffe?* Nervously she stared at him.

"You should report to Sergeant Gillespie," O'Keeffe said. "We shall move out directly."

Marty blinked, wanting to ask the question, but unable to form any coherent thought.

"I will go with you," O'Keeffe said with a smile.

"I advise against that, sir," Dr. Johnson said. "The ball is in your kidney, Lieutenant. Travel, I fear, will kill you."

"Flint . . . ," Lacey began, but O'Keeffe cut him off.

"Staying, I fear, will kill me," he said. "What mercy would Bloody Bill Cunningham or Zachariah Gibbs give a Patriot officer? I shall not be left here, gentlemen, defenseless, to be butchered by some avenging Tory. No, I will return . . . ." Although he addressed Colonel Lacey, O'Keeffe grinned again at Marty. "I have a strong reason to live, Edward. A home to find, a life to build."

Chapter Twenty-Two

"You carried a firelock here," that self-righteous turncoat named Shelby told the gray-haired man standing in front of Stuart Brodie. "And, damn you, you shall carry one away with you."

With that, Shelby slapped the man's shoulders with the flat of his sword, knocking him to his knees. Without comment, Brodie helped the old man up, picked a light carbine, and gave it to the prisoner, who shouldered the weapon and marched quickly away, falling in single file behind the other Loyalists being forced to carry muskets, their flints removed from the locks, off King's Mountain.

Cinders from the burning wagons stung Brodie's eyes as he grabbed a musket.

"You appear stout enough to carry two," Shelby told him. "One on each shoulder."

Brodie bit his tongue. Healthy? Rebel balls had torn through his right hand and thigh, cut off his left earlobe, pierced his left shoulder, singed his right armpit, and put a dent in his skull an inch above his right eye. He hefted one musket over his left shoulder and a fowling piece over his right, refusing to give Isaac Shelby the pleasure of hearing him grunt. Nor would he stagger off like that old man. He stood erect as he marched across the ridge and down King's Mountain.

Overseen by rebel guards, a handful of prisoners remained behind, still burying the dead. It would take them the rest of the day, and maybe into the morrow, Brodie figured, to accomplish that task. He wondered if, once the last body had been buried, the guards would kill the prisoners, then scatter like leaves to avoid Cunningham, Gibbs, and Tarleton. Dr. Uzal Johnson, who had not slept all night, worked diligently on the more severely wounded, Whigs and Loyalists alike. The rest of the rebel wounded, those unable to walk, lay on litters being pulled behind horses and mules. Mountaineers had chopped down young trees, stripping off branches to make poles that they secured to each side of a saddle, then fastened a blanket or ripped section of tent to form a kind of bed. Not the most comfortable ride, Brodie imagined, but they feared anyone left behind would be killed. Having ridden with William Cunningham, Brodie knew the Whigs were right.

I should be dead, he told himself.

* * * * *

It had been a suicide, riding toward the rebel line after the Bulldog had been mortally wounded, waving that dirty white shirt tied to the gun barrel. He didn't remember being shot, just waiting for death, seeing the *banditti* take aim at him. For once, the cowards proved poor marksmen. Oh, they had hit him, sure enough, put a ball in his shoulder and nearly shot out his eye, and they had killed the mount he had been riding. The head wound had knocked him cold, and, when he came to, he had peered over the dead horse and witnessed those butchers. He could hardly stomach what they were doing to the major's body. Indecent. Barbarous. Remembering the musket he had been given had been charged and primed, he had brought it up, steadying the barrel against the withers, aiming. *If I can kill just one of those Myrmidons*, he remembered thinking.

Well, he had even failed at that. Put a ball in a lieutenant's back, yes, but the officer still breathed, most likely lying on one of those litters Brodie passed. Besides, Brodie had later learned the man he had shot had been trying to stop the depredations. Shot in the back, too, although that had been a mistake. Brodie had been aiming at another pig, but the officer had stepped in the path of the musket ball. Almost immediately, the rebels had caught him—not that he could have escaped, wounded as he was, surrounded by butchers—and dragged him to the woods, where already Loyalists had been executed.

Bound for the cord, his mother had always told him, and the rope had gone around Brodie's neck. Yet he had been granted another reprieve. First, a wiry little reb had tried to save him, with no luck, but the renegades had listened to a Whig colonel when he had threatened them with their own hangings. What Brodie could not fathom was this: the rebel lieutenant, shot in the back by Brodie, had pleaded for Brodie's life to be spared.

* * * * *

So he was alive—for now. Still, he would not put anything past these brigands. Likely they would massacre the prisoners when they felt safer, when they were farther from Lord Cornwallis's grasp.

Early that afternoon, the column was stopped. A Whig colonel named Williams had died, and Brodie figured now the rebels would rise up one more time and start up the slaughter. Only they didn't. After a brief rest, they continued the march, stopping at a plantation along the Broad River. The prisoners stacked their weapons in piles, then were hustled off to a corral— the bullpen, the rebels called it—and bedded down for the night.

A good King's man named Matthew Fondren owned this plantation, but had fled the advancing army. Whigs ripped apart Fondren's fences for fires, and ate the last of his sweet potatoes. The prisoners were given nothing to eat, just water, not even allowed a place to answer nature's call.

The next morning, the over-mountain men buried their dead colonel, fired a volley over his grave, and continued the march. Once again, that stern Colonel Shelby made the Loyalists walk past him, his sword raised, and pick up weapons from the stacks and move on. Again, Brodie shouldered two muskets, although, this time, he grunted when he lifted the Brown Bess pieces, and staggered forward.

For two days, they continued, hours flowing murkily like the Broad River, camping in the woods, stumbling on, toward Gilbert Town. More rebels joined the army at the Cowpens, mostly infantry and men with inferior mounts. The numbers amazed many prisoners, who had believed the Bulldog when he had laughed at the reports of this Ghost Legion. Better than 1,800, they were, although only half that number had fought in the battle. Of course, Brodie had known the Patriots' true strength. So had Ensign Yarbrough and Saul Pinckert. Ferguson should have retreated straight to Lord Cornwallis. Too late to think about that now, though.

Convinced they would eventually be slaughtered, a handful of Loyalists fell back, and the guards, equally exhausted, did not pay them much attention. Six men escaped, and the rebels refused to send soldiers after them. *They are scared*, Brodie knew, *scared of Tarleton, scared of His Majesty's retribution.*

Just below Gilbert Town, another Loyalist dropped his pair of muskets in the woods and crawled under a pile of leaves. An Irish colonel spotted him, however, hauled him out of his hiding place, and ran him through with a sword.

That evening in Gilbert Town, the Virginia commander named Campbell issued an order, which he had nailed across the settlement, including the gate of the bullpen.

I must request the officers of all ranks in the army to endeavor to restrain the disorderly manner of slaughtering and disturbing the prisoners. If it cannot be prevented by moderate measures, such effectual punishment shall be executed upon delinquents as will put a stop to it.

Colonel William Campbell
Commanding

"Do you think the barbarians will obey?" a young boy asked Brodie.

Brodie didn't reply. A guard answered for him, telling a Loyalist woman who had just asked about the prisoners' fate: "We are going to hang all the damned old Tories, and take their wives, scrape their tongues, and let them go."

Both the Loyalist woman and the young soldier sulked away, whimpering.

They moved slowly, covering maybe forty miles in a week. For the next two days, the prisoners marched without food, only water, but Brodie had to concede that the rebel soldiers had little to eat. The glory of their victory had faded. Now they suffered almost as much as Ferguson's men.

On Cane Creek, the Loyalists finally ate—green pumpkins and some corn. Guards tossed in the food, cackling like hens, calling out at the prisoners as they would while luring hogs in to eat. Brodie ignored those taunts, and no one seemed to care, not even Captain DePeyster. For the Loyalists, this was a feast. They ate with relish until hearing news that at Fort Ninety-Six, just a few days earlier, eleven Whigs had been hanged.

Soon, Brodie heard the guards talking, could see the hatred returning to their eyes, smell their lust for revenge.

The next day, they covered four or five miles, arriving at Bickerstaff's Old Fields, better known as the Red Chimneys. Before the insurrection, it had been another thriving plantation. Now the barns and houses lay crumbling, the main building nothing but charred timbers and red chimneys that rose from the ruins like tombstones. A couple of cabins had recently been erected on the property, ramshackle buildings really, just enough shelter from wind and rain. Campbell, Shelby, and Sevier claimed the larger of the cabins, while the second was turned into a ward for wounded officers. After stacking the weapons one more time, the Loyalists, as usual, were marched into the remnants of a large corral.

In the bullpen, Brodie watched the commotion. The number of guards had been doubled, and ropes with hangman's nooses were soon tossed over the huge limb of a stout oak. Rebel soldiers and civilians, some women, paraded past the prisoners, pointing at a few, whispering. Whig officers took notes and nodded secretly. A handful of words reached Brodie's ears: house-burners—trial—Buford—horse thief—assassin—magistrates.

"So this is where it ends," he said softly, and waited.

* * * * *

The colonels had relinquished their cabin, turned it into some court of law. *Brigands law*, Brodie thought as they ushered him inside, hands tied behind his back. A fat captain explained the proceedings to him as he stood facing a jury of twelve traitors, fiends who had risen against King George, men who had killed his brother, cowards who had the gall to try him for crimes against North Carolina.

According to colony law, two magistrates could summon a jury, conduct a trial, and, if needed, execute convicted offenders. Cloaked under legality, these snakes in the grass would be free to kill their enemies. The magistrates, now wearing powdered wigs, had fought at King's Mountain along with the jurors, all officers, some of them showing wounds they had sustained in the battle.

"A mockery," Brodie whispered.

Never had he witnessed a trial, let alone been tried, but his father had told him of what he had seen back in England. Poor wretches being hurried into a court, dazed, petrified. Often, before they even realized what was happening, they had been tried, convicted, and sentenced.

The magistrate named Cleveland, a rebel colonel, informed Brodie that he had been charged with breaking open two score houses, which were then burned, of leaving defenseless women and children homeless, of killing men and boys in the most ruthless, cold-blooded fashion.

"I have done no such," Brodie said. "I have fought honorably, to avenge my brother you Patriots flogged, brutalized, and hanged."

"Then you deny that you rode with Bloody Bill Cunningham?" A man leaped from his seat, pointing a gnarled finger at Brodie. "You were there, damn you, on the Pacolet River!"

Colonel Cleveland demanded order, and, as if somehow detached from his body, Brodie observed the cabin as a young ensign escorted a frail woman to the front. Although she looked ancient, Brodie understood that she must be in her early thirties. A second later, he remembered her so vividly, pictured her again, sobbing in front of Bloody Bill's Legionnaires at that farm, the dog wailing near the well, begging for the butcher to spare the lives of her two young sons caught manufacturing ammunition for the rebellion. When interrogated by Cunningham, she had said the pewter balls were for hunting, a lie. This time she admitted that the balls would have been given to the boys' father, her husband, a gallant sergeant who rode for liberty with Elijah Clarke. "Had ridden," she corrected herself, weeping harder. He had been among those prisoners hanged at Ninety-Six.

"Now I have no one," she cried. She revealed the scar on her throat, the mark of a bayonet, and barely made it through her account as she told the assembly how Cunningham's Legionnaires had raided their farm, knocked her out, and left every building burning. They had stolen the horses, slaughtered her pigs, even killed the dog, then poisoned the well. She had had to bury her two boys, chopped beyond recognition, with her own hands.

"The darky was with them," the woman said feebly.

Brodie could not deny it. He had been there, had watched the butchery, had not tried to stop it, although he had saved another woman's life, had almost beaten Lieutenant Abel Hart to death later on Brush Creek. Cunningham would have killed Brodie then if Major Ferguson had not arrived. Maybe that would have been a better end for Stuart Brodie.

The jury found him guilty, and Magistrate Colonel Benjamin Cleveland sentenced him to hang. "'For they sow the wind,'" Cleveland said, quoting Hosea just as Brodie had back on the Pacolet, "'and they shall reap the whirlwind.'"

* * * * *

Bound for the cord. Of the thirty-six Loyalists tried by this mock jury of rebel trash, only four had been acquitted. Midnight had passed by the time the magistrates passed the last death sentence, and the wind sighed as hundreds of Whigs escorted the convicted to that large oak tree. One man tried to break free, only to be clubbed down by the throng, four or five deep, singing, chanting, waving pine-knot torches. Two Loyalists helped the man to his feet.

"Bear up, old man," one said. "Do not give these brigands the satisfaction. We are men. They are animals."

They stopped a few rods from the oak, listening as a rebel preacher said—screamed, to be precise—a few words about the fire of Hades, the candle of the wicked, God's mighty arm and freedom.

"Three at a time," an officer ordered, and the first row of condemned men were led forward. Hands bound behind their backs, they were helped onto wobbling chairs and offered blindfolds.

"I shall prefer to watch you cowards," said Colonel Ambrose Mills, shaking his head, "so that I might recognize your faces when I see you in the pit."

A handful of Loyalists cheered their colonel, despite the knowledge that they would join him shortly. Those hurrahs fell silent when the chairs were kicked from underneath the three men. Captains James Chitwood and Walker Gilkey died instantly. Colonel Mills was not so lucky, and dangled helplessly, kicking savagely for minutes before giving a final shudder, then soiling himself.

Moments later, three more stepped forward.

"Damned efficient," the man standing beside Brodie said softly. He kept his head up, stiff, but tears welled in his eyes, his Adam's apple bobbed, and beads of sweat, reflecting eerie light from the torches, rolled down his forehead.

"Come on, ye sons-of-bitches," one of the savages demanded, "take ye medicine!"

Within seconds, the number of bodies stretching from the oak had doubled.

"Next three!"

The hangmen moved rapidly. Now, nine men hanged from the limb. The killers would soon be out of room, would have to move their gallows to another limb, mayhap even another tree.

Laughing, a man in buckskins pushed a limp foot dangling from the tree with his rifle butt. "Would to God every tree in the wilderness bore such fruit as that!" he said.

"Amen," another blackheart agreed with a chuckle.

"Next three prisoners, step forward!"

In unison, Brodie, the sweating man, and a third Loyalist took their places underneath the oak. Two men lifted Brodie onto the seat of the dirty chair. The body of Augustine Hobbs brushed against Brodie, and he trembled uncontrollably at the savage light reflecting in the dead man's bulging eyes. He regained control, would not let these murderers recognize his fear. Brodie steadied himself.

So be it, Brodie thought as a white-haired, tall outlaw called Folson tightened the noose around his neck. *Finis.*

Chapter Twenty-Three

In the cabin, she bathed in a copper tub, a canvas partition separating her from the makeshift hospital, scrubbing herself furiously, a woman possessed, trying to remove all the dirt and grime, gentle only around the gash in her hand, which had been stitched up at King's Mountain by the Tory surgeon, and the scar across her ribs. The sight of the latter wound, healing but puffy, raw, and rugged, shocked her, but not as much as the filthy water when she finally climbed out of the tub.

As muddy as the Catawba River during spring run-off.

After toweling herself off, Marty looked at the wardrobe. Colonel Sevier had brought it in last night, a gift for Lieutenant O'Keeffe, he said, to present to that lady friend he had been talking so much about in his sleep. The clothes had been found with Ferguson's traps. "Your share of the spoils," Sevier had told O'Keeffe with a smile. "Your lady fair will be one much admired, Mister O'Keeffe, so you had better heal quickly to fend off all her suitors."

O'Keeffe had smiled weakly, and, after the colonel had left, he had asked Marty if she would put on the clothes so that he might see how truly beautiful she was. Marty had blushed. No one had ever called her beautiful. She certainly didn't feel pretty.

Now, she looked at the clothes. She put another strip of bandage across her side, then slipped on the linen smock. The petticoat and chemise were quite ornate, laced, delicate. Marty had never seen such clothing, couldn't remember the last time she had worn a dress. *Have I ever worn a dress?*

The skirt was billowing, the bodice beautiful, but the shoes wouldn't fit. Leather things would pinch her too much anyway, so she pulled on her moccasins, and laughed in spite of herself. *A fancy outfit, probably the rage in London or Charles Town, and deerskin moccasins. Don't I look proper.* She combed the tangles out of her hair—tried to, that is—and peered around the curtain.

The last officer to remain in the cabin, Flint O'Keeffe lay on a cot. Others had healed enough that they were sent home. One had died.

Although she wondered how she looked, Marty felt too afraid to find a mirror. Cautiously she stepped behind the curtain and went to O'Keeffe's bedside, praying no one would enter until after she had put on her smelly hunting frock and breeches. Late as it was, dark as it was, and with the trials proceeding at the other cabin, Marty didn't worry too much about any intrusion. She gripped O'Keeffe's pallid hand, and his eyes slowly opened. Biting her lip, Marty tried not to cry.

At the Cowpens, O'Keeffe had been improving. He even had gotten off the litter unassisted, walked around for a couple of minutes, proclaimed that he was on the mend. Marty knew better, although she wanted to believe. The ball remained in his kidney, and, by the following morning, fever racked him. He couldn't keep any food down, not even water. A Sullivan County man named Welchel, who said he had doctored many a man, had made a poultice for the wound and forced a smelly broth down O'Keeffe's throat, which he promptly threw up. Another self-anointed healer later suggested that they bleed the poison out of the lieutenant's body with leeches, but Marty had never held with such notions. Desperate, though, she had relented, and the

Wilkes County man attached the leeches. O'Keeffe had grown weaker, however, so she had halted the treatment, hoping they would find a doctor—a real doctor—in Gilbert Town.

The closest they could find, though, was a midwife named Mrs. Cash. "There is nothing to be done," she had told Marty. "He is in God's hands."

He had slept fitfully the past couple of nights, and, when he had been able to talk, Marty had heard death's rattle in his throat. Finally he had slipped into a deep sleep. Marty wasn't sure he would wake up.

Yet he did, eyes adjusting to the candle-lit room, and he spoke in a hoarse, barely audible voice. "Why, Martha Anne McKidrict, you are fetching."

She shook her head.

"I wonder," O'Keeffe said, "why Ferguson . . . ?"

Placing her fingers on his lips, she told him to save his strength, not to talk. She remembered the red-headed woman, shot in the head, remembered the Negro prisoner saying that they should bury her with Major Ferguson. She knew why Ferguson had carried this wardrobe. She knew whose clothes she was wearing. They were too big for her, really, but felt so comfortable, not as itchy, not as filthy as what she had been wearing for so long. Her breasts seemed to appreciate no longer being strapped down to hide her sex.

He tried to lift his hand, but couldn't, so Marty helped him, guided the hand into her wet hair. O'Keeffe stroked, but the very effort left him exhausted.

"You are beautiful," he whispered.

"I am no such . . . ."

"Find a looking-glass, please," he said. "I want you to see yourself. See yourself for the first time."

Reluctantly Marty rose, remembering one of those fancy ladies mirrors that had been left on a corner table. She grabbed a candle, crossed the room, found the mirror, but didn't have the courage to look at herself. Mirror in hand, she was crossing the hard-packed dirt floor again when Teever Barnes burst through the door.

"Hey, Lieutenant!" Barnes yelled. "We are about to hang that darky! The one that shot you. Hanging the lot. You shall be avenged . . . ."

She had not seen Barnes much since the battle. The last time she had really noticed him had been on the mountainside, when he had been cradling his dead Tory brother in his arms, bawling like a newborn calf. Barnes must have blocked out that memory, for now he was his old, revengeful, repulsive self.

At the sound of breaking glass, he spun, his eyes widening, face paling, as if he had seen a ghost. He stared at Marty, uncomprehending, began to stutter as he backed away, then whirled around, and knocked Edward Lacey off his feet as the colonel crossed the threshold. Barnes tripped himself, skinning his knees, but bounced back to his feet and ran scrambling into the night, yelling something lost amid the cacophony of voices from outside the other cabin.

Dusting himself off, Edward Lacey rose, cursing the fleeing Barnes for his clumsiness. A second later, he saw Marty from the corner of his eye, checked his tirade, and quickly removed his cocked hat, apologizing for his offensive language. Lacey bowed, looked up again, and dropped his hat.

From his bed, Flint O'Keeffe let out a weak laugh.

Marty ignored the colonel. She had dropped the mirror when Barnes startled her, smashing the glass. O'Keeffe's laugh died suddenly, and the sound of voices outside rose, angry shouts, and the words of Teever Barnes must have finally registered, for O'Keeffe tried to lift himself off the cot, only to fall back with a groan.

She knelt beside him, wiping perspiration off his face.

"How many?" he asked, his voice suddenly strong. "How many are they hanging?"

Marty bowed her head. *I don't know*, she mouthed, unable to speak. Tears stained her cheeks.

Lacey stood at the foot of the bed. O'Keeffe redirected his question.

"More than thirty," Lacey answered. "But this was done by jury and magistrates. A legal proceeding."

"You must stop this," O'Keeffe said.

Lacey shook his head. "There is nothing that can be done. The man of color was not charged with shooting you, Flint, but of riding with William Cunningham's cut-throats. That is why he shall hang."

"No!" O'Keeffe clenched both fists.

"Flint . . . ," Marty began.

"Damnation!" he roared. "Why are we fighting, Marty? Is this what liberty means? This is murder. Murder in the dead of night. We are no better than Tarleton or Gibbs if this is allowed . . . ." He sank deep into the cot, too weak to continue, and drifted back to sleep.

"It is too late," Lacey said, although O'Keeffe could not hear him.

"No."

Marty didn't realize she had spoken, but suddenly she stood. Her gaze caught Lacey's eyes momentarily, then she lifted the hems of her skirt and raced outside. For the second time, she ran to save this Negro, although she knew it was more than just him. O'Keeffe was right. Hanging men like this, guilty or not, under the cloak of midnight—this was not justice, not the act of Patriots. If she allowed this to happen, if the Whigs allowed this, they would be despoilers—as evil as Seb McKidrict.

She pushed her way through the crowd, shouting to be heard above the rough voices. A torch singed her, and she smelled the stench of burned hair.

"By God," someone said at last. "This is a woman!"

They had lifted the Negro and two other men onto chairs, and Marty gasped at the sight of the nine others, nine men she was too late to save.

"Stop this!" she yelled, but a rough hand threw her on the ground. Marty looked up. Ryan Folson's eyes blazed in the firelight. He lifted a hand as if to strike her, then the arm fell at his side.

"It's . . . ." He peered closer. "My . . . McKidrict?"

She pulled herself up. "Are we butchers?" she demanded. "Let these men go!"

"They have been convicted, you damned harlot!" someone shouted from the crowd. "They are Tory sons-of-bitches . . . ravishers . . . barn-burners . . . murderers . . . the scourge of God!"

In the distance, thunder rolled. The breeze picked up.

"By Jupiter, that is Marty McKidrict! He's a woman!"

"McKidrict! It cannot . . . thunderation, it is!"

"Nine men have been hanged," Marty said. "Is that not enough of a warning? Flint O'Keeffe lays in that cabin yonder, dying, and it is his request that these lives be spared. It . . . ."

"This nigger is the one that mortally wounded Lieutenant O'Keeffe!"

Her lips trembled as she tried to think of something to say. "Has not there been enough killing?" she asked timidly. "Are we . . . should not we be the ones that cherish life, even the lives of our enemies? Are . . . are we no better than Tarleton? That's what Flint O'Keeffe wonders . . . . That's . . . ."

"'Tis my brother who stands next to the darky," another man said. "My brother, a Tory, a man I hate, an enemy I despise . . . but still a brother . . . a brother I love. I beg of you to spare his life. Ferguson has been whipped. Let the bloodshed end . . . tonight."

Fingering his cross, Ryan Folson bowed his head, and no one moved. The wind turned suddenly cold. Slowly two figures stepped forward, and helped one of the condemned men out of the noose and off the chair. Colonel Lacey and Colonel Cleveland, Marty recognized them in the flickering light. Cleveland, the magistrate, announced a pardon. The Negro came down next, then the last man, his knees buckling, teeth chattering.

"Return the prisoners to the bullpen," Cleveland said. "All of them. They shall be marched with the others to Hillsborough."

She didn't wait to hear the rest. Raindrops began peppering her face as she hurried back to the cabin. She grabbed Flint O'Keeffe's hand, told him that the hangings were over, that Colonel Cleveland and Colonel Lacey had stopped it, had pardoned the condemned men, that it was over, thanks to him, thanks to Flint O'Keeffe. She squeezed his hand tighter, hoping he would respond, but he didn't.

Blubbering now, she buried her face in his chest. She told him that she loved him, that he had to get better, that she wanted to find that place of his, that special home, that she wanted to be with him . . . forever. Rain began falling in sheets. Reluctantly Marty stood, wiping her face, and hurriedly crossed the room and closed the door.

O'Keeffe's breathing was ragged when she returned, his face white, his flesh cold. She held his hand all night, till two hours past dawn, when Sergeant Gillespie came inside, hat in hand, and begged forgiveness for the intrusion but needed to inform her that Colonel Campbell had requested her presence immediately. Gillespie stood uncomfortably, and not because of his rain-soaked clothes.

It was Sunday, October 15, 1780.

Marty bent over, kissed O'Keeffe's forehead, and folded his hands across his chest. She rose stiffly, looked at him again, and followed Sergeant Gillespie into the cold, wet morning. It didn't matter. Not now. Not any more.

Lieutenant Flint O'Keeffe had been dead an hour.

Chapter Twenty-Four

That Sunday downpour must have washed away the rebels' urge to kill. The rain began long before sunrise, not that anyone could see the sun, slacking only twice, then coming down steadily, drearily. Despite the weather, the Ghost Legion broke camp that morning, leaving the Red Chimneys, pressing on urgently to cross the Catawba before the river flooded.

Brodie couldn't understand these *banditti*, especially the woman who had intervened, had saved his life. Finally he stopped thinking about them. In spite of the deluge, they traveled better than thirty miles that day—nearly doubling the distance they had traveled the previous week—reaching Quaker Meadows well past sunset.

The militiamen had lost interest in the war, it seemed, but mostly in the prisoners. Maybe they just wanted to go home now. Perhaps they had accomplished their goal. They had crushed Major Ferguson, had killed the Bulldog, annihilated the western flank of Lord Cornwallis's army. It would take a miracle, Brodie realized, for the British and Loyalists to recover.

It struck him as he wandered into the forest: *The war is lost.* The Whigs would win. No matter what happened, they would beat England into submission. Cornwallis and Sir Henry Clinton might claim a few more battles, but they would never be able to suppress men like Sevier, Shelby, Campbell, Clarke, men like Sumter, Pickens, and Marion, and all of their followers. A new nation would be formed, partly because of what had happened on King's Mountain.

Escape proved almost effortless. The mountaineers just didn't give a whit any more. Several prisoners had gotten away fording the Catawba. Others had disappeared into the woods that evening. At Quaker Meadows, Brodie just got up to relieve himself and kept walking.

Already the mountain men were disbanding. The Whig named Lacey had taken his followers back to South Carolina. Sevier and Shelby planned to trek back across the Blue Ridge. Others were bound for Virginia. A few remained behind to escort the prisoners to Hillsborough, but the number of prisoners kept shrinking. Brodie would not be surprised if only a handful remained for exchange by the time they reached the next bullpen.

Stuart Brodie would not be among them.

He had not seen the woman since the night at the hanging tree. Brodie wondered about her. He wondered about the lieutenant he had shot. Word was that the officer had died, had been buried back at the Red Chimneys. *A pity*, Brodie thought. His feelings surprised him. *What now?*

Rain had not only cleansed the Whigs of their blood lust. Brodie no longer felt he had to avenge Ezekiel. Maybe he had already done that, fighting at King's Mountain and Musgrove's Mill. He had done all anyone could ask, yet he was a Loyalist, and a far-sighted man. After the final battle of this brutal insurrection, not all Patriots would be forgiving as the woman at the Red Chimneys oak. Loyalists would be abused. Some, like Cunningham, deserved such scurrility, but others . . . .

He could try to find Lord Cornwallis, fight on, but what was the point?

No, Brodie wanted to put all of this behind him, so he turned westward. Across the Cumberland Gap, he thought, back into Kentucky. A man could start over there, even a Loyalist, leave his past behind him in the colonies, find a new beginning, a new country, a new hope. Should England somehow win this war, he could always return to the Carolinas, but he doubted it.

Moving with confidence despite his aching joints, Brodie quickened his pace.

Yes, he told himself, *Kentucky*.

Chapter Twenty-Five

"Mayhap Colonel Sevier finds your behavior amusing," Colonel Campbell said stiffly, "but I see no mirth whatsoever. You should be ashamed of yourself, acting like a termagant. I will pray for your soul, McKidrict, if that truly be your name, but I will not allow your presence in our army one more day."

Marty had expected this, so she stood silently in the cabin, listening more to the rain pelting the roof than the Virginian's tirade. The tall commander shook with rage, but could not look Marty in her eyes.

"Colonel Sevier," Campbell continued, "says he will settle accounts with Madam Lewallen."

Bewildered, Marty cleared her throat. "Madam Lewallen?" she asked.

Thunder rolled, and Campbell's eyes narrowed. He did not like the interruption. "The Cherokee woman at Sycamore Shoals who gave you the old stallion you rode. Rode like a man! Shameless." He looked away. "I can provide you an escort to Gilbert Town. 'Tis the Christian thing to do. That is all I shall do."

"I sha'n't be going to Gilbert Town," she said firmly, and held his eye when he glared at her. Again, he looked away before dismissing her.

"Then take your horse and be gone."

She walked into the rain, back into the cabin. She would leave when she was ready, after they had buried Flint O'Keeffe.

Marty picked the spot, a nice place, she thought, and far enough away from the Gallows Oak. Colonel Lacey said a few words over the muddy grave, but Marty didn't pay attention. Lacey even offered his condolences before departing, the only soldier who dared speak to her. Folson, Barnes, Vance, and others, even Sergeant Gillespie, avoided her—John Sevier did not even attend the funeral—treated her as if she were some leper. Marty preferred it that way.

The army marched out in the rain, prisoners still carrying captured firelocks. Ghost Legion, Ferguson had called the force of mountaineers, and Sevier and Shelby had adopted that name. Fitting, too. Ghost Legion. A legion of ghosts. Edisto Bickley—James Williams—William Chronicle—many she didn't know, or barely knew—and Flint O'Keeffe. Marty didn't watch. She just stood at the grave until the rain slackened.

"Good bye, Flint," she said at last.

Back in the cabin, she exchanged the drenched pretty clothes for her gamy frock and breeches. She thought about waiting out the storm, but that wouldn't do. Marty wanted to put as much distance between the Red Chimneys and her as she could. So she tossed a blanket over her shoulders and went outside. Abimelech waited patiently.

Rifle in hand, Marty found the stirrup, pulled herself into the saddle, and kicked the old stallion into a trot. She gave Abimelech plenty of rein, keeping him pointed westward, toward the silhouette of the mountains. And then?

Marty had no place to go, no home, not really. She didn't really know where she was bound, and yet, oddly enough, she did. The thought comforted her. When she closed her eyes, she could picture it, just the way Flint O'Keeffe had described it. All she had to do was find it.

And she would find that place, the one Flint O'Keeffe had dreamed of. His words echoed through her mind, clearly, so alive, as she loped through the fallen leaves.

There's a place where the meadow is green in the summer, the creek bubbles to life. Not too big, not too small, and the mountains are blue in the distance, not too close, not too far. It's a place where you respect the land, and the land respects what you offer. It's not an easy place to live, but it's not impossible to make a living. I can't think of a place better to see one's sons and daughters grow.

THE END

Author's Note

The Battle of King's Mountain (or Kings Mountain, depending on your preference) proved to be the turning point of the American Revolution, followed shortly by the decisive American victory at nearby Cowpens and a costly British victory at Guilford Courthouse, North Carolina, that sent Cornwallis's blooded army to Yorktown, Virginia, and George Washington and the Continentals to destiny.

For research help, I owe thanks to the staffs at Kings Mountain National Military Park near Blacksburg, South Carolina, Cowpens National Battlefield near Chesnee, South Carolina, Sycamore Shoals State Historic Area in Elizabethton, Tennessee, the Overmountain Victory Trail Association, and the late Frank Handal.

Father of my best friend at the University of South Carolina, Frank Handal was Brooklyn-born, but we native Sandlappers never considered him some carpetbagger. After all, as owner and president of Sandlapper Publishing Company in Orangeburg during the late 1970s and '80s, Mr. Handal helped keep interest in South Carolina's Revolutionary War history alive by publishing many of Robert D. Bass's histories, including *Ninety-Six: The Struggle for the South Carolina Back Country* (1978). That book began fueling my desire to write a novel about King's Mountain and the over-mountain men.

Surprisingly the definitive historical account of the Battle of King's Mountain remains Lyman C. Draper's 1881 book, *King's Mountain and Its Heroes: History of the Battle of King's Mountain, October 7th, 1780, and the Events Which Led To It*, reprinted in 1991 by The Overmountain Press. I plan on coercing fellow South Carolinian Walter Edgar, author of *South Carolina: A History* and *Partisans & Redcoats: The Southern Conflict That Turned the Tide of the American Revolution*, to tackle this subject and update Draper's monumental narrative.

In addition to the works by Bass, Draper, and Edgar, other sources—of a varying range of information and credibility—for this novel include: *One Heroic Hour at King's Mountain* by Pat Alderman (The Overmountain Press, 1990); *The Road to Guilford Courthouse: The American Revolution in the Carolinas* by John Buchanan (John Wiley & Sons, 1997); *King's Mountain: The Defeat of the Loyalists, October 7, 1780* by J. David Dameron (Da Capo Press, 2003); *South Carolina and the American Revolution: A Battlefield History* by John W. Gordon (University of South Carolina Press, 2003); *Southern Campaigns of the American Revolution* by Dan L. Morrill (The Nautical & Aviation Publishing Company of America, 1993); *A Battlefield Atlas of the American Revolution* by Craig L. Symonds (The Nautical & Aviation Publishing Company of America, 1986); and the 1991 National Park Service publication *With Fire and Sword: The Battle of Kings Mountain 1780* by Wilma Dykeman. An excellent language source was *Colonial American English* by Richard M. Lederer, Jr. (Verbatim, 1985).

Martha Anne McKidrict, Flint O'Keeffe, Stuart Brodie, and Saul Pinckert are fictional characters, but many others, including Patrick Ferguson, John Sevier, Edward Lacey, and Isaac Shelby, are historical figures who fought at King's Mountain. James

Crawford and Samuel Chambers did desert the "Ghost Legion" to warn Ferguson, but the flight, capture, and execution of the fictitious Seb McKidrict and Willie Duncan are my own inventions. Also, Virginia Sal and Virginia Paul, according to legend, remained with Loyalist forces (and may have been Ferguson's mistresses). Sal was killed during the battle, and Paul was probably sent to Charlotte.

The trial of prisoners at the Red Chimneys also is true to history. Nine Tories were executed, then left hanging from the oak's limbs, before the others were pardoned. The tree earned the name The Gallows Oak after the incident.

In 1815, Dr. William McLean, a former Patriot, led an effort to clean up the battlefield and re-inter the dead, many of whom had been uprooted and eaten by animals. It's even said that, after the war, hunters often trekked to King's Mountain, where wolves were abundant and fat. Approximately 55,000 people attended an anniversary celebration at the battlefield in 1855, and twenty-five years later a monument was unveiled on the small mountain top in observance of the battle's centennial anniversary. In 1931, Kings Mountain National Military Park was established.

As far as the principal historical figures depicted in this novel are concerned, Dr. Uzal Johnson returned to New Jersey and resumed his medical practice until dying in 1826 at age seventy. John Sevier and Isaac Shelby became powerful government figures, not to mention living legends. Sevier and Shelby were the first governors of Tennessee and Kentucky, respectively. Shelby died in 1826; Sevier, in 1851. While serving at Yorktown in 1781, William Campbell suffered an apparent heart attack, only a couple of months before the British surrender, and died at age thirty-six. Edward Lacey moved to Tennessee and later Kentucky after the war, but at age 71 on March 13, 1813, he was thrown from his horse into Deer Creek and drowned. Legend has it that a Gypsy told Lacey's fortune when he was a boy: he would survive many battles but would later drown.

Many Loyalists, including Captain Abraham DePeyster, fled to Nova Scotia after the war. DePeyster died in 1799. Bloody Bill Cunningham, who is believed to have died in 1787, faded from history—but not before executing more than a dozen Patriot prisoners in retaliation for King's Mountain after a skirmish at Haye's Station, South Carolina, in November 1781. Likewise, ruthless Tory leader Zachariah Gibbs also disappeared into obscurity.

And Patrick Ferguson? His body remains buried at King's Mountain, not far from where he was killed in a last-ditch effort to break the Patriot resistance in the Carolina Backcountry.

Johnny D. Boggs
Santa Fé, New Mexico

About the Author

Johnny D. Boggs has worked cattle, shot rapids in a canoe, hiked across mountains and deserts, traipsed around ghost towns, and spent hours poring over microfilm in library archives—all in the name of finding a good story. He's also one of the few Western writers to have won both the Spur Award from Western Writers of America (for his short story, "A Piano at Dead Man's Crossing," in 2002) and the Western Heritage Wrangler Award from the National Cowboy and Western Heritage Museum (for his novel, *Spark on the Prairie: The Trial of the Kiowa Chiefs*, in 2004). Another novel, *Ten and Me,* was a Spur finalist in 2000. A native of South Carolina, Boggs spent almost fifteen years in Texas as a journalist at the *Dallas Times Herald* and *Fort Worth Star-Telegram* before moving to New Mexico in 1998 to concentrate full time on his novels. Author of twenty-seven published short stories, he has also written for more than fifty newspapers and magazines, and is a frequent contributor to *Boys' Life, New Mexico Magazine, Persimmon Hill,* and *True West.* His Western novels cover a wide range of topics. *The Lonesome Chisholm Trail* is an authentic cattle-drive story, while *Lonely Trumpet* is an historical novel about the first black graduate of West Point. *The Despoilers* and *Ghost Legion* are set in the Carolina backcountry during the American Revolution. *The Big Fifty* chronicles the slaughter of buffalo on the southern plains in the 1870s, while *East of the Border* is a comedy about the theatrical offerings of Buffalo

Bill Cody, Wild Bill Hickok, and Texas Jack Omohundro, and *Camp Ford* tells about a Civil War baseball game between Union prisoners of war and Confederate guards. "Boggs's narrative voice captures the old-fashioned style of the past," *Publishers Weekly* said, and *Booklist* called him "among the best Western writers at work today." Boggs lives with his wife Lisa and son Jack in Santa Fé. His website is www.johnnydboggs.com.